The

A Patchwork of Rivers, Volume 1

Rosie Williams

Published by Purple Trunk Press, 2021.

This is a work of fiction. Similarities to real people, places, or events are entirely coincidental.

THE FACE OF IT

First edition. June 22, 2021.

Copyright © 2021 Rosie Williams.

ISBN: 978-1-914607011

Written by Rosie Williams.

To Roe, without whose encouragement this book would never have been completed.

To Rob, who read it first.

And to Charlotte, for supporting me in everything I do.

Thank you to Greg, who is a very patient editor, and to Dad, who is an even more patient proof-reader.

CHAPTER ONE
Bad Good News

PAIGE

A thin panel of shatterproof glass embedded in her office door neatly framed Dr Paige Spencer as she worked at her desk. She tucked her shoulder-length auburn hair behind her ears and scowled at the computer screen that displayed this year's class schedule. Her desk was under the lone, high-level window, while bookcases inhabited most of the other wall space. The books were stacked two deep which made the shelves bow slightly in the middle. Additional towers of books were piled on top of the bookcases, some of them precariously forced over the edges by the odd pot plant or framed certificate. A giant, well-worn beanbag occupied one corner of the room, surrounded by note cards and different colour highlighter pens. Extensively annotated journals lay open in front of it, as if in audience. The office was quiet; term did not start for another fortnight. There was only a smattering of staff traversing the hallways, and over-eager freshers nervously making small talk in the courtyard below.

Dr Spencer closed her class schedule and opened

Facebook. She was immediately greeted by a video of a dog and two children playing in a pile of leaves, her elder brother Brandon and his wife laughing behind the camera. A little further down her sister Jenna had checked into a posh hotel in London with the hashtag 'blessed'; the accompanying photograph of her and her now-fiancé strategically taken so as to draw attention to the engagement ring.

A few scrolls later and Dr Spencer had caught up with her news feed. Thomas, her younger brother, hadn't posted an update in months. He was probably too far down the rabbit hole with his photography again; he had been enthralled by it since the first time he held a camera. Paige was reminded that she hadn't posted in months, either, or even spoken to Thomas in that time. She sent him a quick text requesting proof of life. The next conversation in the app was the group chat the four siblings had with their parents, with Jenna and Brandon valiantly keeping the conversation going with little help from the other two siblings. Jenna had been talking about her latest career change, and Brandon about a new hobby that had taken his fancy. The rest of the chat was taken up by pictures of Brandon's children.

The latest picture of her niece and nephew grinning at

the camera was suddenly replaced with a shrill ring and a green button demanding she answer.

'Hey, Maya. You know how I feel about phone calls,' Paige chastised her by way of greeting.

'I know, lovely, I'm sorry, but I'm driving so I didn't really have a choice.' Dr Spencer could hear the faint noise of an indicator in the background, and Maya's distracted voice sounded distant and electronic. 'I just wanted to let you know I'm running a bit late, my meeting overran. I should be able to make it for half seven?'

'OK, no problem. Drive safely'

'I always do, Paige,' Maya laughed, before hanging up.

Paige and Maya had known each other for over a decade. Maya had crashed into Paige's life only a few days after Paige moved into her university halls of residence. Maya had come through the front door carrying too many boxes and not paying much attention to the room numbers. She didn't notice she was in the wrong room until she dumped the boxes on the bed, only for the bed to yelp in response - Paige had been lying there reading one of her new textbooks. Maya's way of making up for her mistake was to persistently entice, cajole, and bribe the disinterested Paige to leave her room and attend every freshers' event. Paige in turn had made sure Maya got home safely from the freshers' parties. Maya had helped her inexperienced friend with the rules of dating and romance as best she could for a then eighteen-year-old, and had introduced Paige to her first girlfriend.

Maya almost dropped out near the end of her second year. Her spring term tutor had taken an instant dislike to her, and his constant cruelty and criticism were almost too much. Paige sat with Maya in their shared flat, night after night, drying her tears, eventually convincing her to put in a formal complaint, and holding her hand the entire way through her meeting with her head of school. They attended each other's graduations, both of them graduating near the top of their classes, and their excited cheers for each other could easily be heard above the polite clapping in the auditoriums. Maya celebrated graduation by going travelling for a few months, though only after making Paige promise to pursue her dream of becoming a professor despite the saturation in the field. She sent Paige postcards from every new city and country she visited. Upon her return she got an entry level job at a computer software start-up in a city several hours away and began working her way up the corporate ladder. Her current job was in health software and less than an hour away from Paige. The upper management position she held at the international health software business allowed her some flexibility with her hours, so the friends were able to meet up regularly; though this evening's type of delay wasn't unusual.

Paige leaned back in her chair, stretched, and rubbed her eyes; she wasn't going to get any more work done today. She got up from her desk, glanced at the handwritten notes scattered over the floor, and shook her head. It was a paper monument to her failure. Her application for internal research funding had been turned down. Again. Although her predominantly male colleagues accepted that women's contributions to the French Resistance in World War II were invaluable, they thought there were enough books on the subject already. Their conceptualisation of the project only extended as far as imagining fact-laden textbooks and dry repetition of names and dates, like the works they churned out. Paige had not been able to communicate her idea of bringing these historical figures to life in a way they could understand. She had already started preparing a fresh application on the same subject, which she hoped would be ready for the next round of funding. This was the second time the panel had rejected her idea and seeing her notes sprawled across the floor just reminded her of her defeat. She really needed that drink with Maya.

Paige turned off the lights as she left her office, and locked the door behind her, and smiled politely at the few people she passed on the way to the lift. Her office was on the fifth floor of the university's Silverton building, a structure which the History department shared with Journalism and English. There was a large cafe on the ground floor that served good food and was popular with the students, including those studying in the neighbouring smaller buildings. Paige always tried to avoid it at lunch times, but would sometimes grab a tea refill in the mornings, before too many people had arrived.

Once outside, Paige walked past her car in the car park, deciding instead to walk to the pub where she was meeting Maya. It was only about two miles along the river and there was still enough light; the autumn sun was only just starting to paint the sky with pink and orange hues. She used this footpath regularly during the summer, immersing herself in the serenity of the babbling river, and the fresh air always made a welcome change from her stuffy office. This evening a few fallen leaves welcomed her as she strolled along. A couple of gentle rapids serenaded her as she walked past; the sound of moving water was sometimes the only thing that could calm her frantic mind. On another night the musical waters might have been adorned with the bright colours of university kayakers paddling in their waves, and in the summer she would often see the vibrant swim caps of the open water swimmers who trained upstream of the white water. Regardless of the human presence on the river, Paige could count on the company of various animals for whom the river was either home or hunting ground. Even when deep in thought about her latest paper or journal article review, she never failed to appreciate the beauty of the herons, the skittishness of the squirrels, or the cuteness of the ducks. However, it was the owls that were her favourite, even though (or perhaps because?) they were the most elusive. Even on the rare occasions when she decided to walk along the river *and* had left work late enough, there was never a guarantee she would hear an owl, let alone see one. But there was always that enticing chance.

About halfway towards her destination Paige tried to refocus her thoughts on her research project. The niggling doubts she always carried with her threatened to claw their way to the surface. Had she been too direct in her delivery? Too blunt in her defence of her project? She knew that people often bristled at her abrasiveness. Her first girlfriend had broken up with her over it. Paige didn't understand why someone would ask a question if they didn't want an honest answer, and how she was expected to know that her girlfriend had actually meant the *opposite* of what she had said? At the time she had consoled herself by burying herself in her studies, the one thing she knew she excelled at. But now it felt like the academic side of her was being questioned; her whole existence was under attack. Maybe Maya would be able to translate again.

'So sorry I'm late, Spence!' Maya apologised as she stumbled through the pub door, quickly spotting her best friend in the corner they had claimed as forever theirs. Maya had dragged Paige to the pub's open mic poetry night in their first year, and they had been in love with it ever since. The mismatched furniture was all reclaimed or upcycled, and there was an open fire that was perfect for warming cold toes; especially for students who prioritised drinking money over paying to heat their draughty student houses. An old-fashioned jukebox completed the atmosphere. It was full of songs from before the friends were born, but that didn't stop them feeding it fifty pence and dancing away, much to the bemusement of the older patrons.

Maya sat down at the table, her large white wine ready and waiting, courtesy of Paige.

'Traffic was a nightmare and there were roadworks getting out of the city centre,' Maya continued.

'It's fine, it gave me time to walk here instead of drive. Clear my head a bit.' Paige let out a barely audible sigh. The fresh air of the river hadn't helped blow away the dark cloud that had followed her from her office.

'What's up?' Maya probed.

'Just the research funding thing again.' Paige had texted Maya earlier that week, as soon as she'd been told about her latest funding rejection, on the verge of tears and feeling like she might explode. 'It's stupid. Rejection happens. It shouldn't get to me this much.'

'Just because it happens doesn't make it hurt any less, lovely,' Maya soothed. 'How're you getting on with the new application?'

'It's going about as well as you'd imagine,' Paige said, scowling slightly at her gin and tonic as if it was the reason she was failing.

'Have you thought that maybe you're going about this the wrong way?' Maya asked.

'What d'you mean?'

'Well, you want to tell the stories of these women,

right? So why not actually write their stories?'

'I still don't understand,' Paige stated with a furrowed brow.

'Well…' Maya trailed off, before taking a big breath in and rapidly spouting, 'I know you're an academic through and through, and that it's important to you to talk about these people in an academic way, but why not write historically accurate novels about them? Outline their lives, their triumphs and losses, in a story that even an average Joe like me can understand?'

'There is nothing average about you, Maya.' Paige chuckled.

'Well, obviously. But aside from that. What do you think?'

'I don't know. It would be interesting to see if the research committee responded better to a more… human approach.'

'I didn't mean to submit it as a research proposal, lovely. I meant write a book. Get it published. Or publish it yourself? Tell these women's stories and screw what some dusty old academics think.'

'It's a misconception that all academics are old, and I'm sure they all practice good hygiene,' Paige said.

Maya rolled her eyes. 'The point is,' she continued

patiently 'you have the content already, you have the drive to do it, so to hell with what they think and just do it anyway!'

Paige stared into her glass whilst fidgeting with her beer mat. She had no experience with novel-writing. But these stories... they were so vivid to her, as vivid as one of Thomas' photographs. She was about to respond, voicing her concerns about her lack of ability, when they were interrupted by a tall man casting a shadow over their table.

'Hi... I was wondering if I might buy you a drink?' he asked politely, looking directly at Paige.

'No, thank you,' she said curtly.

'Paige!' Maya scolded. 'Sorry, what she meant to say was that she isn't looking for a relationship or hook-up right now, but would gladly extend a hand of friendship.'

'No, that's not what I meant,' Paige corrected bluntly. 'I don't make a habit of befriending strangers in pubs.' The man skulked away back to the bar, ordering a lone drink before disappearing around the corner and out of sight.

'You could have been a bit nicer to him,' Maya said.

'Being honest is being nice. I wouldn't want to give him false hope,' Paige stated, before adding, 'If you roll your eyes at me much more, they're going to fall out your head.'

'I'm just saying, you should be more open to potential relationships, platonic or otherwise. Who else do you hang out with, aside from me and your family?'

'I speak to people in work, and at the climbing club.'

'Work doesn't count, and half the time at climbing you're up a wall or belaying someone who is. Do you ever go out socially with the climbers?'

'Sometimes,' Paige answered, and Maya cocked an eyebrow. 'Probably not as often as I should, but I don't really have time.'

'You should make time -' Maya began, before her phone started ringing. 'Sorry, lovely, I've got to take this, do you mind?' she asked, already standing up. Paige shook her head and Maya headed outside.

The idea of writing a novel, of becoming an author, was alien to Paige. She hadn't exactly excelled at creative writing in school, but then, the topics they were given never really interested her. This would be different. She didn't have to come up with a complicated plot, or intricate back stories, or any of that stuff, she just had to give life to the characters that already existed in history books as footnotes. That's what had started this whole crusade. One of her reference texts mentioned a Resistance fighter and 'his wife'. She wasn't even named in the book, just mentioned as the property of the man. As if her contributions weren't valuable enough to even recall her name. But she had helped mothers escaping with their children by providing food and clothing for them and getting them safe passage. She had even acted as a midwife when necessary. Paige only knew all this because she had spent weeks trying to find out this woman's name, so at least someone would know it, would know her; Emilie. During her research on Emilie she came across many more like her: just mentioned in passing in the books, or not even mentioned at all.

Maya thumped back down into her chair, snapping Paige out of her thoughts.

'Everything OK?' Paige asked.

'Yes, fine. Great, actually.' Maya answered. 'But you're not going to like it.'

'Like what?'

'That was my boss's boss, offering me the job I interviewed for earlier this week. I got the job.'

'You didn't tell me you had an interview! Congratulations!' Paige exclaimed.

'Wait, Paige, that's not the whole story… Our company is setting up new offices in Japan and they want someone to go out there and oversee the process. I'll be moving there for six months.'

Paige was silent. All she could hear was the heavy pounding in her chest. She just stared at her friend. Tears burnt in her eyes, her throat closed up, and her ribs felt like a constrictive cage. Over the years Paige had constructed a reassuring routine for herself and it suddenly felt like the foundations of it were being ripped away, that everything was just hovering over a void, about to break apart as it fell in.

Maya had been her rock, her constant, for more than ten years. When the world confused her beyond belief, Maya was able to translate it. Most of her happiest memories involved Maya. They texted nearly every day, and saw each other almost every week. It had become a rhythm, and all of that was changing. It was all changing and going wrong and it was too much…

'I need to go home now,' Paige forced out, stumbling to her feet and making her way towards the door. She turned back briefly when she touched the handle. 'I am happy for you, Maya, I really am. I just –'

'I know, lovely,' Maya said gently as she watched her best friend dart out of the door.

Paige locked her front door behind her and leant back

against it, head back, eyes closed, breathing deeply and deliberately. She knew she had not handled that very well.

Her suburban townhouse was right on the edge of the city; she could even see the forest and hills from her bedroom window. It was more space than she needed given that she lived alone. She had bought it so that her family could come and stay without having to spend a fortune on hotels. Her niece and nephew loved sleeping over and would often trek up to the forest to build forts and dens, with Paige in the thick of it, playing the role of the dastardly pirate or the army general. The decoration downstairs was clean and simple. White walls contrasted with the odd splash of colour provided by historical items she had collected over the years. The kitchen was quite small but well organised, optimised for maximum efficiency. But one of the spare bedrooms looked like it had been haphazardly transplanted into the house by Dr Frankenstein. Brightly coloured walls supported shelves loaded with games and stuffed animals, waiting in silence for their owners. The superhero bedding clashed horribly with the walls, but the children had been so happy when they picked it out. Paige tended to keep the door to that room shut when her family weren't staying; the clash of decor felt like someone was playing the cymbals in her head. Her favourite room in the house was her office, which doubled as a library. It had the best views across the fields towards the forest and the window had framed many a spectacular sunset. Much like her office at work, there were books piled everywhere, but instead of a bean bag she had an old, beaten-up, fold-out sofa along one wall. She'd fallen asleep on it numerous times with a book still in her hand, and woken up with pain in every joint, but she still couldn't bring herself to get rid of it. It was one of the first things she'd bought when she got her own place after her undergraduate degree. It had been second-hand and pretty worn even back then, but it was hers. It had seen her through her masters, her PhD, a couple of break-ups, and many, many job applications. It was almost a historical object in itself.

Gathering the energy to detach herself from her front door, a still dazed Paige wandered into the kitchen to make a cup of tea. Her mum would always tell her tea fixed everything, and while she wasn't sure it actually worked, she found the nostalgia comforting. Her cat Sooty stretched lazily on the sofa, jumped down, and followed her into the kitchen purring. His purrs were so loud they echoed around the tiled room. Paige filled up his food bowl and gave him some scratches behind the ears. He licked her hand in appreciation before digging in to his dinner. The kettle clicked off and Paige poured the water, leaving the chamomile tea bag in the cup and taking the whole thing with her back to the living room. She curled up under a blanket on the sofa and put something mindless on the television; her eyes still glazed over. Her brain slowly started re-booting. She had coped just fine before Maya came into her life. She had coped when Maya went travelling after they graduated. She had coped when Maya moved away from the city they both studied in, even though that had been unexpected, too. Logically, she knew she could cope with this. She just wasn't sure how.

As if psychic, her phone vibrated in her pocket - it was a text from Maya.

'How're you doing, lovely?'

'OK,' she messaged back. *'Calmer now.'*

'Do you need me to come over? I'm still in the city...'

'No, it's OK, thank you though. I really am happy for you, Maya. I'll speak to you tomorrow.'

'OK, lovely. Sleep well xxx'

Paige put her phone face down on the table and tried to focus on the television; a random nature documentary about penguins. But it didn't take long for her brain to wander back to their conversation at the pub. Maybe trying to make new friends wouldn't be such a bad idea, especially with the prospect of Maya moving away for a while. Sooty interrupted her thoughts by jumping on her lap and demanding attention, rubbing his head against her hands.

'Ah-ah! Careful!' she scolded him before putting her tea down on the table, out of his reach. He hadn't paid any notice to her mild telling off and flopped ungracefully down onto her lap with a thud, still purring. 'At least I know you'll never change.'

CHAPTER TWO
Home Comforts

Paige got up early that Saturday morning, as always. She could hear the birds exchanging dawn gossip as she stretched in her driveway. Her run would take her over the top of a nearby hill, gifting her with panoramic views of the forest below. Her whole body felt restless, like each muscle fibre and nerve ending had an itch. She put her earphones in and started her watch. The route she had chosen was a tough ten-kilometre route with a fair bit of incline, but as thoughts of Maya moving away flickered across her mind like a picture book, she picked up the pace.

The well-worn trail gradually thinned as other routes splintered off; each step caused leaves and twigs to brush her calves, and every now and again she would have to duck under a low-hanging branch. Each step took her further away from the university, the city, and life.

Maya had planted a seed in her brain and it had taken root. It had germinated to the point where the vague structure of a book was visible. She had been wondering, hypothetically, who she would write about. There was also the small issue of a novel being a very different style of writing compared to that of academia, her native tongue. She didn't know if she was actually capable of creative writing.

Her chest tightened slightly as she headed towards the final and steepest descent. It seemed like every step she took sent small stones tumbling down the trail, but she did not slow down. Way ahead of her personal best, the adrenaline rushed through her veins, allowing her to push on despite the burning in her legs. Suddenly, a brown rabbit jumped out of the bushes right into her path. Avoiding it broke her stride and destroyed her concentration. Her foot slipped on a particularly muddy patch of ground. She stumbled sideways, then toppled forward, limbs flailing as she desperately tried to stay upright to no avail. Knees, arms, and face all hit the rough and muddy ground as she slid downward.

Eventually her crumpled body came to a stop.

'Damn it!' she shouted, lifting her head out of the mud. A new personal best had been within reach!

She sat up gingerly, carefully scanning each limb for any obvious deformities or severe bleeding. Nothing seemed sprained or broken, she just had minor cuts and grazes. 'Screw it,' she thought, scrambling to her feet. She took a few exploratory steps before launching herself back into her run at an even faster pace than before, ignoring the dull throbbing that seemed to have overtaken every inch of her body. One wayward rabbit was not going to deny her a personal best.

The ground began levelling out for the final stretch and Paige started sprinting. Her lungs desperately tried to suck in more air, as if that would put out the fire that now burned inside them. It only fuelled it. She was so close to the end. Fifty metres to go. Twenty. Ten…

She slammed her fingers down on the stop button of her watch as she passed her finish line, chest heaving and legs about to give way. Her vision drifted in and out of focus as she tried to read the digits on her watch. Vindication! She sat down on the grass and interlaced her fingers behind her head, fighting to inhale as much oxygen as she could. She had beaten her personal best by over forty seconds. That feeling of triumph was worth the scrapes and inevitable bruises that would appear in the next few days.

Eventually, Paige felt she had enough control of her limbs to drag herself to her feet and begin the short walk back to her house, allowing her muscles to cool down from the run. Her legs complained painfully that she had been sitting down for too long and the lactic acid hadn't been able to clear. She kept going, motivated by the thought of a well-earned shower - and the need to find some antiseptic cream and plasters.

That afternoon, Paige went to her favourite coffee shop. The barista did a double take when Paige got to the counter. She could understand why - she had a graze on her forehead, another above her left eye, and a cut on her cheek. She had bandaged her left forearm, wrist, and palm in an effort to keep the extensive grazes there clean.

'What...' he said, eyes flicking between her face and her arm, 'what can I get you?'

'A pot of tea, please,' she responded chirpily. 'Could you possibly bring the tray over for me, please? Because, y'know...' she trailed off, gesturing with her bandaged arm. The last thing she needed was to spill scalding hot tea on the broken skin.

'Y-yes, yes, of course,' he stammered sheepishly, not making eye contact.

Paige smiled, paid, and made her way to her usual corner. The soft armchair gave her clear views of both the entrance and the counter, and she could see out of the front windows to the street. From this vantage point she could observe people coming and going. For example, the two people who had just walked in. Paige guessed they were siblings by their similar features and the playful way the woman nudged the man's arm.

TAYLOR

'Ow! That hurt!' the man said teasingly. 'You *clearly* don't know your own strength, Taylor!'

'Yeah, yeah,' Taylor replied. 'Whatever, Dylan. You give as good as you get.' She emphasised her point with a slight shove.

'What do you want to drink?' Dylan asked. 'I'm buying, it's the least I can do for you helping me move this weekend.'

'A mocha would be great, thanks. And one of those little cakes would express your gratefulness too, a *sweet* thank you to your big sister…'

Dylan rolled his eyes. 'You're only nine minutes older than me!' he protested. 'And your puns are awful.'

'No they're not, and don't you forget it, little bro,' Taylor said, smirking and dodging past him. 'I'll go and get us a table.'

Taylor weaved her way between the chairs to a table by

the back wall. The coffee shop furniture was mainly plush cotton and real wood chairs, with a few dark red sofas around the edges of the room. The red fabric seemed richer when framed by the dark tones of the stained oak. She chose a particularly soft-looking sofa and sank into it gratefully, muscles aching from lifting boxes all day. The smell of coffee filled the air as she leant further back into the chair, closing her eyes and resting for what felt like the first time in an age. Between her prep work for the start of term, and helping Dylan move into a student flat on the third floor of a building with no lift, she felt like she hadn't slept in days.

The clunk of the tray as Dylan placed it on the table caused her to open her eyes again, just in time to see the woman in the corner looking away. Had she been staring at her? Taylor shook her head. She was tired, probably just being paranoid.

'I asked for the biggest slices of the chocolaty-est cake they had,' Dylan said proudly, handing her the plate and a fork. 'I don't understand how you can drink and eat chocolate at the same time.' Dylan had opted for a plain cappuccino, his first sip giving him a foamy moustache where the skin before had been bare. Taylor chuckled and wiped her own top lip meaningfully. Dylan got the hint and applied a napkin.

'When do your lectures start?' Taylor asked in a faux nonchalant way.

'Oh, don't start now,' Dylan said, his jovial expression slipping slightly.

'What do you mean?' she questioned with feigned ignorance.

'I don't need you keeping an eye on me, or hounding me, or nagging me about whether I've made any friends yet like it's my first day of school. Mum and Dad are already doing that. I'll be fine, Lor, you don't need to worry.'

'I'm your sister. I always worry! But OK, I'll try and back off a bit. You'd better not shirk on our lunch dates though, just like when we both lived at home? I've been looking forward to those.'

'I know, me too. I won't, I promise.'

Taylor glanced past her brother's ear at the woman in the corner. This time she was sure she'd caught her looking. Maybe the strange woman was just daydreaming in their direction. She was quite an unusual sight, shoes kicked off and legs tucked underneath her on the chair, peering over a laptop screen with a pot of tea nearby. She looked a little like a hermit who had been transplanted into a coffee shop and the shock hadn't quite worn off yet. A very accident-prone hermit, Taylor thought as her eyes roamed between the various injuries present on the woman. And that was just the ones she could see; Taylor was sure there would be more elsewhere.

Dylan noticed her slight distraction and snapped his head around to look, seemingly scared of missing out.

'What're we looking at?' he said loudly.

'Shhhhhhh!' Taylor hushed, smacking his arm. 'Don't be so obvious!'

'Oh, OK,' Dylan said, turning back around. 'Is it the chick with the messed-up face you're staring at?'

'No… she's the one who's been staring at me. Or at least I think she has.'

'Maybe she likes you?'

'Ha, don't be stupid'

'OK then,' Dylan said, changing tack, 'how about…' And with that he did the most over dramatic yawn and stretch she had ever seen, during which he turned around to gawk at this poor woman. 'She works for MI5 and you're under surveillance. Her face got all busted up on her last mission, so they've assigned her something more mundane, such as following you around.'

'Oh, ha ha!'

'You should go talk to her. She's your type, right? Brunette, athletic, slightly crazy-looking...' The last bit Dylan said tentatively, already recoiling from the expected retort from his sister.

'Too soon, dude,' she scolded, glaring at him.

'OK, OK' he held his hand up in apology. 'But you should still go talk to her. Get back on the horse, or whatever they say.'

'I've got enough going on, like helping my muppet of a brother move to a new city.'

'Hey! I'm the muppet of a brother who got accepted into one of the best journalism schools in the country, thank you very much. If you're going to insult me, at least use my full title.'

Taylor rolled her eyes. He was right though. The university where she worked, and at which he was now a student, had an exemplary School of Journalism. She was so proud of him when he had gotten accepted. She had offered for him to come and live with her as soon as he got his acceptance letter, supposedly to make life easier for him - but really, she just wanted to keep an eye on him. He had politely declined her offer for that exact reason. He didn't need his sister 'cramping his style', apparently. The engineering building wasn't far from the journalism department though, so they could easily have lunch together, unless her teaching schedule was too hectic. Taylor looked across at her brother and smiled. He was looking so much healthier than he had last year. His eyes had that sparkle again, rather than that sunken, hopeless look. His clothes fitted him now rather than hanging off him. But she still worried.

'We should probably head off soon,' he said, taking another gulp of his coffee. 'Those boxes aren't going to unpack themselves!'

'You're on your own with that one, I have plans tonight,' Taylor replied.

'Ooooooh, does Taylor have a date?'

'Yep, a date I've been looking forward to all week. I'm spending some quality time with Mr Ben and his friend Jerry, and we're viewing an amazing cultural phenomenon known as a televised baking competition. You should try it some time!' She laughed. 'Come on, I'll drive you back.'

'If you haven't got a date, that means I can slip the MI5 agent your number, right?' Dylan teased as they stood up.

'Not if you want to retain the ability to have children.'

Taylor had been lecturing in the engineering department for a few years now. She had previously worked in the industry, but it always felt like something was missing. She would read about new technological advances a few weeks or months after they were published, and it was like she was being left behind. When one of her old lecturers, now a professor at her current university, contacted her telling her about a new, fully funded PhD project he was putting together, she jumped at the chance to return to university. The research was on adapting existing mechanical engineering solutions so they could be employed in areas of extreme poverty with the resources they had available. Part of her contract required she teach for a manageable number of hours a week, but her teaching commitments were fast taking over, and she was falling behind on her research.

Taylor helped Dylan carry the last few bits from her car up the three flights of stairs that felt all too familiar now. He was sharing with a few other people, none of whom had moved in yet. The university tended to house the mature students together, so she at least knew they would all be in the same boat. The worn furniture looked odd in Dylan's shared living room, like it had never really belonged there in the first place. They'd done their best to make his bedroom feel more homely, with photographs of their family adorning the walls, blankets on the bed, and even a small plant on one of the shelves. The slightly flickering fluorescent light didn't do the whole set-up any favours.

'Are you *sure* you don't want to come and live with me?' Taylor said, glancing around the room as she put the box she was carrying down on his desk. 'I mean...' She trailed off. She didn't want to criticise his new home too aggressively, but even he couldn't pretend it was a comfortable place to live.

'I'm sure. This will do me good. And it's a hell of a lot better than The Grove was...'

'That is true. Well, let me know if you need anything, OK? I'm always at the other end of the phone.'

'I know. You ring me often enough that it's not something I could easily forget.'

Taylor embraced her brother in a tight hug, and whispered in his ear, 'I love you and I am so proud of you, Dyl.'

'Thanks, Taylor.'

They both pulled back and tried to pretend their eyes weren't watering slightly.

'Well, I'd best be off. I have a fun day of planning tomorrow, and I can't keep Mr Ben and his friend Jerry waiting!'

Taylor slipped out of the front door, superstitiously crossing her fingers as she stepped over the threshold. This had to go well for him. It had to.

The drive back to her house took around fifteen minutes. The roads were fairly quiet at that time on a Saturday evening. She only passed a few groups of drunk students, most of them already inside the various clubs and bars hosting freshers' events in preparation for the start of term. She wondered what kind of students she would get this year. She'd been lucky so far and not had any major problems with any of her undergraduates. She'd heard of other faculty members having to report students for lack of attendance or turning up to class inebriated, and even less-than-gently suggest a student left the course before they were failed.

Typically, it started raining just as Taylor pulled into her street. She lived in an average-sized terraced house close enough to the university to give her a very short commute, but far enough away that she wasn't surrounded by students. Most of the people living on the street also rented, but there were several families that she recognised by face, even if she didn't know their names. She always waved to the children when they passed her window.

She hadn't spent a fortune on furnishing her house. Going back to university to teach and do a PhD had been quite a step down salary-wise so she had carefully saved as much as she could from her last few pay cheques, and wasn't about to blow it all on furniture. Her previous accommodation had come fully furnished, so she owned very little herself. It had made her multiple moves over the last few years easier, but it also meant that the various flats and houses she lived in never really felt like home, just somewhere she was passing through. Maybe this time would be different, especially now Dylan was here too. Maybe.

CHAPTER THREE
Climbing the Walls

'Pleeeeeeeeeease!' Dylan pleaded over the phone, making his voice extra whiny just for the benefit of his sister.

'I told you, I have lesson planning to do today,' Taylor said as she ruffled through some of the papers spread all over her desk. Truthfully, she was quite well prepared for this coming term, but she wanted to get a few extra planning hours in. She hoped that if she was extra prepared, it might allow her more time to work on her actual research.

'I know, but I'm climbing the walls here. Haha, geddit? Climbing the walls?'

'Oh, very funny. If this whole journalism thing doesn't work out for you, you could go on the road with your one-man show.'

'It's Sunday, the buses are awful on Sundays. It'd do you good to get out the house too. It'd be just like when we were kids, going to the centre and scaring Mum and Dad half to death with how high the climbing walls were.'

Taylor didn't say anything, but Dylan must have known he was wearing her down. Some of their favourite childhood memories were of their time spent at the local climbing centre. They would race each other up difficult routes, seemingly barely touching the holds. Or they'd dangle precariously from overhangs before nailing some difficult move or falling several metres before the rope caught them, the other twin on the other end of the belay, laughing.

'Fine.' Taylor conceded. 'But you're going to have to work out the bus schedule eventually, I can't do this every week. I'll pick you up around one?' She pulled the phone away from her ear as her brother shouted down the line at her with glee, before hanging up, shaking her head. It was years since she had been climbing. She wasn't even sure where her gear was - probably in one of the many still-packed boxes in the spare room. 'Maybe it's a good thing Dyl didn't move in,' she thought as she waded through the cardboard mountains trying to find the one containing her sports equipment. 'Sorting through this lot would've taken ages.'

Taylor manoeuvred herself around a particularly precarious tower, catching sight of the one she was searching for. Grabbing her keys out of her pocket, she used her parents' house key to slice through the packing tape on the box. The layer of dust that had formed on the top of it made her cough as she pulled it open. A photo of her and her brother was lying on the top, both with winner's medals around their necks. They had won their county's under-sixteen categories in indoor climbing that year. Their happy faces beamed out of the picture. She could still feel her brother grabbing her hand and thrusting it into the air as they posed for the picture their parents insisted on taking. Taylor smiled as she put the picture aside, only to find the medals underneath. Dylan hadn't taken his with him when he moved out of their parents' house, and Taylor had grabbed it when it was at risk of being thrown out in the process of her parents having a clear out. She picked up the medals and gently ran her finger over the engravings. The smell of chalk and sweat filled her mind as she put the medals aside with the picture. Her old harness stared up at her from the box. Her half open chalk bag had coated it with a fine layer of white powder, as if it was a cake that had been recently decorated. She checked her watch; she had a couple of hours before she needed to pick Dylan up. Grabbing the rest of her climbing gear she left the room, leaving the medals and photograph out to bathe in the sunlight they hadn't seen for many years.

Taylor dropped her gear off by the front door and

returned to the living room. Her old laptop was complaining loudly under the pressure of having multiple programs open. She tucked her feet under her and picked up her coffee mug, sipping the now tepid liquid. Staring at the computer screen all morning hadn't helped her come up with a solution for her scheduling dilemma. Her contract only required her to teach for eight hours a week, which on paper left plenty of time for research. But the preparatory work needed for those teaching hours easily took the same amount of time again. She closed the laptop in resignation. The living room, which was sparsely furnished, could have done with a good clean, and there was a sink full of dishes in the kitchen begging to be washed. Taylor sighed and reached for a nearby blanket, pulling it all the way up to her chin and tucking her legs up in front of her. She leant back and closed her eyes, thinking about her life before she came back to university. Out in industry she could get her hands dirty. While the work was exhausting, there was a sense of satisfaction in coming home covered in grease, aching from head to toe, knowing that you had created something from nothing.

The loud ring of her phone woke her up with a start. Bleary-eyed, Taylor picked it up and fumbled for the answer button.

'Hello?' she said, mildly confused.

'I thought you were picking me up at one?' came Dylan's voice, patient as ever.

'Damn it! Sorry, Dyl, I'll be there in five,' Taylor said, scrambling to her feet and nearly tripping over the blanket that was now coiled around her ankles. She ran up the stairs two at a time and quickly changed into a loose-fitting T-shirt and tracksuit bottoms, before bolting back down the stairs, grabbing her harness and climbing shoes on the way out.

To say the climbing centre was vast would be an understatement, thought Taylor. The cavernous room was filled with colour, like a toddler had been let loose in an art shop. Each wall was decorated in a different theme, like volcanoes or lightning, with different climbing features to negotiate. The main sources of light were fluorescent strip lights that ran around the ceiling like train tracks, intersected by the high rope course walkways. In one corner there was a bouldering area; the walls there were much lower, only about four metres high, and surrounded by crash mats. When the twins walked in their eyes were immediately drawn upwards to the massive triple overhang which faced the entrance to the climbing room. There were no ropes on it currently; the only way to climb it would be a lead climb. There was a young girl and her dad at the bottom of this wall now, the dad double checking the daughter's harness before letting her set off. The girl climbed slowly and methodically, each re-positioning of a hand or foot well thought out and cleanly executed. She ensured she had a solid grip on the wall before reaching down for her rope and clipping it in to the evenly spaced carabiners.

On a wall to their right the twins could see a teenage boy utilising the auto-belay, scampering up the wall hastily and falling off with even more speed, laughing all the way down, knowing the auto-belay would guide him gently to the floor. In the back right corner there was a group of people who seemed to be climbing together. The people on belay were chatting amongst themselves while carefully watching their charges ascend the wall.

Much to Taylor's surprise, a well-bandaged arm on a belay stood out; it was the woman from the cafe. Her hair was tied back in a small bun, her vest top revealing that Taylor had been right about there being more bruises. You could see the purple marks on her shoulder, collar bone, and the top of her arm. She was wearing leggings which perfectly outlined the shape of her legs.

'...Earth to Taylor...' Dylan said, tapping Taylor on the arm, snapping her out of her reverie.

'Sorry, what?'

'I was saying, shall we go introduce ourselves?'

Taylor swallowed hard, her throat suddenly and inexplicably dry.

'Sure. You go first?' she said, half offering and half pleading.

'It's not like you to be shy, Lor?' Dylan said questioningly as he looked over at his sister, who looked slightly flushed.

'I know, but this is going to be your club, not mine. I'm just here playing taxi.' Just then the secret agent glanced over at them and smiled, before focusing back on her climber.

'Uh huh' Dylan said knowingly under his breath. They made their way over to the group, Taylor walking half a step behind her brother. They waited patiently, watching the climbers already on the wall.

'Good job, Danny!' the secret agent said as her climber topped out. 'Ready when you are,' she informed him, at which point he started bouncing down the wall.

'Now that Danny's done showing off... Hi, my name's

Paige. Are you new to the club?'

'Yeah, I've just moved to the area and my sister hasn't climbed in a while. I'm Dylan Watkins, this is Taylor, my sister.'

'Nice to meet you,' Paige said, offering her hand in a rather formal manner. Dylan shook it clumsily, whereas Taylor took her hand gently, as if she expected an electric shock.

'Have we met before?' Paige asked, staring slightly.

'You were in the coffee shop yesterday. I wouldn't normally have remembered but you kind of stood out…'

'Ah, yeah. This would be my excuse for not climbing today. Still a bit sore. If you haven't climbed in a while, maybe I can give you a refresher?'

'Oh no, it's OK, I'm only here to belay Dylan really, I don't have much time to climb nowadays.'

'OK,' Paige shrugged. 'Dylan, do you need a refresher?' she asked innocently. Dylan stared a couple of seconds too long at his sister, before turning his attention to Paige.

'No, I'm OK, thanks, I climbed quite regularly back home.'

'OK then, I'll let you two get on with it. I'm sure the rest of the guys will introduce themselves when they get a chance,' Paige said, before turning back to the wall where a different climber had tied into her belay. She checked his knot before allowing him to set off.

Taylor and Dylan made their way to a free wall near the group. Dylan introduced himself to one of the other people belaying while setting up his own, giving Taylor little choice about whether she was going to climb today or not. She dipped her hands into her chalk bag and coated her palms with the white powder; they were sweating more than one would expect in the vast, chilly space. As a result, she chose one of the easier routes on the wall, dragging Dylan's attention away from the pretty redhead he had been talking to.

'If you could concentrate long enough not to kill me, I'd appreciate it...' Taylor said to him before setting off. The holds were rough against her hands. The calluses she'd formed climbing as a teenager were long gone, and her grip was nowhere near as strong as she remembered. But a few metres off the ground she remembered why she used to love climbing so much. It was just her against the wall. She became hyper-aware of her own body and its location relative to the holds around her. Looking up she planned her route and pushed on, feeling a little bit more confident with every move. It wasn't long before she was approaching the top. She could no longer hear the people below her or anyone else in the room. The feeling of getting both hands on the topmost hold of a climbing wall for the first time in years was all-consuming.

Quietly triumphant, she shouted down to Dylan. 'Ready?' she said, looking down over her shoulder at her brother, who had the biggest grin on his face.

'Ready!' he hollered back. Taylor slowly walked herself down the wall, her face aching slightly from beaming.

'That was great!' she said to Dylan as she reached the bottom.

'See? I told you you'd enjoy it.' He said, giving her a one-armed hug and making her tumble slightly; he hadn't given her quite enough slack for her to take her own weight fully, so the small contact was enough to make her spin on the rope. 'Oops! Sorry!' he said, letting out more slack and helping Taylor regain her balance. Taylor had only just managed to untie herself when Dylan snatched the rope out of her hand and began tying in, throwing the belay device vaguely in her direction.

'My turn!' he exclaimed eagerly.

Taylor had just finished clipping in when a pair of hands came out of nowhere to check her harness.

'What the -' Taylor exclaimed, registering the bandaged arm and the dark hazel eyes within a millisecond of each other.

'You said you were out of practice,' Paige said, without further explanation or apology. Taylor just stared. 'You're good to go.'

Dylan smirked as he looked quickly between Paige and his sister. She just glared at him. He quickly busied himself by starting his ascent of the wall. It took all of Taylor's willpower to keep her eyes on her brother, and not glance at the woman who was standing that bit too close behind her. Thankfully, Dylan provided a welcome distraction. He had of course chosen the most difficult route on the wall and kept attempting quite challenging dynamic moves, often only just making them. Each time he leapt or threw himself at the next hold, Taylor braced, ready to catch him if he fell.

'He is quite… fearless, isn't he?' Paige said, her words spoken almost directly into Taylor's ear. Taylor shivered slightly.

'Yes, well, Dylan isn't one to do things half-heartedly,' Taylor laughed awkwardly, just as Dylan topped out on the route. She still wasn't used to women swooning over her brother.

'Woo-hoo!' he shouted, bouncing sideways off the wall with his arms outstretched above his head, legs kicking back and forth. He ended up bouncing off the holds and features on the way down, but he didn't seem to care.

'Muppet,' Taylor grumbled as Dylan landed on the floor on his backside, still celebrating.

Paige had slipped away unnoticed, and was tying back in to a different wall to belay someone else. Taylor couldn't help staring, as she had been unable to get any kind of read on her. Dylan followed her gaze, rolled his eyes, and walked towards Paige, whispering as he passed his sister.

'Well, if you're not going to talk to her…'

'No, don't!' Taylor said, trying to grab him. But he twisted out of her reach with a cheeky grin. There was nothing she could do as she watched her brother waltz over to the mysterious woman.

'Hey, Paige. As I'm new to the area, I was wondering if you'd be willing to show me around?' he said sweetly.

'Why? Don't you have maps on your phone?' she asked, deadpan.

'Ha, yeah, I do,' he acknowledged, scratching the back of his head 'but it's not quite the same as local knowledge, is it?' he said. 'I mean, my sister has lived here for a while but I'm sure you could show us –'

'Sorry, I'm rather busy at the moment' Paige answered, not really paying attention. She turned her back towards him to focus on her climber, making it clear that the conversation was over. Dylan walked slowly back towards Taylor.

'Well, I tried,' he shrugged.

'Tried to scare her off, you mean? You appear to have succeeded.'

'Well, maybe you should try talking to hot women rather than relying on your brother to be your wingman?'

'I didn't *ask* –'

'I know I know, but you haven't even been on a date since you and she-who-must-not-be-named broke up'

'Yeah? Well, I've had other priorities,' Taylor said pointedly. Dylan flushed red and looked sheepish. 'Let's just climb.'

CHAPTER FOUR
Paige's City Tours

PAIGE

A few weeks later university life was in full swing. The previously quiet corridors were filled with chatting students and slowly fraying faculty. Paige stood at the front of the lecture hall and over a hundred faces stared back at her; a sea with eyes. That morning's text conversation with Maya was still playing on her mind. Maya had nagged her once more about trying to make more friends, reminding her yet again that she was moving away soon. As if Paige needed reminding. The debate had continued when Maya asked about Paige's weekend plans, and Paige had said running and reading, the same as usual. She could almost sense Maya pulling her hair out on the other end of the line.

'Any questions?' Paige asked, bringing herself back to the present. The class had already started packing away their things and getting to their feet, the noise almost drowning out her voice. Paige gave up. It was only their third week of university and as she had just pumped their brains full of facts and dates, she doubted they could phrase a question coherently even if they wanted to. So she joined them in packing up and went back to her office. It hadn't changed much in the last few weeks - there were still books threatening to fall on someone's head and papers spread all over the floor - but the whiteboard that hung above the beanbag had been replaced by a series of Post-it notes, arranged haphazardly in a spreadsheet-like table made of brightly coloured tape. It was the skeleton of her novel idea. Or ideas. She still hadn't decided exactly what, and more importantly, who she was going to write about yet. She grabbed her rucksack and peered inside, only to discover she had forgotten her lunch.

'Oh, crap,' she sighed, resigning herself to braving the cafe at lunch time. Her stomach rumbled, a war cry. Paige closed her eyes and gathered herself, then marched determinedly out of her office. There were a few people already waiting for the lift, so she decided to take the stairs.

The cafe was packed by the time Paige got there. Dozens of students milling around, queuing at the tills, and sitting in groups. She watched from afar. The hair-netted cafeteria workers were dishing out the warm food as fast as they could, but the queue still snaked back on itself and into the hallway. Digging out her headphones Paige decided to wait the horde out. There was a group of soft chairs not far away, so she nestled there and observed the throng. It was easy to identify the new students; they took longer than the others to order their food, still not certain of all the options the cafe had to offer. The older students were nowhere to be seen; they had the sense to bring their own lunch or visit the cafe at a quieter time. Paige did not have that luxury as her schedule for the day was packed with teaching, meetings, and tutoring. Part of her duties involved being a personal tutor for the postgraduate students. She had yet to meet all of this year's charges, though her schedule was filling up rapidly. Paige was staring vaguely in the direction of the cafe when a hand touched her on the shoulder. It felt like she had been electrocuted. She simultaneously whipped her earphones out and jumped to her feet.

'Oh er - hi - sorry, I didn't mean to make you jump' Taylor apologised, taking a half step backwards.

'No problem, though for future reference I don't appreciate being crept up on.'

'Noted,' Taylor said, smiling. Paige's face remained expressionless. She'd seen the woman at climbing a couple more times since they'd first met, but they hadn't spoken. She wasn't entirely sure why she was making the effort to speak her now.

'I'm meeting Dylan for lunch,' Taylor offered without prompting.

'In a university cafe?'

'Yes. This is the Silverton building, isn't it? Journalism?' Taylor said, looking around, as if hoping for some kind of sign that she was in the right place. Or maybe she was just looking for an escape.

'Yes, it is,' Paige reassured her.

'Oh, OK. Good. Dylan has just started here.'

'Isn't he a bit old to be an undergraduate?'

'Ha, yeah, he is a bit older than most of his peers. It was a last-minute calling. Do you study here?'

'I teach History.'

'Ah, a sister in arms,' Taylor said with a slight nod, before explaining. 'I teach Engineering.'

'At this university?'

'Yes, for a couple of years now. Part of my PhD contract.'

Paige attempted a smile, not quite knowing how to respond. The women stood in silence, occasionally making eye contact before smiling awkwardly and looking away.

Paige stole glances at her companion when she could, making mental notes on various aspects of her appearance. She was a brunette like Paige, but a darker shade, and wore her hair much longer than Paige would have been able to tolerate. She didn't dress like most of the lecturers Paige knew either. Most of them wore smart suits or dresses, or if they were feeling particularly daring, just smart trousers and a shirt. Taylor was wearing jeans and what looked like a band T-shirt. She didn't appear to be wearing any make up but did have her ears pierced in multiple places.

'How is your arm doing now?' Taylor asked, breaking the silence.

'Oh, much better thank you. No bandage anymore,' Paige answered, offering her arm for inspection. Taylor's gaze flicked up to her face, at the traces of the cut and grazes that were still discernible. She opened her mouth to speak again just as Dylan turned up.

'Hey, Lor,' he said, wrapping his sister up in a bear hug. 'Dr Spencer,' he nodded politely at Paige.

'The formality is unnecessary,' Paige said by way of acknowledgment. She'd spoken to Dylan at most of the climbing sessions held over the last few weeks, and ever since she'd let slip her official title, he had made a point of using it whenever he could.

'Shall we go?' Dylan said, turning to Taylor, barely hiding the laugh on his face.

'You don't want to eat here?' she asked, confused.

'Err, no?' he said, gesturing sarcastically towards the packed cafeteria.

'Right, yeah,' she replied, as they started walking away. They'd gone about ten metres before Taylor stopped. Turning back around, but hesitating. Dylan watched her for a few seconds before rolling his eyes.

'Paige, would you like to join us for lunch?' he asked politely.

'No thank you,' she said without looking at them, still watching the swathe of students in the cafeteria. Dylan looked at his sister and gave a slight shrug, as if to say 'Sorry, I tried'.

They were about to walk away when Paige continued, 'If you still would like someone to show you around, I know a few places which aren't quite as... busy' she said pointedly.

'That'd be great! Here...' he said, practically running back towards her, digging in his pocket. 'Can you put your number in my phone?'

Paige took his phone and created a new contact for herself, heart-rate increasing and chest tightening. She wasn't used to giving strange men her number.

'There you go,' she said, handing the phone back to him.

'Thanks! See you soon, then, I guess?' he said happily.

'Sure,' she replied, turning her attention back to the cafe. It had shown no signs of getting quieter.

Paige had let Maya get under her skin, talking about needing to make new friends and how she was at risk of becoming a hermit once Maya moved to the other side of the world. She barely knew this guy, yet here she was, agreeing to 'show him around'. She hoped that wasn't another double entendre she wasn't aware of.

Paige made it back into her office with a sandwich and some crisps, but before she tucked in, she decided to call Maya.

'Hey, lovely, what's wrong? What's happened?'

'Nothing's wrong?'

'But you're calling me. You never call me.'

'Oh. Well. It appears I am trying lots of new things today then.'

'Oh?'

'Remember that guy at climbing I told you about? I just offered to "show him around".'

'That's great, honey! Well done!'

'Please don't be patronising, Maya.'

'I'm not being patronising, lovely, I'm genuinely happy for you. You're trying something new.'

'Well, yes, but anyway, I was hoping you could come along. I promised I would show him some places that aren't frequented entirely by students, but I don't want him to get the wrong idea.'

'Hmmm…' Maya said. Paige could hear the scroll of a mouse wheel in the background. 'I can do Friday?' she suggested.

'Sure. I'll run that past him.'

'OK, great. Look, lovely, I've got to go, I was just going into a meeting when you called. Text me later?'

'OK. Bye,' Paige said before hanging up. She leant back in her chair and covered her face with her hands. She really hoped she wasn't making a mistake.

Friday came around all too quickly for Paige, who had experienced increasing levels of anxiety as the days went on. She had seen the twins at climbing in the interim and made more of an effort to be sociable with them. But at climbing, like at work, she had faith in her competence. She didn't expect to win a history prize or become a world champion climber, but there were rules and expectations that she understood and could easily follow in both those scenarios. Spending time with a person she just met in an effort to make a new friend wasn't something she had really done since she was a child. Maya hadn't given her a choice in the matter; they were going to become friends whether Paige wanted to or not, so that didn't count.

Paige decided the easiest way to show Dylan around was to walk between a few of her favourite haunts. The coffee shop he already knew about as he had been there with his sister, but there was also a small cafe tucked up a side street and a pastry shop not much further along. It wasn't the quietness of the pastry shop that warranted making it a stop on the tour, but because their bread and pastries were so good that there was often a queue out the door, even at seven in the morning. The last stop of the tour was both Maya and Paige's favourite pub. Maya was already there when Dylan and Paige walked in.

'Hi, lovely,' Maya said, standing up to hug her friend. Paige squeezed her back, tighter than usual, before sliding past her to sit in the corner. Paige tried watching Dylan's reaction to see if any kind of disappointment registered on his face, but if it did she either she missed it or he did a very good job of hiding it.

'After a wonderful evening walking around the city it seems only fair that I get the drinks in. What'll you have?' he said, looking at Paige.

'A gin and tonic, please,' she said, closing her handbag and placing it under the table.

'And for the lovely lady?' Dylan said, looking at Maya. Maya pointedly looked between Paige and Dylan, slightly jerking her head in his direction.

'Oh, sorry! Dylan, this is my best friend Maya. Maya, this is Dylan, who I told you about.'

'Should I be worried?' Dylan said, only half joking.

'No, you're OK,' Maya said. 'I'll just have a shandy, I'm driving,' she explained, picking her car keys off the table and jingling them at him.

Dylan was about to go and order the drinks when Paige suggested to Maya, 'Why don't you stay at mine tonight? Have you got anywhere you need to be tomorrow morning?'

'Eh... nowhere that can't be re-arranged.' She pondered for a few seconds. 'Twist my arm, why don't you. In that case, I'll have a whiskey and coke, s'il-vous plait.'

'Coming right up!'

Both women watched him head to the bar, making sure he was out of earshot.

'So, he seems nice,' Maya observed. 'Do you like him?'

'Yes, he seems quite fun to have around. Sometimes it goes too far and becomes silliness, though.'

'A bit of silliness never hurt anyone, Spence.'

'I know a fourteenth-century -'

'I know, I know, some historical muppet at some point in time somewhere proves you're right and I'm wrong,' Maya said in good humour. Paige just laughed.

The wait at the bar was longer than usual on account of it being a Friday night. There were many suits dotted around the room who had loosened their ties, or shed them all together. There were a couple of groups that looked like parents visiting their offspring; offspring who had the sense to take them somewhere off the beaten track, rather than somewhere their usual revelry might be revealed. The jukebox was humming out some sixties classic and the fire was roaring away, doing a duet with the music as it crackled and burned. Paige relaxed more into her seat, less anxious in familiar territory.

The bell above the door chimed as it opened, causing a cold draught to dart around their ankles. The person who came in was so well wrapped up that their eyes were barely visible from under the hat, scarf, and coat. They briefly scanned the room before clearly recognising someone and making a beeline for them. Paige was surprised when the person they headed towards was Dylan, and it quickly became clear, as woollen items were removed, that the cocooned figure was Taylor. Dylan and Taylor hugged, with Dylan leaving his arm around her shoulder before putting in an extra order for her drink.

'Girlfriend?' Maya questioned, without taking her eyes off the pair.

'Sister,' Paige said, causing Maya to sit up a little straighter and start peering at the woman.

'Maya!' Paige said, tapping her friend on the leg

'What? Can't a girl be curious?'

'Sure, but at least be subtle about it!'

'Really? You? *You're* telling me to be subtle?' Maya said, laughing.

'Shhh! Here they come,' Paige said, trying to arrange her face into one of nonchalance.

The twins sat down, Taylor opposite Paige and Dylan opposite Maya.

'Maya, this is my twin sister, Taylor,' Dylan said, waving his glass in the vague direction of his sister.

'I always wanted to be a twin!' Maya said. Taylor and Dylan rolled their eyes in unison.

'So have a lot of other people,' Dylan said. 'Taylor was in the area so thought she'd swing by.' He explained, and Paige thought she saw a brief shadow pass behind his eyes.

Paige melted further back into her seat, not really contributing much to the conversation. She watched as Maya flirted outrageously with Dylan and it was more than reciprocated. Maya was laughing a little too loudly, causing Paige to shuffle away slightly out of embarrassment and discomfort. She loved her friend dearly but that shrill laugh in her ear was painful.

Taylor was joining in the conversation a little, but was mainly just observing, seemingly aware that she had gatecrashed her brother's social event. She kept fidgeting with the sleeves of her jumper, alternating between having her hands on the table and on her lap. She also seemed to not quite know where to look and flinched at any excessively loud laughter or drunken exclamation.

'Another round?' Maya said, standing up.

'Sure'

'Yup'

'Yes please.'

'I know Spence will have another gin and tonic, what about you guys?'

'A lemonade would be great, thanks,' Taylor requested.

'Ginger beer for me!' Dylan said jovially.

'You can't *both* be driving!' Maya mused.

'Haha, yeah, something like that,' Taylor said awkwardly, while Dylan suddenly went quiet.

'Alright then, my purse certainly isn't complaining,' Maya joked as she went to the bar. Dylan pulled out his phone and became engrossed in something on the screen, leaving Taylor and Paige to make small talk without the input of their more outgoing companions.

'How long have you known Maya?' Taylor asked.

'Since our first week of university. She assaulted me with some boxes.'

'What?!' Taylor laughed. Paige's stomach jolted. It was the first time she'd heard Taylor laugh properly and it caught her off guard. She tried to push down the butterflies in her stomach. She was there to try and make friends with Dylan, not to hit on his twin sister of all people.

'Let's just say her spatial awareness, or more to the point, who might be occupying those spaces, isn't that great,' Paige continued, her laughter contrasting with the slight blush that had crept across her face.

The rest of the night continued in much the same fashion, with the quartet staying until closing. The landlord knew Paige and Maya from their university days so let them stay until he was done with his closing up routine, giving them a few extra minutes before he had to turf them out into the cold. The four got to their feet, with Maya stumbling slightly as she did so, nearly tripping over the strap of her handbag. Dylan managed to reach out and steady her in time. Maya held on to him all the way from the table to the door outside, with Taylor and Paige walking behind, the former replacing her scarf and hat as she went. The wool was the most brilliant turquoise, Paige noted, the kind of colour you only see at Mediterranean beaches.

The pairs separated outside, the twins going left and the best friends going right. Maya offered hugs to the siblings while Paige just gave a slight wave, before dragging her friend away before she made a fool of herself. Paige subtly interlinked their arms to ensure Maya stayed upright on the journey home. She was also grateful of the extra warmth; the cold air misted in front of their faces as a slight breeze heightened the chill that hung in the air.

'That was fun!' Maya said, giggling.

'Uh huh,' Paige said, not because she didn't agree, but because she was concentrating so hard on keeping them both upright.

'You don't have to worry about that Dylan fella... he's

not into you.'

'How do you know?'

'Because he gave me his number!' Maya giggled again, waving her phone in Paige's face.

'But he gave me his number too? That's how we arranged this,' Paige said, confused.

'Not the same thing, honey,' Maya laughed. 'That Taylor though… you should totally try and get in her pants.'

'They probably wouldn't fit,' Paige responded.

'Not what I meant!' Maya half yelled almost directly into Paige's ear. 'I meant… you should ask her out.'

'OK, Maya,' Paige said, humouring her.

'What? You should! You haven't even been on a date in aaaaaaaages,' Maya said, drawing out the last word in that annoyingly whiny voice that only tipsy people have.

'Whatever you say,' Paige said, fumbling with her keys while trying to keep Maya upright. 'Come on, get inside.' Paige left Maya in the living room while she dug out a spare pair of pyjamas, got her a clean toothbrush, and made sure there weren't too many trip hazards between her room and the bathroom.

'God, sweetie, it looks like a carnival threw up in here,' Maya said from the doorway, just as Paige was placing the pyjamas on the bed. Her normal house guests were a good deal younger than her best friend; the other spare bed was currently covered in washing waiting to be put away, and Paige couldn't be bothered to clear it.

'I'll just go and get you some water and then I'll turn in. Do you need anything else?'

'Nah, I'm good,' Maya said as she fumbled with the buttons on her shirt, not bothering to wait for Paige to leave.

Paige went back downstairs and filled a bottle with water; she didn't trust her friend not to spill a glass everywhere in her inebriated state. Rooting around in the utility room she managed to find some painkillers for Maya's inevitable headache in the morning. By the time she had made it back up the stairs she could already hear her best friend lightly snoring. She tiptoed into the room to place the bottle and tablets on the nightstand. Maya had fallen asleep on top of the duvet, half undressed, so Paige grabbed a blanket and carefully laid it over her, tucking her in. As she left she paused in the doorway to look at the slumbering form. She couldn't imagine what it was going to be like not seeing Maya every other week, which was the pseudo-routine they had fallen into over the last few years. She gently closed the door behind her.

Paige quietly got ready for bed, even though she thought a bomb going off wouldn't wake Maya. She lay down and closed her eyes, expecting sleep to come quickly like it usually did. Instead, Maya's drunken suggestion about Taylor kept playing around in her mind. She got the familiar twinges in her stomach that indicated her anxiety was about to flare up, so she forced herself to think of something else. Her niece and nephew would be coming to stay soon, so she started planning various walks for them to go on, and different fairy tales she could tell them about the forests they were exploring. As she drifted off to sleep her head was filled with thoughts of woodland elves and monsters hiding in felled trees, and happy little children exploring and trying to catch sight of them.

TAYLOR

Taylor had driven Dylan home. She had intended on just dropping him at the door and heading home herself, but he had been conspicuously quiet during the drive, so she invited herself up. Dylan didn't protest, but she wasn't entirely sure she was welcome. She followed him through the first set of doors and up the winding stairs in complete silence. The only sounds were their footsteps on the tiles and the tinkling of the keys in Dylan's hand.

'You alright?' Taylor asked when they finally got to his front door.

'Fine,' Dylan said unconvincingly. But still, he held the door to the flat open for his sister.

'Tea?' he offered politely.

'Have you got any decaf coffee?' she asked. He glared at her in response.

'Of course I do, I always have some knocking around in case you visit. I don't know how you can drink that stuff,' he muttered, turning his back on her and beginning to make the drinks. The white tiles of the kitchen felt cold under the fluorescent light, with the blue walls adding to the chill of the room.

'Are you sure you're OK?' Taylor asked, pressing.

Dylan didn't answer straight away. Instead, he carried on making his tea and her coffee, giving the drinks all his attention. He stirred the sugar into his tea quite vigorously. Once he was finished, he unceremoniously shoved Taylor's mug into her hands, before blurting out, half angry and half hurt, 'You don't trust me, do you?'

'What do you mean?' Taylor asked with feigned ignorance.

'You don't trust me to be able to go into a pub and not drink. Were you really in the area or were you just hovering?' he asked, more aggressively than he meant to.

'I was really in the area,' Taylor said softly. 'I finished late in work, and by the time you told me where you were, I was basically back at my car.' Dylan glared at her some more. 'But yes, I was probably hovering too,' she said quietly. Dylan huffed and put his drink down on the table with force, slopping tea everywhere. He grumpily got some paper towels and began clearing it up.

'I just worry about you, alright! I know how hard you've worked to stay sober, and I want to do everything I can to support you with your sobriety. I don't even drink anymore!'

'I never *asked* you to stop drinking! I never asked you for any of this! You're not my parent, or a support worker, you're my sister! Can't you just be my sister?' he said pleadingly, before trailing off, deflated.

'This *is* me being your sister. Sisters worry. It's in the job description,' she said, trying to appease him.

'I know, just… Stop hovering, OK? I can take care of myself,' Dylan said, calming down.

'OK' Taylor said gently, 'OK, I hear you. Backing off. But I'm always going to worry, OK? I'll always worry about you. I love you.'

'I love you too,' Dylan mumbled under his breath, looking at the floor. Taylor stepped towards him and embraced him tightly. He half-heartedly hugged her back, before returning the squeeze full force and picking her up, making her scream.

'Hey! Just 'cause you're bigger and stronger than me!'

'Brother's prerogative?' he said with a sheepish grin as he put her down. She slapped him lightly on the arm while smiling. There was that pain in the arse she knew so well.

The siblings said their goodbyes and Taylor let herself out, leaving Dylan by the sink washing up the mugs they had just used. Listening to the echoes of her footsteps down the stairs, she re-played what he had said in her head. She didn't want to smother him, but watching him go off the rails last time had broken her heart. Their parents had found an excellent treatment facility for him, but he hadn't exactly gone willingly; they'd given him an ultimatum, it was that or he would be kicked out. She could still feel the hurricane she'd felt in her stomach when the intervention started. She could still remember the look of betrayal on his face when it became her turn to speak. That expression would be etched in her mind for the rest of her life.

Taylor sighed as she got back in her car, watching the light go off through his kitchen window. She needed to let him stand on his own.

CHAPTER FIVE
Helped Back on the Horse

Taylor stood in the entrance to the climbing centre, folding and unfolding her arms. Every now and again she would take a few steps and glance out the door or up at the clock on the wall. Dylan was supposed to have met her here twenty minutes ago, having finally decided to brave public transport. The windows into the climbing area revealed that the climbing club was in full swing. People were pairing up and starting their climbs. She was just starting to worry when Dylan finally replied to her text:

'*Missed the bus sorry, should be there in half an hour. Start without me.*'

Taylor sighed and put her phone away in her bag. Easy for him to say. He'd already learnt the names of everyone in the club and even had in-jokes with some of them. She told herself that the only reason she was there was to make sure Dylan actually managed to get there by bus. Taylor toyed with the idea of relocating to the cafe, but she'd already eaten that evening and didn't want to buy a drink just for the sake of it. Then again, she felt awkward just standing there in the foyer. Thankfully, she remembered the existence of the auto-belay and headed in to the climbing wall. It took a few seconds for her to acclimatise before registering that the auto-belay was in use. A few chairs scattered in one corner provided a safe retreat. She tried wasting time, rummaging in her bag and dawdling when putting her climbing shoes on, but the auto-belay remained occupied. Sitting there alone somehow made her more conscious of her body and her breathing, and the sight lines of everyone else in the room, so she slipped quietly over to the bouldering wall.

The smaller enclosed space felt safer. Several of the bouldering walls sloped inward, providing a greater climbing challenge, and affording Taylor somewhere to hide. There were a couple of young children climbing horizontally around the walls, rather than up one particular route, giggling as they chased each other. Taylor waited for them to pass before surveying a route, mentally going through the moves she would need to use. It was something she used to do a lot as a teenager, and the rusty cogs were slowly grinding into life. The route grading cards normally stuck to the bottom of the wall seemed to be missing She knew she hadn't picked the easiest route, but her steady improvement over the last few weeks gave her confidence to try. Climbing regularly with Dylan meant she was getting some of her old form back. The last part of the climb involved almost crouching on two foot holds, with her hands on a third, and launching herself at a large hold with a concave top, known as a jug. The lip of the jug would allow her to wrap her fingers over it, giving her enough purchase to handle her momentum from the jump.

Happy with her plan, Taylor arranged her limbs into the starting position and began to climb. She had barely got a metre off the ground before questioning her route. She could feel a trickle of sweat between her tense shoulder blades as she hauled herself up to the halfway point, making a mental note to work on her grip strength. She scolded herself almost instantly - she was only here for Dylan, she wasn't going to take up climbing again, so didn't need to work on her grip strength, or anything else for that matter. Steadily she navigated her way to top of the bouldering wall, a slight burning in her forearms telling her she hadn't used her legs enough. Finally, she positioned her hands and feet like she had planned and set up for the dynamic move; a coiled spring ready to launch. Taking one last steadying breath she leapt from her position, up, arms outstretched, towards the giant hand hold at the top of the wall, and just as she made contact with it she realised her terrible mistake. The hold was not, in fact, a jug. It was just a regular hold. For regularly training climbers this would have been no problem; but Taylor's experience alone wasn't enough to make up for how out of practice she was. She scrabbled at the coarse surface, her momentum causing her legs to keep going, swinging her up to an almost horizontal position before her hands slipped off the hold. The top of the wall rapidly grew distant. In a split second Taylor landed on the crash mat, flat on her back. The unmistakable slapping sound her body made as it hit the material drew the attention of everyone in the vicinity. Taylor blinked a few times, trying to re-orientate herself. She had managed to avoid landing directly on her head, which was something. But then she tried breathing, and nothing happened. She tried again. Still nothing. Finally, after what seemed like an eternity she took a giant rasping breath in and began coughing, still lying prone on the crash mat.

'It's OK, you're OK,' a voice said from somewhere above her. She could vaguely see the almost fluorescent green shirts of the staff in her periphery; but it was Paige who had got to her first, kneeling on the crash mat beside her and helping her into a sitting position.

'Easy now,' Paige said gently with her hand carefully

placed on Taylor's back. The dark spots that had started appearing in front of Taylor's eyes were slowly abating as her breathing steadied. Once she had fully regained control of her diaphragm, her brain seemed to divert all its energy into turning her face bright red as she became aware of the crowd of people starting at her. She tried to scramble to her feet, but Paige held fast on to her arm.

'I think we're OK here guys, thank you. I'll call you if we need anything,' she said to the staff members authoritatively. Taylor didn't hear them respond but the fluorescent green in her periphery faded away.

'I wouldn't try standing just yet, give yourself a few minutes.' Taylor felt like her vocal cords were paralysed, so she just nodded in response. The draught of air from her crash landing had caused the lost grading card to reappear, flipped the right way up. Catching sight of it, Taylor groaned. The route she had attempted was much harder than she anticipated.

'Are you hurt?' Paige asked in response to the noise. Taylor shook her head. The slight crimson on her cheeks changed to a deep red.

The rest of the climbers had gone back to their own activities, and Taylor felt the paralysis on her vocal cords ease. 'Sorry, I didn't mean to interrupt your climbing.'

'I know. I was only watching though. Dylan asked if he could climb with me as you weren't coming tonight, so I hadn't partnered up with anyone. I'm glad you were able to make it in the end.'

'Yes,' Taylor said through slightly gritted teeth. 'I'm glad I could make it too.' Paige didn't seem to register her sarcasm. 'I feel OK now' Taylor said, slowly getting to her feet. Paige was still holding on to her arm, and Taylor wasn't sure her close proximity was helping with her balance. She was planning on making small talk just long enough to be polite before leaving, never to return. Paige didn't give her that chance.

'Would you like to do a rope climb? To, err... get back on the horse?' Taylor was unsure if Paige was asking her the question, or questioning her own idiom. 'I'd be happy to belay you. I would have offered sooner but I didn't notice you were here.'

Taylor smiled politely back, but her insides squirmed at the thought of having Paige solely focused on her as she climbed, considering she had just scraped her up off the crash mat.

'How about I belay you?' Taylor suggested. 'You've been letting everyone else climb while your arm healed, it's definitely your turn.'

Paige paused before responding. 'Sure, I'd like that.' She smiled.

The two women unsteadily made their way off the soft crash mats and onto the climbing room floor. They made a quick detour to retrieve Taylor's harness before Paige made a bee-line for a feature in the back right corner. Three walls, heavy with inset features and dark but detailed colour, created a small chimney-like void that went almost to the ceiling. Taylor hadn't tried any of the routes here, but Paige seemed to know it well; she didn't even glance at the grading cards. Taylor knew that the way the walls twisted and undulated meant she would have to be hyper-vigilant when belaying, as she wouldn't always be able to see Paige. Her stomach started twisting into knots. Paige however was already tying in. Taylor watched as Paige's nimble fingers deftly made the figure-of-eight knot popular with climbers. Eventually she unhooked the belay device from the side of her harness, threaded the rope through it, and re-attached it to a loop on the front. She double and triple checked everything was secure.

'Ready?' Paige asked

'R-ready,' Taylor stammered back. Her days of climbing multiple times a week seemed a very long time ago.

Without a second look Paige made her way into the chimney, bracing her hands on the two opposing sides and finding her first foot hold. To Taylor's great surprise, Paige was not using any of the various colour-coded routes. Instead, she was climbing the chimney solely using the features and the three walls. Taylor's hands moved quickly on the belay, making sure she always had one hand on the rope and that she kept her eyes focused on Paige. It meant that she was almost directly underneath as the secret agent seemed to bound up the walls, the form-hugging leggings allowing her to contort her body into a variety of positions.

Taylor gave herself a mental shake as she took in more of the rope.

PAIGE

Paige repositioned her legs, giving herself a better angle to brace her arms. She was just a metre or so from the top of the wall now and her limbs were starting to burn a little. 'The Chimney' was her favourite climbing wall in the centre; being surrounded on three sides blocked out the outside noise, and it almost felt like she was being embraced by the walls. The lack of external stimuli allowed her to concentrate much better, meaning that in this small space she became a better climber. She had climbed like this several times before, but she enjoyed challenging herself to do it faster or with less rests. A massive grin stretched across her face as she put both hands over the top lip of the wall; something she quickly realised was a mistake. When she lifted them back up again they were caked in dust. Taylor began lowering her to the ground, and Paige carefully walked herself down the wall, using one hand to hold on to the rope and the other to make sure she didn't hit her head on any of the holds or features. She was both smiling and grimacing when her feet touched the ground., and she quickly wiped the dust from her hands on the sides of her legs.

'Do you want to have a go at this one?' Paige asked Taylor, quickly untying and offering her the rope.

'No, thank you, I couldn't do anything that impressive,' she said, laughing awkwardly.

'It's not fair on you for you to compare yourself to me, you're out of practice. I come here most weeks.'

'No, I know. But I'm competitive enough that I'd probably take it too far and... well... you saw what happened earlier,' Taylor said, blushing again. Paige noticed that every time Taylor was embarrassed, she looked down and to the right, trying to hide her tell-tale cheeks. It was not very successful.

'OK, how about that one?' Paige said, pointing at a much easier wall in the middle of the room.

'Yeah, that'd be a good -'

'Hey, sorry! I'm sorry I'm late!' Dylan interrupted, bounding over. 'The bus timetable I was using was out of date and then by the time I got to the right bus stop the next bus wasn't until -'

'It's fine, Dylan, don't worry about it,' Taylor said, holding her hand up to shush him. 'I did some bouldering and just belayed Paige, it's fine.'

'Oh, good. You guys seem all sorted, I'll leave you to it. The auto-belay is free and it's my own fault -'

'No it's OK,' Taylor said conspiratorially, 'I know you planned to climb with Paige so I'll go use the auto-belay, I know you *weren't expecting me* tonight'. Dylan just looked confused at his sister for a few seconds, and then his eyes went wide. He opened and closed his mouth several times, but no sound came out. 'Have fun!' Taylor said, flicking a smile at Paige before walking away. Dylan was still doing his impression of a fish.

Paige stayed silent and watched Taylor walk away. She found herself feeling disappointed that Dylan had made it;

she had enjoyed the brief time she'd spent with Taylor, and her near-constant blushing had been endearing.

'Did you guys have fun without me?' Dylan asked while tying into the chimney rope.

'Yes, I think so. I know I did anyway.'

'Oh?'

'I got to climb, that's always fun,' Paige said, clipping in ready to belay.

'Sorry, did you want this climb?'

'No it's OK, I just went, you go.'

Paige watched as Dylan began climbing one of the more difficult routes in The Chimney. It wasn't long before she was tempted to scan the room for Taylor, but as she currently had her back to the auto-belay, it wouldn't have been safe to do that while belaying Dylan. The more she thought about Taylor, the more she thought it would be nice to climb with her again. As a more experienced member of the climbing club, she was often asked to watch the others, or coach them up the more difficult routes. She didn't always have much time to just climb. Taylor had allowed her that, which was nice. And Paige was sure that she could help Taylor with her technique, if she wanted it…

She was suddenly jolted upwards as Dylan missed his

footing and slipped off the wall, falling a couple of metres.

'Everything OK?' Paige shouted up to him, bracing a foot against the wall and locking off the rope.

'Yeah, all good,' Dylan answered, already back on the wall. Paige knew she needed to force her brain to focus solely on him. He made it to the top quite quickly, though he did have a few more near misses.

Once Dylan was back on the ground they made light work of untying, before having a brief conversation on where to go next. They chose a wall with a slight negative incline so Paige could practice fighting gravity that bit more, with her goal of completing the new routes on the triple overhang in mind. It was a short walk to that wall, but before they began tying in Paige paused.

'Is Taylor interested in climbing?' Paige asked

'I dunno,' Dylan said, clipping into the belay. 'I expected her to only come with me to the first meeting, but she's been a few times now. I guess *something* must keep drawing her back...' He trailed off, leaving his words hanging in the air.

'So she *is* interested in climbing?' Paige asked again.

'Yeah. Climbing,' Dylan said with a slight chuckle. Paige still hadn't started clipping in even though he was all set. She just stood next to the wall, holding on to the rope.

'I was wondering if she would like some pointers?'

'I don't know, you'd have to ask her.'

'I would but...' Paige paused, looking past Dylan, 'she appears to have left already.'

Dylan turned around and surveyed the room for his sister. He could just see the area where all the climbers dumped their bags when they came in, and hers was gone. He sighed.

'I can give you her number when we're done, if you like? You know, so you can give her some pointers,' Dylan said, his voice with a slight intonation of mirth.

'That works.' Paige said, before tying in.

Later that night, once Paige was back in her own house, she pulled out her phone and pondered, thumb hovering over the text icon. Would Taylor be offended by her offering climbing advice? Would it be rude to text her out of the blue like this? Would she be annoyed at Dylan for giving out her number? She didn't want to get Dylan in trouble.

Paige locked her phone and put it back in her pocket. Sooty jumped up onto the arm of the sofa she was sitting on and started purring loudly, rubbing his head against her arm.

'Hey, buddy,' she cooed at him, giving him lots of scratches behind his ears. He placed his two front paws on her lap and stretched lavishly, before walking across to the other side of the sofa and jumping down, heading into the kitchen. When Paige didn't follow, he meowed, loudly.

'OK, OK,' she said, easing herself to her feet. She had done the most climbing she'd done in a while that night and was already aching for it. She decided to feed Sooty, make herself a cup of tea and go for a bath to try and ease her aching muscles. She leant on the counter as the kettle boiled, waiting to pounce on it when it was done. The steam swirled up into the air creating a light mist, similar to the night she and Maya had walked home from the pub after meeting the twins. The reminder of that night made Paige take her phone out again. She wrote and re-wrote the message several times, sometimes just changing a word here and there and other times deleting a whole sentence. The kettle clicked off and before she could change her mind, she pressed send.

Once upstairs, Paige threw her phone onto the bed and grabbed a clean towel. She decided to allow herself the luxury of a bubble bath and didn't want her phone to distract her or cause anxiety with any potential replies or work emails.

The soothing smell of lavender filled the air as she poured the blue bubble bath into the water. She lit the candles she had surrounding the bath and turned the lights off. The hot water bit at her feet as she stepped in, feeling like it was burning her skin until her body acclimatised. She sank down and let out a long sigh. The warmth of the water wrapped her up like a blanket and soothed her aching muscles. Twisting around to get her tea, she took a sip and closed her eyes, trying to relax. Images from the day flashed across her mind - had she done the right thing by rushing to Taylor after she fell? It wasn't really her place as she didn't work there, but it had been instinctual; it was quite a high fall. Should she have tried to stop Taylor going to the auto-belay, and therefore have stopped her leaving? Dylan was the one who was late, technically he should have been the one to miss out. Or they could have climbed as a trio? All of these thoughts raced through her head as she squished the bubble bath foam between her fingers, relishing in how soft it felt against her skin. The faint popping of the bubbles and occasional squeak of the bath as she adjusted were the only sounds. Eventually, the silence, candles, and lavender bubble bath slowed her brain down enough that she could finally relax.

CHAPTER SIX
Labels

The following day, Paige had two meetings and several hours of lecturing scheduled, but she still managed to squeeze in an hour of research for her novel first thing. The life of one particular Resistance fighter had caught her interest; her name was Anna. Her mother had died when she was young, and her father had been conscripted into the French army when she was still a teen, and was killed in action not long afterwards. World War Two had fractured so many families, and German occupation had resulted in her grandparents and an aunt being moved out of their house to make way for high-ranking Nazi officers. Anna had no idea where they had gone, or if they were even still alive. Her family had been openly unsympathetic to the Nazis when they arrived. Yet the more Paige read about her the more it seemed she joined the Resistance not out of desperation, but for revenge. Anna had accomplished many things throughout the war, but her story had been lost from the history books; information on her was scattered and piecemeal.

After lunch Paige had a meeting with the rest of the

postgraduate personal tutors in the History department. The postgraduate students always started their courses a few weeks after the undergraduates, to stagger the load on the faculty. This meeting was to discuss the incoming students and who was assigned to which member of staff.

Paige was the first to enter the meeting room. It was a clean and clinical space overlooking the park. One entire wall was made of glass, giving unobstructed views to the grassy area opposite the building. The leaves on the trees glowed gold in the low evening sun. Dappled light fell through them like water trickling in a stream. The conifers stood proud and defiantly green, daring the approaching winter to do its worst. The other walls of the room were a stark white, which reflected what little light came through the north-facing windows at this time of year. Cheap plastic chairs huddled around a square central table. The room had an overhead projector, but that wasn't used much anymore; most presentations could be conducted using the flat screen TV mounted to the wall at one end of the room. It was only the older members of the faculty who still insisted on using the projector, much to the annoyance of some of their colleagues.

Other faculty members started trickling in, greeting Paige as they did so. Some of these people were the same people who had rejected her funding application, and they did not quite meet her eye when they greeted her. The head of the department arrived and promptly started handing out the necessary paperwork, even though they had all received it via email already. She fumbled the paperwork, dropping half of it on the floor with nearby colleagues then helping clear it up.

Each page contained a brief summary of each student. These meetings were a great way to run through the teaching schedule to ensure the taught information was presented in a coherent and sequential manner. There was no point in running the research skills session in the second term. Before the meeting started, the department head came over and crouched down next to Paige's chair, placing a hand on her arm. Paige immediately winced and tried to move away as much as she could without actually leaving her seat. She hated people touching her. The contact between the woman's hand and her arm made Paige feel like she had shoved a fork into a electrical socket and held on.

Paige stared at the table as the feeling overwhelmed her. She was vaguely aware of the department head's mouth moving but couldn't hear a word she was saying. The unexpected physical contact was all-consuming.

Eventually, after what felt like an eternity, Paige managed to rip her arm away. A tidal wave crashed over her as all of her senses returned at once. She took a few steadying breaths before forcing her gaze to flick towards the department head, briefly making eye contact, then looking somewhere vaguely past her ear.

'Sorry, what were you saying?' Paige asked, carefully attempting to hide the tension in her voice.

'I was *saying*' the head said, a little impatiently, 'I hope you don't mind me giving you the masters student who is, you know, *on the spectrum*.' She whispered the last words, like it was a dirty phrase. 'I just figured you would be able to… ah… *relate* to them better than anyone else.'

'I don't understand.'

'Well, as you yourself are… well, you're quite set in your ways, aren't you?'

'So?'

'So you'll be able to help them in ways the rest of us couldn't,' the head said quickly. She seemingly instinctively went to pat Paige on the arm as she stood up, but noticing Paige's flinch, thought better of it.

Paige barely registered anything else that was said in the meeting. Her senses were still firing on all cylinders; she could hear the electric hum of the television even though it was off, could smell the cafeteria food despite being three floors up, and the chair cushion was clawing at her legs through the backs of her trousers. And on top of all that, she was angry. The department head didn't have to ask that question, or word it like that, as if autistic people were some kind of burden to be tolerated. The word 'autistic' had been whispered around her since she was a child. One of her sixth form teachers had gently mentioned it to her parents one parents' evening, and another teacher had chimed in saying she couldn't possibly be autistic because she was a girl.

The shuffling of chairs brought Paige back to the present. The meeting had finished and she had no idea what had been discussed; she hoped someone had been minuting it. She dawdled while putting her papers in her bag to allowed everyone else to leave first, before dashing out. She walked past her office door and down a long corridor towards the back of the building. There was a rarely used stairwell which descended to a card key-controlled door; people only tended to use it in the evenings and at night, when the main doors were shut.

The heavy fire door closed behind her as she entered the stairwell, almost sealing her off from the noise of the rest of the building. She paced backwards and forwards, fingers haphazardly hitting her phone screen as she typed out a message to Maya, explaining what had happened and begging her to call. It wasn't long before her phone started ringing.

'Two phone calls in as many months? It must have been bad,' Maya said when Paige answered the phone.

'I felt like I was being crushed and couldn't breathe. I had nowhere to go. Then she started talking about this autistic student and how I am "set in my ways" and -'

'I didn't think you had a diagnosis?' Maya interrupted.

'That's irrelevant.'

'Well I can understand why you're overwhelmed. What do you need, lovely?'

'Distract me. Talk about your day,' Paige asked, her pulse rate already slowing down due to the comforting familiarity of Maya's voice. She continued to pace as she listened to Maya explain how there was drama in her office as two of her colleagues had been secretly dating, and how someone had caught them kissing in the kitchen and now it was all anyone could talk about. Eventually a calendar alert sounded on Paige's phone, dragging her back to the real world and the responsibilities that came with it.

'Thank you, Maya. I have to teach a class now.'

'OK, Spence, text me later, OK?'

'I will. Thank you. Bye.'

Paige unclenched her jaw, pulled her shoulders down from her ears and walked back to her office to grab her laptop. She still had fifteen minutes before the lecture started. She mentally ran through her pre-lecture checklist, physically miming out each stage to make sure she had everything she needed. Just as she locked her office door on her way out, her phone pinged again. Paige was surprised when it wasn't Maya sending a thoughtful text like she expected, but was in fact Taylor responding to the text she had sent her last night. The feeling of being overwhelmed threatened to creep back in as she stared at her screen. She shoved her phone back into her pocket and made her way to the lecture hall. She'd reply properly later.

At home that evening, Paige was curled up on the sofa with Sooty nestled down in the awkward gap between her head, shoulder, and the back of the sofa. He really did not understand personal space. She had ordered a takeaway pizza as soon as she got home, before feeding Sooty and making a cup of tea as usual. She hadn't turned any of the lights or the television on, and she'd seen the delivery driver hesitate before getting out of his car. He'd seemed relieved when the porch light came on and she came to the door. The half-empty pizza box was still open on the table and the mug of tea was most definitely cold. Sooty yawned lazily before going back to sleep, his little paws and fine whiskers twitching as he dreamt.

Paige carefully pulled her phone out her pocket and stared at the text from Taylor.

'Hey, yeah sure, climbing pointers would be great. When would you be free? x'

It felt like a flutter of butterflies had awoken in her chest. She had tried to make friends with people before, by offering them help with something or giving them something she thought they would enjoy. Most of the time they smiled politely and never spoke to her again. She rationalised this by deciding that their friend quotas must be full - there was no way people could have the mental energy for an infinite number of friends, right?

Paige opened the calendar app on her phone and tried to find some free time where she could meet with Taylor. Her phone helped her keep her life organised, reminding her where she needed to be and when, the map apps giving her confidence to go to new places, and the music was so vital in drowning out the rest of the world when everything got too much. Before getting a smartphone, Paige had struggled to leave the house without getting extremely anxious, to the point where she almost stopped trying, other than for work. It meant that she often had to turn to her siblings or Maya for help when forced to travel for conferences or guest lecturing at an unfamiliar university. Modern technology had given her so much more independence. But right now it wasn't helping her work out how to respond to this text.

Eventually she was able to compile a list of suitable times and dates to send across to Taylor, covering the next four weeks. Message sent, she sat up, put her phone aside and pulled her laptop towards her. Sooty opened his eyes, glared at her a little, and moved to the other end of the sofa to lie on the blanket. Paige opened up a web browser and her fingers hovered over the keyboard. What information was she actually trying to find out? Eventually she typed 'How to tell if you are autistic'. One of the results that came up corrected the phrasing of her question to 'How to tell if you *have autism?*' and linked to a multiple choice questionnaire she could take, where her score out of fifty would indicate whether autism was likely or not. She began reading the instructions at the top of the page, shaking her head now and again when the page called autism a 'mental health condition', or made sweeping generalisations about autistic people being good at maths. She reminded herself it was just an online quiz; it was never going to be the epitome of scientific accuracy. The quiz required her to decide to what degree she agreed or disagreed with certain statements. Some of the options confused her - of course she was interested in dates, she was a history lecturer at a university, it was her *job* to be interested in dates. And wouldn't anyone get upset if they couldn't pursue something they were interested in? Everyone she knew through the climbing club was always a bit unhappy when an injury or illness kept them at ground level. Surely that was just human nature?

She had made it as far as question thirty when her phone started ringing; it was Taylor. She stared at the screen, eventually managing to pick it up on the eight or ninth ring.

'Err, hi, I hope you don't mind me calling, I thought it would just be easier to discuss dates over the phone.'

'Hmmm? Oh, right, yeah' Paige said, still scrolling down the quiz and holding the phone a few inches away from her ear, as if it might burn her.

'I could do Thursday next week, but it wouldn't be until later as I have a lecture that doesn't start until four. I can't imagine I'll be done any earlier than six.'

'I can do six,' Paige said absentmindedly.

'Well, I wouldn't be at the climbing centre by six, I probably wouldn't be able to get there until seven. Is that alright with you?'

'Yes, that's OK with me.' Paige said, finishing the quiz and paying a bit more attention to the phone call. 'We can start with a bit of a warm up then go through some of the basics so I can get an idea where you're at, and take it from there.'

'Sounds great' Taylor responded. There was a long pause where only Sooty's quiet purring could be heard.

'Well, if that's all -'

'I was wondering if we could grab a coffee afterwards, my treat,' Taylor blurted out. 'My way of saying thank you for your help.'

'I don't really drink coffee,' Paige said obtusely.

'Oh, well… um, OK, well -' Taylor spluttered.

'I could have some tea if that's OK?'

'Oh, yes! Yes, of course.'

'OK then, I will see you Thursday,' Paige concluded.

'See you then!' Taylor said before hanging up. Paige took the phone away from her ear and looked at it for a little while. She wasn't exactly sure what had just happened.

The results from her quiz had finally loaded. She had scored forty-six, which was supposed to indicate it was highly likely she was autistic. Paige looked at the screen for a while before snapping it closed and standing up, heading to the kitchen. Sooty, thinking he was getting fed again, followed. Paige made herself a cup of herbal tea, distracting herself with the familiarity of the routine. It had been a strange day and she couldn't work out how she was feeling. Was she sad? Happy? Angry? She was definitely feeling something but had no idea what. It felt like she had one of those hospital pain charts with the faces on, only it was spinning around in front of her, and she was unable to get the chart to stay still for long enough to pick which face was closest to how she was feeling.

Sitting back down on the sofa, she turned the television on to create some background noise, and texted Maya. Maya responded by initiating a video call. Paige considered the screen with a slightly disgusted look on her face. But she still answered.

'Err, hello?'

'Hi, lovely! Great to *see* you' Maya said cheerfully.

'What are you doing? We don't video call.'

'I know, Spence, but with me moving away we're going to have to find alternative ways to communicate.

Don't tell me you could go six months without seeing this beautiful face?' Maya said, putting her hands under her chin in a V shape and fluttering her eyelashes.

'I mean, I could,' Paige replied 'but it wouldn't be very pleasant. I would miss you.'

'I know, sweetie, and that's why we're video calling now. So you can get used to it.'

'That makes sense,' Paige admitted, without looking at the phone screen. It felt very strange to be holding her best friend's virtual head in her hands. She quickly put her phone down on the table, propped up against her mug of tea. Maya winced a few times as the act of Paige putting her phone down created loud bangs and thuds at her end of the line.

'Take it easy there, Spence,' Maya said, rubbing her ears.

'Oh, sorry.'

'So what's new?' Maya asked, before looking away from the screen. She was sat in front of a mirror and was busy applying make up. Her tightly curled dark hair had already been pulled back into a bun.

'My head of department thinks I'm autistic.'

'You said earlier. So?'

'So I don't have a diagnosis so she couldn't know that.'

'Sweetie, most people who meet you know you're a little bit quirky.'

'But that doesn't make me autistic.'

'And if it did? Would it matter?'

'Not really. It's not a bad thing. I just think she overstepped the mark, that's all.'

'She probably did.'

'I am going climbing with Taylor on Thursday, to give her some coaching. She would like to buy me a cup of tea afterwards to say thank you.'

'Uh-huh,' Maya said patiently, 'so you've got a date with the hot climber chick'

'It's not a date. I'm coaching her.'

'But it's just you two? And she wants to spend time with you, on your own, afterwards?'

'Yes. She said it was to say thank you.'

'You know people don't always mean what they say, lovely.'

'So she doesn't want to say thank you?' Paige asked. Maya laughed a little.

'No, lovely, she doesn't want to *just* say thank you. She's into you.'

'She hasn't said anything if she is. Should I ask her?'

'You can't just ask her outright. Flirt with her a little,

see how she responds.'

'But I don't even know if she's gay.'

'Trust me, lovely, the way she looked at you the other night; she's gay.'

'If you say so,' Paige said, rolling her eyes.

'I saw that!' said Maya.

'Oh, sorry. I forgot you could see me.'

'Clearly,' Maya said, exasperated. 'Will you ring me afterwards, let me know how it goes?'

'If you want?' Paige said, confused.

'Thank you. Look, lovely, I have to go, I'm going out with the work lot tonight to celebrate me getting the Japan job. I'll speak to you soon, OK?'

'OK,' Paige said. Maya picked up her phone so she could speak directly into her camera.

'Remember, lovely, no matter what your boss thinks, you are a wonderful person. A label doesn't change that, or you. Love you,' she finished, blowing Paige a kiss.

'Love you too,' Paige said, and they hung up.

CHAPTER SEVEN
Rain and Sparks

Paige arrived early at the climbing centre so she could do a lap around the walls, planning the routes she would suggest Taylor tried. Easier ones if she needed them, and progressively harder ones if she wanted to push herself. There were a couple of families there for the evening, which made Paige think about her niece and nephew coming to stay next week. It was their half term break, so she had made sure she didn't schedule any meetings or tutorials that week. It was also reading week for the students, so she had no lecturing commitments. She was looking forward to getting up in the hills with the kids, getting some fresh air, and just generally not worrying about real life for a while. A few members of the climbing club greeted her as she walked around, making small talk about the difficulty of the routes, or about missing the summer months and being able to climb outdoors. During winter the rock faces tended to be too wet for all but the most avid climbers. It was pitch black outside already, so the room was lit solely by the fluorescent lights on the ceiling. Rain hammered on the windows and echoed around the room slightly, making it sound like there were a bunch of tiny people tap dancing on the roof. As others arrived at the centre they came in in various states of dampness. Paige decided to head back out to the entrance to wait for Taylor, only to see she was already there - and thoroughly soaked. Someone on reception had given her a towel and she was patting her hair dry when Paige walked up.

'Hi!' Taylor said enthusiastically. 'Sorry I'm late.'

'You're soaking,' Paige stated, confused. 'Are you OK?'

'Yes I'm fine, I just got drenched when I left work. It didn't look like it would rain this morning, so I left my umbrella at home. I see now that that was a mistake.' Taylor's top looked several shades darker than it was meant to, due to how damp it had gotten, and her hair still looked like she was fresh from the shower, despite her attempts to dry it.

'Do you still want to climb?' Paige asked.

'Yes, of course! Unless you've changed your mind?' Taylor questioned, her eyebrows rising slightly and worry in her eyes.

'I haven't. I thought we'd do some bouldering to warm up and then get started on some routes?'

'Sounds great!'

Taylor handed the towel back to the receptionist with thanks, and the two women made their way into the climbing room. Taylor made quick work of changing into her climbing shoes and they headed over to the bouldering area. Paige quickly identified a route for them to warm up on. Taylor hesitated, standing at the edge of the mat, watching. Paige made quick work of the first part of the route. About halfway up she paused and looked over her shoulder to see how Taylor was doing, and saw that she hadn't moved.

'Are you coming?' Paige asked gently. Taylor smiled and quickly made her way to a secluded section of wall, out of Paige's eye-line. Paige mentally shrugged and carried on climbing. Climbing allowed her to clear her head in a way she hadn't been able to replicate anywhere else. She could feel each individual element of the rough texture of the holds under her hands while her climbing shoes squeezed her feet just the right amount; not enough to cause her pain, but enough to give her the feeling of close contact with the wall. The smell of chalk and sweat reminded her of days at the beach as a child. The sound of rope moving through a carabiner reminded her of her mother zipping up her coat. She loved being able to share her passion with other people and always hoped that they got even a tenth of the pleasure out of it that she did.

Ten minutes later Paige got to the top of another route. After she topped out, she jumped off from the wall and gracefully landed on her feet, bending her knees to absorb the force from the jump. As she stood up she brushed a bit of excess chalk off her hand and went to check on Taylor. She had chosen quite a technical route. It did not contain any dynamic moves, but it did require some pretty exact body positioning and weight distribution. Paige watched Taylor unnoticed for a while; her slender figure was balanced quite precariously, with both her feet on one hold. Paige looked on as Taylor made a few attempts to ascend to the next hold, but she could see straight away that her foot position was wrong. She walked over.

'Can I give you a hand?' Paige asked, making Taylor jump so hard she nearly fell off the wall.

'Jesus! You scared me there,' she said, adjusting her grip on the hand holds. 'Help would be great, thanks. I just can't get past this bit.'

'What you need to do,' Paige said, before taking a step forward and putting her hands on Taylor's ankle and foot, 'is get more of your heel onto the hold, like this.' Paige adjusted Taylor's foot into a position where she could get her weight down through her heel, so it was directly above the middle of the hold. It would allow her to almost sit on her ankle as she transferred her weight across, before standing up on to reach the next hand hold. Paige's stomach became fuzzy at the physical contact. She withdrew her hands.

'There you go. Give it another shot.' Taylor did as she was told and easily climbed past that part of the route, all the way to the top. Once she finished she jumped down next to Paige, both of them still looking at the wall.

'Why do I remember this being so much easier when I was younger?' she said, slightly out of breath.

'We tend to over-think things less when we're younger,' Paige said, thoughtfully. She stole a quick glance at Taylor, looking her up and down, before focusing back on the wall. 'Are you ready to move on?'

'I think so.' Taylor said, before adding, 'Just... don't judge me too harshly, OK? I'm nowhere near as good as you.'

'I'm not that good, I just climb a lot,' Paige said honestly.

The two women made their way over to the first wall Paige had picked out earlier that evening. The slight incline would make it easier to practice the more technical moves, and there were a couple of routes that would allow progression. They talked a little about their work while tying in before Paige sent Taylor off on her first rope climb of the night. Watching from below she was able to analyse Taylor's technique and shout instructions and encouragement when needed. They took it in turns, climbing different routes, and the gap between their route gradings decreased as the night went on, until Taylor was climbing only a few grades below Paige. One of them being several metres up in the air for most of the night didn't facilitate much conversation, but Paige did learn that Taylor hadn't always been an academic and that Dylan was her only sibling. She also learnt that Taylor's smile filled her with light, so she did everything she could to make her smile as much as possible.

The cafe was empty when the two women walked in, laughing. Only the person behind the counter was there, cleaning one of the glass cabinets with a cloth. The room was quite cold, like the rest of the building, but Paige didn't really notice. The coffee machine spluttered into life after they placed their orders, and the smell of coffee and herbal tea quickly filled the small room. Taylor had insisted on buying them both a slice of a very rich-looking chocolate cake, saying they had earned it, which was true; they had completed over a dozen climbs each in fairly quick succession. Paige automatically led them to a table tucked into the corner of the room, from which she could see both the entrance to the cafe and the counter. The location of a condiment cabinet meant that it was quiet and enclosed, an intimate space.

'How did you find that?' Paige asked, sipping her tea.

'Amazing,' Taylor said, beaming. 'I remember why I used to love climbing so much.'

'But you're climbing again now? Do you think you will you stick with it?'

'Definitely, that was so much fun! To be honest, I'm stuck behind a desk most of the day with work, so it's nice to get some exercise in and just forget about work for a while.'

'I understand that. I go running up in the hills behind my house sometimes when I need to get away from real life for a bit.'

'Where do you live?'

'On the edge of the Silverton forest.'

'Oh! I've always wanted to go exploring there. It seems like it would be a great place to get lost in for a while.'

'My niece and nephew are coming to stay next week,

and we're planning on going to the forest. You could come with us if you like.'

'Seriously?'

'Yes, why not?'

'I'd love to, thank you!' There was that smile again. It created little dimples in her cheeks and made her eyes seem a little bit brighter. Paige continued studying her, and Taylor blushed a little. It wasn't long before they were chatting away about anything and everything, like they'd known each other for years rather than weeks. Paige found Taylor easy to talk to. She didn't make fun of her little idiosyncrasies or get offended if Paige wasn't staring directly into her eyeballs when she was talking. Looking away helped her listen, and Paige wanted to make sure she heard every word.

Eventually the person behind the till starting making obvious moves that he was packing up for the night, and Paige was amazed to check her watch and see that it was 9:30 already. She grabbed her bag and coat from the floor and got to her feet, still talking to Taylor as she did the same. They got to the door and could see that the rain was still coming down in sheets, battering the walls and windows of the climbing centre. Paige suddenly remembered that Taylor didn't have an umbrella, and her jacket clearly wasn't waterproof. She took off her own coat and held it aloft over the both of them.

'Want to make a run for it?' she asked, smiling. Taylor didn't respond but instead took one half of the coat and pushed the door open. They both ran out, Taylor directing them toward her car, giggling all the way. Paige held the coat for both of them while Taylor dug her keys out of her pocket. In the short time they'd been outside her hands had gotten cold and wet, meaning she fumbled with her keys for a while before managing to unlock the car and open the door. She paused before getting into the car.

'Thank you for today, Paige, I really enjoyed it. It blew away the cobwebs and I learnt loads.'

'No problem,' Paige said, eyes roving around her companion's face before settling on looking at the dimple on her right cheek. She was aware of how close Taylor was. She could clearly see each of her freckles and almost feel the body heat radiating off her.

'I'll see you soon?' Taylor asked, almost in a whisper. Paige just nodded. Taylor dove into the car and shut the door, throwing her bag onto the passenger seat next to her. Paige stood there for a few seconds longer before jogging over to her own car and being very grateful for keyless entry. She wasn't sure she could feel her hands anymore, and not just because they were wet and cold.

Paige watched as Taylor started her car, turned her lights on, and began to drive away, flashing her hazards a couple of times in farewell. She smiled and started her own engine, the car roaring into life and the heated seats beginning to warm up. She sat there a little while longer, staring out through the water-soaked windscreen, unsure exactly what had happened that evening. It wasn't until the staff members came out of the centre building to lock up that she actually put her seatbelt on and drove away.

Paige practically bounced through her front door. Sooty lazily picked his head up from the sofa to see what all the fuss was about. She strolled over and picked him up, holding him in her arms. His eyes went wide with shock, but a few pets was all it took for him to start purring and rubbing his head against her hand. Paige had picked up some reduced price chicken on her way home as a treat for him, and she could swear he somehow knew. She carried him into the kitchen and he gracefully jumped down from her arms to sit knowingly by his food bowl. His impatience led to Paige dropping more than one piece of chicken on his head, as she tore it into manageable pieces and plopped it in his bowl. His loud purring echoed around the room like an engine.

Back in the living room Paige shot Maya a quick text to say that she was back form her climbing session with Taylor and that it had gone well. Almost as soon as she'd sent it Maya was video calling her.

'Tell me everything!' Maya squeaked giddily.

'There's nothing to tell. We climbed and had a drink in the cafe after,' Paige said, but the slight crimson flush that crept across her cheeks betrayed her.

'C'mon, Spence, I can always tell when you're hiding something.'

'I'm not hiding anything! It was nice, that's all,' she said before pausing, then muttering under her breath, 'and she's very pretty.'

'I know she's pretty, lovely, I've met her. Do you like her?'

'Well, yes, or I wouldn't have gone climbing and then had drinks in the cafe with her.'

'*No*, I mean, do you *like* like her?'

'Oh. That. I dunno.'

'Stop the presses, Spence doesn't know something! When does that ever happen?'

'Oh, ha ha.'

'Are you seeing her again?'

'We're going exploring the forest with the kids.'

'That doesn't count as a date.'

'It wasn't supposed to be a date'

'OK, well, you need to go on an actual date. But let her ask you this time, make her work for it a little bit.'

'Make her work for what?' Paige asked innocently

'You, lovely. She should make an effort to show she wants to spend time with you.'

'But if she didn't, why would she agree to go climbing with me today? Or ask me to have coffee with her after?'

'Just trust me, sweetie, let her make the next move, OK?'

'OK…' Paige said, rolling her eyes.

'Video call! Remember?'

'Oh, yeah, sorry…'

CHAPTER EIGHT
The Past in the Present

TAYLOR

The PhD students' workspace was a slightly cluttered conglomeration of desks and furnishings. The three sofas arranged around an oval coffee table were almost always occupied, groups either working together on their projects or just socialising. A bookcase wall partially separated it from the main workspaces. Most of the desks were occupied by students with headphones in, tapping away at their keyboards or staring at the monitors; some thoughtfully, and some with that glazed look in their eyes which indicated they should have stopped for a break hours ago. The room provided hot-desk-style work stations for all PhD students studying under the broad title of Engineering.

Taylor's preferred desk was pushed up next to one of the windows giving views out across the city. Being on the edge of the hive helped her concentrate while still allowing her to feel connected to other people. So far this term she had hardly spent any time there. Her supervisor kept piling on more and more teaching responsibilities, leaving her with less and less time to focus on her research. This dreary Friday afternoon was a rare exception; a seminar had been cancelled at the last minute, clearing a few hours in her schedule. She had filled up a large travel mug of her favourite coffee, got some snacks, and sat down to work at her favourite desk. However, the words were just not flowing. Academic writing was not like riding a bike; she was rusty. Finding her notes from the last time she'd done any work on her research made her stomach lurch; it had been nearly a month. Sighing, she started reading over them. Her memory of the notes was so vague that it was like someone else had written them. Thankfully, that 'someone else' had also left her instructions on what to do next. She silently thanked four-weeks-ago Taylor and began finding the journal articles and books she had made notes on.

The group currently occupying the sofas were laughing loudly on a break from work. She glanced over at them briefly, realising she didn't even know any of their names. That one might have been called Phil? Or Peter? Something like that. Some of the students in the room had only started their PhDs that September so she excused herself from not knowing their names. But she had worked alongside Phil/Peter for two years now. She sighed and went back to searching for the papers she needed. Some of them weren't available online, meaning that she would have to go and dig out the physical copies from the library. The sofa group let out another fit of laughter, distracting her from her work once again. She took that as a sign and headed to the library.

A short walk and a flight of stairs later she was standing in front of aisles and aisles of books on meticulously organised library shelves. The paths through the shelves presented themselves to her like the entrance of a maze. She glanced at the scrap of paper in her hand which contained the reference number for each book. It wasn't a maze, she decided, but a treasure hunt, with a very strange set of clues. Taylor laughed to herself before beginning her search. Sometimes dancing her way around other students browsing the shelves, she successfully managed to collect an armful of books and journals. She carefully navigated to the scanners used to check books out, the stack of books wobbling slightly as she joined the rather long queue. It gave her time for her mind to wander, and for her arms to grow heavier with the weight of the books. She started thinking about climbing with Paige the day before and how it had all just felt so *easy*. Paige seemed to be the type of person who was quite upfront about things; whenever Taylor had made a mistake Paige had told her, but that made her subsequent praise all the more meaningful. Taylor could feel her walls coming down a little further the more time she spent with the secret agent. 'Maybe it's a technique she learnt at MI5,' Taylor thought, joking to herself.

Eventually she got to the front of the queue and started scanning her items out one by one. Just as she re-loaded the books into her arms she felt her phone vibrate in her pocket. She secretly hoped it was Paige, but acquiesced it was more likely to be Dylan or one of her parents. She would have to wait to check it until she had made it back to the workspace.

She dumped the books on her desk with a thud; the noise loud enough to make those in the room look up. She held her hand up apologetically and mouthed the word 'sorry', turned red, and sat down. Hiding behind her computer monitor she took her phone out to check her text. Now her face turned white, and then grey, as she read the message.

'You can't keep ignoring me like this, it's cruel. It's been three years and I miss you. I'm doing better now I promise, I'm sorry for all the things I said. If you ever

loved me, call me xxx.'

It was Daniella, her ex. Suddenly the walls in the study room felt several feet closer and closing in, and her breathing became rapid. Taylor pulled at the collar of her T-shirt and tried to swallow, but her mouth and throat felt like sandpaper. Another text came through while she was still staring at the screen.

'No call then, huh? You stupid bitch, I was too good for you anyway.'

Leaving her phone at her desk, she quickly got up and left the room. It took all of her self control to just walk fast, instead of run and run until she had put as much distance as she could between her and those memories. She trotted down a couple of flights of stairs, not acknowledging the people who greeted her on the way down. Eventually she made it out the main doors, but didn't stop there. She found herself walking, then running, in the vague direction of the Journalism building with no idea why. But she kept going.

It was late afternoon so by the time she got to the cafe in the Silverton building it was fairly empty. Taylor bought herself a bottle of water, not able to speak to the woman on the till or even look her in the eye. Once sat down in the corner she tried to concentrate on her breathing to get it to slow down. Memories kept crowbarring their way into her head. A flash of blue lights as she stood outside A&E. Staying overnight on the ward, dozens of times. The threats Daniella made, to do Taylor or herself harm if she couldn't control every aspect of their lives. How she'd faked a serious illness to manipulate Taylor into staying, and isolated her from her friends and family.

'Lor?' Dylan said softly. He'd called out to her from across the foyer but she hadn't responded, just carried on playing with the lid of the water bottle and staring into space. He now stood directly in front of her. She looked up and saw him, but was unable to form any words.

'C'mon, let's get you home,' He said, helping her to her feet. He looked around on the floor for her bag but couldn't see anything.

'Lor, where -?'

'In the PhD room,' she said robotically.

'OK, we'll go get it, then go home?' Dylan said gently. She just nodded.

The taxi dropped them off outside Taylor's door. She had tried to insist on driving but Dylan had joked that he wanted to live. Dylan thanked the taxi driver and paid him, then started rummaging through Taylor's bag for her keys.

'It always amazes me how much girls carry in their bags,' Dylan said to himself.

'Hmmm?'

'Nothing. Here we go.' Dylan opened the door and ushered Taylor inside ahead of him. 'OK, you? Sit there' he said, pointing to the sofa, 'I'll go make us a drink.' He fussed around Taylor a little bit first, putting a blanket over her and making sure she had the television remote and her phone handy in case she wanted them. Taylor took the phone and put it on the other side of the coffee table, face down. She could hear the kettle begin to bubble away as Dylan moved swiftly around the kitchen. Her mind wandered back to the memories from those years spent with her ex, and she shivered. It was a long time ago, but the wounds were still fresh, not helped by being ripped open by the occasional text or un-answered call from her.

Taylor reached out and snatched at her phone, opening the texts. There must have been upwards of fifty of them from this year alone. They varied from apologies and platitudes, to begging for her to go back, to outright insults and cruelty. Taylor never replied, but they kept coming. She shook herself and exited the text thread. She could see the preview of her most recent text from Paige; she had checked in that morning to make sure Taylor wasn't too sore after their climbing session. She smiled slightly just as Dylan walked back into the room.

'That's more like it,' he said, smiling back at her and handing her a mug of hot chocolate. 'I couldn't find any marshmallows but I did find... these!' He withdrew a pack of digestives biscuits from his hoodie pocket and tossed them onto the middle of the sofa, then sat down, positioning himself cross-legged facing Taylor. She couldn't look at him. She didn't want to talk about it.

'So, what - or who - was making you smile so much when I walked in?' The question threw her - it was not the line of questioning she was expecting.

'Oh, it's nothing. I was thinking about climbing last night, that's all.'

'You went climbing without me?!' Dylan said in mock offence.

'I went with Paige...' Taylor said, resigning herself to the barrage of questions no doubt forming in Dylan's mind.

'Oh, I see... whatever happened to bros before h -'

'Oi!'

'Fine. Brothers before hot secret agents doesn't apply anymore then?'

'She was just giving me some help with my technique.'

'Oh, is that what they call it nowadays?'

Taylor grabbed a pillow from behind her and threw it at his head, striking him square in the face and making him nearly spill his hot chocolate all over his lap.

'Hey! Careful! I'd like the option of having kids one day,' he said, carefully running his finger around the base of the mug to catch up any stray drips.

'It was just climbing, and we got a drink and some cake afterwards. Nothing more.'

'If you say so,' he said, grinning at his sister. She just scowled at him, before picking up the remote, turning away from him, and turning the television on. Dylan didn't adjust his position, and instead just carried on staring at his sister. Eventually, she sighed, muted the TV, and turned to him.

'What?' she demanded, slightly more viciously than she intended.

'You know what!'

'If I block her number, she'll just find other ways to contact me. There's no point. At least this way I know where the contact might come from.'

'That's true, but, blocking her would at least make it harder for her to get to you. How are you going to move on if she keeps dragging you back to that place?'

Taylor didn't respond. She hadn't really thought about moving on before; she'd not had a reason to. Ever since she and Daniella had broken up, she'd not even looked at another woman, not wanting to make herself that vulnerable ever again. Memories of Paige laughing as they ran across the rain-soaked car park filled her mind and warmed her up more than the mug of hot chocolate was doing. Maybe her brother had a point.

'OK, fine,' she said, throwing her phone at Dylan. 'You do it, though. I don't want to have to look at her face.'

Dylan didn't say anything but started going through every form of social media Taylor had and blocking Daniella. He blocked her number too. Taylor just hoped it would be enough. She wasn't sure that her ex would give up that easily - it had been over three years and she was still messaging semi-regularly. Taylor took another sip of her hot chocolate.

'There,' Dylan said, handing the phone back to her, 'all done.'

'Thank you, Dyl,' Taylor said sincerely. 'And thank you for tonight.'

'Like you haven't done the same, and much more, for me?' Dylan asked, turning around so he could sit back on the sofa properly, his gangly legs stretch out in front of him. 'What're we watching?'

'Horror film? That new one... *Chainsaw Redemption* or something... I've got that downloaded'

'Perfect!' Dylan said, settling in for the night.

Taylor spent an uneasy night tossing and turning. Dylan had insisted he was too tired to get the bus home and as taxis were so expensive, he might as well stay the night and they could share a taxi in the morning. Taylor was grateful. But he was asleep on the sofa downstairs. Even if he was in the room with her, he would not be able to protect her from the bad dreams terrorising her night.

In the house she shared with her ex, she sat at the computer typing up a report for work. Daniella stood in the doorway, bathed in darkness. She stood far enough back that the light from Taylor's computer screen only just caught her outline.

'Tay-tay, *please*,' she whined. Taylor didn't even look up from her computer. 'I don't feel well,' she said, trying to force Taylor to switch her attention to her. They had fought earlier, with Daniella screaming so loudly the veins in the side of her head stood to attention and spit started flying everywhere. Taylor had used all of her self-control to keep her voice calm and steady, but this only seemed to make Daniella more angry. She started saying more and more outrageous things, trying to get a rise out of Taylor, who was running through Newton's laws of physics in her head to keep her calm.

'Maybe I should lock us both in the house and set it on fire, would you react then?!' she had screamed in Taylor's face. Taylor had forced herself to walk away; to go to her study and concentrate on her work. She had only been there for about half an hour when Daniella had appeared in the doorway.

The dream skipped forward to a few hours later. It was late at night, and Taylor had done all she could on her report. She very suddenly became aware of how quiet the house was, and dragged herself to her feet to make sure everything was alright. She took a few steps down the stairs, but couldn't hear the television. A few more steps, but there was no sound coming from the kitchen. Another few steps, but she couldn't hear a phone call or a radio. The kitchen door was shut, which was unusual, and Taylor felt a massive sense of foreboding. Maybe Daniella actually had been feeling ill; she knew the chronic condition her girlfriend had came in waves, so it didn't matter that she'd been fine earlier, maybe it had hit her again and she'd had an accident while cooking.

Taylor burst through the door, imagining the worst. But even what she imagined wasn't as bad as what she saw. Daniella was slumped over on the kitchen table, next to a glass of juice and a bottle Taylor had never seen before, which was unusual: she'd memorised the names and doses of all of the medication Daniella was on. She stepped quickly over to her and shook her, shouting her name. No response. She quickly got her phone and dialled 999, unable to form a coherent sentence for the operator. At the same time, she picked up the bottle on the table. It definitely wasn't one of Daniella's regular medications. Underneath the name, which wasn't Daniella's, there was a warning label in big bold letters.

'*WARNING. May cause dizziness, fainting spells, and vomiting. Do not take unless under strict supervision from a medical professional.*'

But this wasn't her prescription. Her doctors had never mentioned it…

Taylor's phone suddenly slipped out of her hand. All of those trips to accident and emergency after she had passed out. All those nights taking care of her when she couldn't sleep because she was vomiting so much. All those family events she had missed because Daniella was ill, and the reprimands she had faced in work when she left site without permission to go and take care of her. Not being able to visit Dylan in rehab. All of that, and she might be doing it to herself....

Taylor picked up Daniella's phone and used the unconscious woman's thumbprint to unlock it, guilt and fear rising through her as she thought about what the consequences would be if Daniella woke up at the moment. Taylor was strictly forbidden from looking at Daniella's phone, but Daniella had full and open access to hers and frequently checked up on her. She started going through the browsing history and came across several dodgy-looking websites that sold black market medication. Taylor threw the phone away from herself as if it burnt her, and started sobbing.

The paramedics arrived and tried to talk to Taylor to find out what was going on, but she couldn't really find the words. She pointed out the bottle to them and explained Daniella might have taken an overdose, before turning around and walking to the other side of the kitchen. She put both hands on the counter to steady herself, as her legs felt like they were made from sand and might crumble at any minute.

Once the paramedics had taken Daniella away, Taylor did the only thing she could think of and called her parents to say she was coming to stay for a while. She forced herself not to think about the shock in their voice from receiving contact from their only daughter, after barely speaking for years. Then she emailed her boss saying she was taking a leave of absence due to a personal family crisis and filled a giant suitcase with everything of hers that she cared about: her jewellery box containing her late grandmother's bracelet, some old birthday cards, and a blanket her aunt had knitted for her. What room was left she filled with clothes. Her laptop fitted into her work bag, and she tossed that over her shoulder while dragging the suitcase down the hall, no longer caring about scratching the walls or the floor. No longer caring about the home they had bought together, decorated together, loved each other in. But it wasn't really love, was it? It was control and being controlled. Well, not anymore.

She got in her car and drove. Her parents rang several times, worried; why was she driving up to theirs so late, at such short notice? It wasn't until she turned up on their doorstep that she finally broke and started sobbing.

Taylor's sobbing jolted Dylan awake. He was dazed for a few seconds, not quite sure where he was. Remembering, he bolted upstairs and into Taylor's room. Dylan ungracefully crashing through the door startled Taylor awake and into a sitting position. She looked at him through watery eyes, not trusting that he was real. She could still hear the sirens of the ambulance and smell the bitter frost on her parents' doorstep.

Dylan crossed the room in two strides and sat next to her on the bed, wrapping her in a tight hug.

'Shhh, it's OK,' he soothed, rocking her slightly. 'You're OK.' Taylor sobbed into his shoulder. Why couldn't Daniella just leave her alone? It wasn't common for her to have nightmares like this, but they were almost guaranteed on the nights where Daniella had made contact. Her acidic words irritating the wounds Taylor still had, stopping them healing.

In the end, both Taylor and Dylan slept downstairs on the two perpendicular sofas, with the side table lights casting an orange glow around the room.

CHAPTER NINE
Forest Fun

Taylor got up before her alarm that Sunday; it was still dark outside as she went downstairs and put the kettle on. She hadn't slept properly the previous two nights, and she hoped that the fresh air and spending time with other people would help her let go of the stress and pain keeping her awake. For their trip to the forest, she had dug out her old work boots, which had been buried in one of the boxes in the spare room. She had also bought a nice warm coat; waterproof but with a soft lining. On the same shopping trip she had bought the niece and nephew a ball to kick around and a magnifying glass in case they came across any creepy crawlies.

She wasn't due to get to Paige's until noon. She ended up pacing around the house, eventually deciding to dust the mantelpiece and the bookshelves, and anything else she came across. The birds all woke up with the sun and began their chorus. She was mainly surrounded by other buildings, so she imagined her serenaders were all pigeons, but she appreciated it all the same. Sunlight slowly filled the room as time went on, until the clear blue sky looked radiant.

At eleven a.m. she couldn't find anything else to keep herself busy, so she made her way out the door. Her car obediently rumbled into life and as she pulled out of the drive, she was immediately transported back to the day before, when she and Dylan had taken a taxi to collect her car from the car park. She remembered feeling like she was made of glass and every pothole or bump in the road might make her shatter. She shook her head, trying to dispel those thoughts.

Paige's house was not what Taylor had expected. It was a large, family-sized dwelling with a sundial and bird bath in the front garden. The bird bath was frozen over, and there were no leaves on the trees and bushes surrounding the lawn, but Taylor could imagine that in the warmer months it was a little green haven for the thirsty birds. She stepped out the car and looked for signs of life in the house, double-checking the text on her phone for the address, and the metal number on the red front door. It was definitely the right house. Before approaching the door, Taylor made a detour via the bird bath to remove the thin layer of ice, topping up the remaining water from the bottle she had brought with her for the hike. Just then, the curtain twitched and two sets of young eyes stared out at her from just above the windowsill. Taylor gave them a little wave, causing them to quickly disappear, and went to the front door. Paige opened it before Taylor had even had a chance to knock, startling her.

'Hi!' Paige said before seemingly registering Taylor's slightly shocked expression. 'Sorry, the kids saw you through the window and got all excited. I don't know where they are now though,' she continued unnecessarily loudly, as she led Taylor into the living room, 'they must be hiding.'

Taylor could see two sets of little feet sticking out from under the curtains on the French doors.

'Oh, we'll have to find them!' she said knowingly. 'Where could they be hiding?'

One of the curtains let out a poorly muffled giggle, as the two women slowly walked over to them.

'I mean, maybe they just upped and left?' Paige pondered out loud. 'Maybe they snuck out the door when I let you in?'

'Maybe,' Taylor said as she carefully placed one hand on the curtain on the right. Paige did the same on the left, and mouthed a countdown.

'One!' she shouted, and they both ripped the curtains back to reveal two giggling children: a boy with dirty blond hair in a dinosaur T-shirt and a younger brunette girl wearing an over-sized red jumper.

'Taylor, this is Cayden and Susie, my elder brother's children. Guys, this is my friend Taylor.'

'Hi, nice to meet you!' Taylor said, crouching down in front of the little girl and holding out her hand. Susie half-hid behind her brother in response.

'I'm Cayden,' he stated, boldly shaking her offered hand. 'I'm seven.'

'Wow, a whole seven?'

'Yup' he said proudly, sticking his tiny chest out. 'I had a birthday last week.'

'And how old are you, Susie?' Taylor asked gently.

'Susie's five,' Cayden answered. 'I can name different types of dinosaurs, they are -'

'OK, let's let Taylor settle in first before we lecture her on dinosaurs,' Paige said, steering Taylor towards the sofa. 'Want a cup of coffee before we go?'

'Yes, please,' Taylor said.

'Can you guys keep her company while I go make us a drink?'

'Sure!' Cayden shouted, plonking himself down next to her on the sofa. Susie still hadn't moved.

Cayden began rattling off thousands of different facts

about dinosaurs. Taylor tried to 'ooh' and 'aah' in all the right places, but if she was honest, it was hard to keep up. Susie just watched them for a while, before joining them on the sofa. She carefully looked Taylor over, before crossing her legs in just the same way - right over left - and folding her hands in her lap just like Taylor had. Taylor smiled at her, and she looked away.

Paige came back in with a coffee for Taylor, water for the kids, and tea for herself. The living room felt cosy with the autumn sun beaming through the window, and Cayden's happy nattering filling the room. Taylor tried to uphold her part in the conversation, but it was hard to get a word in. Paige smiled at her attempts.

'That's brilliant, Cayden. But don't forget your drink,' Paige said, nodding towards his cup. His first sips of water were the first time the room had been quiet since Taylor had arrived.

'How was your weekend so far?' Paige asked.

'Oh, fine,' Taylor lied. 'I took Dylan to do some shopping yesterday, but that's about it. You?'

'My brother dropped these two off on Friday evening, so it's been... busy.'

'Haha, I can imagine!'

Susie got up off the sofa to get her cup of water, and

took it over to where a pile of toys lay sprawled in the corner, as if the toy box had been upended. She found all of the cars and started lining them up in size order, quietly singing away to herself as she did so. Cayden took a big breath as if about to start another speech, when Paige jumped in to stop him.

'Cayden, can you go and find your boots please? And Susie's too. I can't remember where I left them.'

'OK!' he said, jumping off the sofa and starting the search.

Paige whispered to Taylor, 'I know it makes me a bad person, but I hid one of his boots. Should keep him busy for a while.'

Taylor had just taken a sip of her coffee and nearly spurted it out everywhere as she tried to hold back a laugh.

'That's mean!' she said jokingly.

'I know. But he's always so proud of himself when he finds them.'

The forest trail was slick with mud; the recent rains had saturated the soil and the kids were having great fun sliding all over the place. The grown ups gingerly walked on the edges of the path, trying not to end up embarrassing themselves by face-planting the mud. Trees lined either side of the path, bolt upright like soldiers standing at attention. There were pine cones dotted around here and there, and each time Susie found one she would happily trot over to her aunt and deposit it in a bag. This was clearly a regular activity as Paige had come prepared for it. The higher they got up the trail, the redder everyone's cheeks got, until they looked like painted Russian dolls who couldn't stop smiling. The fresh air whipped around them, bringing with it the aroma of the pines. Alongside the squelch of mud under their feet, they could hear a variety of birds chirping, calling out to one another from their perches, high up in the sky.

'How often do these guys come to stay?' Taylor asked.

'Most school holidays. Their parents both work and it just makes sense when my time off teaching coincides with their half terms.'

'Do you not have work to do over reading week?'

'Yes, I try and get some of it done when they go to bed.'

'Auntie Paige, look!' Cayden shouted from about twenty metres further up the trail.

'What have you found?' she shouted back, speeding up her walk. She then said quietly to Taylor, 'If it's a dead animal or something, we might need to prevent him "investigating" it.'

'Look!' he said, pointing at the leaf of a small bush he was stood almost in the middle of. Only the top of his torso and head were visible, the rest of him had been swallowed up by the plant. He was pointing at a dark brown beetle that almost looked like a mini leaf in itself. It had spindly, orangey-red legs and Taylor could see why he had stopped to admire it.

'Here,' Taylor said, rooting around in her pocket, 'You can use this to have better look!' She handed him the magnifying glass and his face lit up as he snatched it out of her hand.

'Cayden, what do we say?' Paige said sternly.

'Thank you!' he said without looking away from the bug, whose face was now amplified through the magnifying glass.

Paige leaned in and whispered to Taylor, 'A magnifying glass? Why didn't I think of that! Do you just carry one on you or something?'

'No, I bought it when I was out shopping the other day. I thought it might be useful for young explorers.'

Paige smiled gratefully at Taylor. 'It's brilliant, thank you.'

As they approached the crest of the hill, the clouds that

had been hovering cleared, allowing the autumn light to bathe the area in a warm glow. Paige found a felled tree trunk and sat down, placing her rucksack on her lap. The kids were both playing a few metres away; Cayden was looking for more bugs to analyse with his new magnifying glass, and Susie was happily playing with some of the twigs and stones that littered the floor, creating patterns in the mud.

'Kids! Food!' Paige yelled, and they both stopped what they were doing and came running. Susie stood in front of Paige, bouncing up and down on her tiptoes and flapping her hands in excitement. Cayden started lecturing them all on the different bugs he had seen, and how he was going to look them all up on the internet when they got home. Taylor was surprised when after handing the kids their lunch boxes, Paige pulled out another one and handed it to her. She hesitatingly took it, looking confusedly at Paige.

'You don't like sandwiches?' Paige asked, worried.

Taylor smiled and shook her head as her cheeks turned faintly more pink, before thanking Paige and sitting down next to her. She quickly looked away to where the line of the tree tops dipped below the crest of the hill, and over to the city beyond. From here the roads almost looked like veins branching out, carrying the oxygen the city needed to thrive. The buildings standing to attention either side were a barrier to protect the vital routes from the people and the nature that was watching, waiting. In comparison, the forest had criss-crossing paths of various sizes and inclines, with no real rules or boundaries restricting where you could go. Here the oxygen flowed freely, with people and nature synchronised and existing in harmony.

Taylor took a bite out of the jam sandwich Paige had made her and let the sweetness spread around her tongue. The fruity taste reminded her of her grandmother's baking. Warm thoughts of baked delights fresh from the oven filled her up as she sat on the windswept hilltop. The children's laughter penetrated her memories and she realised Paige had been staring at her again. The secret agent hadn't looked away quickly enough this time, and her own cheeks turned crimson, knowing she had been caught. Paige quickly busied herself with the rucksack again, this time pulling out two silver thermos flasks, and handing one to Taylor.

'Don't worry, it's coffee,' Paige said with a smile. Taylor took the flask, which had colourful tape wrapped around it to distinguish it from its twin. She set her lunchbox down beside her, before unscrewing the top of the thermos, pouring herself some of the warm liquid, and taking a sip.

'For someone that doesn't drink it, you make a damn good coffee.'

'My parents both drink copious amounts of coffee. I mastered the skill at a young age,' Paige responded, laughing.

'Remind me to thank them if I ever meet them,' Taylor laughed, before blushing once more. If Paige noticed, she didn't make it obvious. Instead, she carried on watching the children play with a wistful look on her face, smiling the entire time.

Eventually Paige got to her feet, offering a hand to Taylor who was struggling to stand up; all the climbing she had suddenly started doing combined with the hike this morning meant her legs were no longer her friend. She took the offered hand and felt immediate heat flood through her body as if she had been wrapped in a warm blanket. Taylor pulled herself to her feet, and held on to Paige's hand for a couple of seconds longer than necessary. They began walking again and the kids ran after them, with Cayden chatting away and Susie happily singing to herself.

When they started their decent Paige made the children hold her hands. Susie kept trying to pull away, but Paige wouldn't let her go.

'I'm sorry, Susie, but I don't want to risk you falling. I fell here when I was running the other week and I got baddies all over my arm and face, and it really hurt. I don't want you to get hurt. Do you understand?'

Susie nodded and stopped pulling on Paige's arm.

'Is that how you hurt yourself?' Taylor asked.

'Huh?' Paige replied.

'When I first met you your arm was bandaged and your face was all messed up.'

'Oh, right. Yes. I was out running that morning and a rabbit startled me and I slipped.'

'A rabbit?' Taylor said, laughing.

'What's so funny?' Paige said with a slightly hurt tone in her voice.

'I'm sorry, it's just… when we first saw you in the coffee shop Dylan gave you this whole back story about being a mysterious MI5 agent' Taylor said, trying to stifle her laughter long enough to get her words out. She took a deep breath and tried again, 'A secret service agent who hurt herself on a dangerous mission, and it turns out instead that your injuries were due to… due to a cute little bunny rabbit.'

'Haha, yeah, can see how that would be funny.' Paige

chuckled.

'Sorry. I'm not laughing at the fact you got hurt,' Taylor said, going a bit red and looking sheepish.

'I know, it's OK.' Paige's arm moved in a way that suggested she was trying to reach out to Taylor, but she was still holding tightly on to Cayden's hand and so all she ended up doing was nearly pulling him over.

'Careful now!' Taylor said, catching his other arm. The four of them walked down the slope together, holding hands and laughing like a human daisy chain. Once they were on the flat, Paige simultaneously let go of both the children's hands and shouted, 'Race you!', pretending to sprint off towards a lamppost further ahead. She let both the children go in front of her, and when it became clear Susie was falling behind, she scooped her up and ran with her, so that all three of them reached the lamppost at the same time.

'It's a draw!' Taylor declared, trailing behind.

'Well done, you two!' Paige said, ruffling the children's hair.

Taylor looked on at the trio and smiled, thinking she had completely underestimated Paige. She had assumed that she would have been just as awkward with the kids as she seemed to be with everyone else. Instead, she watched as Susie took Paige's hand, gently running a gloved thumb up and down it, and as Cayden bounced around them, never letting them out of his sight. This hidden side to Paige only made the jitters in Taylor's stomach increase. Taylor's cheeks went red again and she tried to push those thoughts out of her mind, not wanting to make the seedlings of affection obvious.

It was starting to get dark as the four adventurers got back to the house. Taylor started to make her excuses to leave, assuming she would be in the way of bedtime routines, but Susie surprised her by grabbing her hand and leading her inside the house. Paige made them all hot chocolate and put the fire on. She let the kids pick out a film to watch while she went upstairs, returning with a massive pile of blankets in her arms, which she dumped directly on top of the children, making them giggle. Susie sat next to Taylor on the sofa and, sucking her thumb, tucked herself into the nook of Taylor's arm. They didn't even make it to halfway through the movie before Susie fell asleep. Cayden kept himself awake by talking almost all the way through, spouting off any tangential facts he knew about whatever was happening in the film at the time. Taylor looked over at Paige every now and again; she was just staring at the television and not saying a word. Her eyes had glazed over a little, as if her mind had gone in to sleep mode like a computer. The fire crackled away in the corner, occasionally letting off a loud pop that would rouse Paige a little. She would adjust her position or pull the blanket a little tighter around Cayden, before drifting back off into her slightly dazed state. Taylor let the heat of the fire wash over her as if she was sinking into a warm bath, and she felt her eyelids getting heavier.

Eventually the end credits started rolling and Cayden sprang to his feet, making both Paige and Taylor jump. Susie slept through it.

'Another one?' he asked Paige hopefully.

'Definitely not, it's past your bedtime, mister,' she replied.

'Aaaaaaaawh,' he whined, but he didn't put up too much of a fight. Taylor tried to wriggle out from under Susie, but every time she moved the little girl gripped the blanket, which was wrapped around both of them, tighter.

'Here, let me get her,' Paige whispered softly. She gently scooped up the sleeping girl and started making her way towards the stairs. Susie nuzzled into her but didn't seem to wake. Taylor remained in the living room with Cayden, who was quietly looking through the rest of the films that Paige had laid out for them. After a few minutes they heard Paige creeping back down the stairs. Cayden seemed to have made a decision, and picked out one of the films.

'Tomorrow?' he asked, his eyes going wide and his smile making him look cherub-like.

'Maybe, if you're good,' Paige said. 'Now, go and get ready for bed, and try not to wake your sister,' she said gently, and he scampered off upstairs. After a few minutes they heard the floorboards in the bedroom creak as Cayden crept into bed.

'Well, that was a long day,' Paige said honestly.

'Fun, though,' Taylor said, standing up and grabbing her coat. 'Thank you for inviting me'

'No problem. To be honest, it was nice to have adult company. There are only so many conversations about dinosaurs you can have in one week before your brain gets fried.'

'That... is understandable' Taylor said with a laugh. 'Well, I'd best be off. See you soon, I hope?'

'Yes, definitely,' Paige said, showing Taylor out.

'Bye, then.' Taylor gave a half wave and smiled. She thought about going in for a hug but wasn't entirely sure how Paige would react, so she decided on just stepping out of the door and not looking back.

Once in her car she let out a huge sigh. It had been a lovely day, she had seen the forest she had been wanting to see for a long time, had had fun laughing with Paige and playing with the kids, but she still had no idea if her small stirrings of romantic feelings were mutual. She couldn't read Paige at all.

Taylor started her car and turned the heaters on full, pulling her coat tighter around her as she waited for the car to warm up. She could see her breath in front of her face and her car windscreen had started to frost over. She wished she was still inside, warmed by the fire and surrounded by the affection that the family had for one another.

CHAPTER TEN
The A Word

PAIGE

Brandon and Lucy would be arriving any minute for lunch, after which they were taking their children home. Paige stifled a yawn as she stood in the kitchen cutting a cucumber. Cayden and Susie were 'helping'. Cayden was chattering about his new favourite topic: insects. His forays with the magnifying glass had finally diverted his attention from dinosaurs. Susie was the first to hear the car pull up. She dropped the tomatoes she was holding, sending them rolling all over the counter and onto the floor. Alerted by Susie's dash to the front door, Cayden narrowly avoiding stomping on a stray tomato as he rushed to join his sister. Paige wiped her hands down, retrieved the stray tomatoes, and went to greet her brother and sister-in-law. Neither child could reach the keys to unlock the door, so both were just bouncing up and down excitedly, Susie quietly clapping her hands and Cayden tapping the sides of his legs.

'Mind out the way now,' Paige said as she got the keys

from the hook and unlocked the door, struggling to open it with two small, excited bodies in the way. Their parents were already on their way to the front door when Susie darted out to meet them in just her socks.

'Hey, Susie-Bug!' Brandon exclaimed, scooping her up in his arms and giving her a snuggle. 'What have we said about going outside without shoes on?' Susie didn't answer, she just giggled as her farther tickled her.

'Hey, Paige,' Lucy said before offering her a hug. Paige accepted and the two embraced, with Cayden watching on, still bouncing. 'And how's my favourite boy?' she asked Cayden, offering him a high five. Instead, he dashed forward and wrapped his arms around his mother's hips. Lucy's expression changed to one of pure bliss as the little boy hugged her.

'Maybe you guys should go away more often!' Brandon joked as he squeezed past his immobilised wife into the house.

'No thank you,' a little voice said from his arms. Brandon squeezed Susie a little tighter.

'Mmm, what smells so good?' Brandon asked before wrapping Paige up in a one-armed bear hug, and saying into her ear, 'Good to see you, P.'

'We made salad!' Cayden shouted in response, causing

the adults to laugh.

'Yes we did,' Paige replied 'but we also made lasagne, didn't we?'

Cayden didn't hear her. He had taken his mother by the hand and was leading her into the living room, where his new magnifying glass lay atop his new book on creepy crawlies. Susie had wriggled out of her father's arms and was now trotting along behind them.

'I just need to finish the salad,' Paige said, gesturing with her thumb over her shoulder, towards the kitchen.

'I'll keep you company,' Brandon proffered, indicating that she should lead the way.

Brandon settled himself onto one of the breakfast bar stools and watched his sister work, with his elbows on the table and fingers all meeting in line with his lips. Paige had her back to him as she worked, relating all the activities they'd got up to in the last week.

'I'm glad you had a good time,' Brandon said, interjecting.

'Yes, it was lovely to have them. My friend Taylor came with us on one of the hikes, they seemed to like her.'

'*Friend?*' Brandon said pointedly. Paige rolled her eyes.

'Just a friend, Bran,' she said, exasperated. 'I think she

now knows a lot more about dinosaurs than she did last week.'

'Ha, yeah, he's really into his dinosaurs right now.' Brandon smiled.

'Not anymore, now it seems to be insects.'

'Lucy will love that!' Brandon laughed, then paused. He seemed to be wrestling with himself, before finally speaking. 'Have you noticed anything... different, about him? About either of them?'

'What do you mean?'

'I dunno. Like... anything unusual, like you wouldn't expect a child to do?'

'I have limited experiences of children, so I have no expectations,' Paige stated, still chopping up some cucumber.

'It's just... the school wants to get them assessed.'

'Assessed?'

'For autism.'

'Ow!' Paige said loudly. She'd cut her finger while slicing up the cucumber and now she was getting blood everywhere. 'Damn it!' she said, sticking her finger in her mouth and sucking the blood away. 'Can you get me a plaster?' she mumbled without withdrawing the digit. Brandon hopped down from the barstool and began searching the utility room.

'Where are they?' he shouted back at Paige.

'In the big cupboard, top right.'

'Got them.'

Once back in the kitchen he extracted a plaster form the box and carefully peeled off the back. Paige offered the injured finger, and he carefully wrapped the plaster around it, taking care to keep her knuckle joint free from restraint. Paige thanked him, but didn't go back to the chopping board.

'Why do the school think they're autistic?' she asked.

'I dunno,' he said, 'they say that they like putting things in order, aren't doing too well socially, and their communication is a bit delayed.'

'Really? How can they say that? Cayden even talks in his sleep!'

'I know, I know, that's what I thought. But if you listen to him, he's not actually making conversation most of the time. He's speaking *at* you, not with you.' Brandon sighed, got to his feet, and started pacing around the kitchen.

'I just… why do they have to put a label on it? They're just kids. They'll grow out of it,' he said, raising his voice slightly.

'But what if they don't?' Paige asked gently. Brandon

didn't reply. 'It's been suggested, recently, that I might be autistic.' Brandon remained silent, but sat down again, putting his head in his hands. 'Now I'm no psychologist, but as far as I understand it, it isn't something a person grows out of.'

'I know that,' Brandon said, picking his head up. 'Don't you think I know that? But I'm their dad, I'm supposed to protect them from the bad stuff. I can't protect them from this, from how the world won't be kind to them because they're a bit different.'

'No, you can't,' Paige said, walking over to her brother and putting a hand on his shoulder. 'But you can help them learn how to deal with it, and teach them that they are great, just the way they are.'

'They are pretty great, aren't they?' Brandon said with a soft smile. 'Thank you, Paige.'

He stood up and gave his sister another massive hug, almost squeezing the air out of her. She tapped him pointedly and he let her go, and she went back to chopping vegetables.

'Do you think you're autistic?' Brandon asked after a few minutes of silence.

'I've not really thought about it much. I did an online thing which suggested I might be, but what does it matter if I am? I've got this far.'

'You're right, it doesn't matter. But don't you want to know, for sure?'

'It would be nice. To have an explanation for my little "quirks", as my department head called it.'

'She said that?'

'Yeah.'

'It's a good thing I wasn't there, she'd have had a piece of my mind,' Brandon said angrily.

'I don't need you to fight my battles, Brandon.'

'I know, and you know I wouldn't, at least not without speaking to you first. But it's not just my kids I feel like I have to protect. I'm your big bro, I've always got your back.'

'I know. Now,' Paige said, picking up a damp sponge and throwing it at him, 'do me a favour and make a start on the washing up.'

'Yes, boss!' Brandon said with a wink.

The two siblings worked quickly, and soon they were just waiting on the lasagne. Paige leant back against the counter and looked at her brother. He had always had this overprotective streak and she worried it would go too far, when it came to the kids, if they did turn out to be autistic. She hoped that Lucy would balance him out with her more practical mind. She suddenly stood upright again.

'Where are my manners!' she exclaimed. 'Do you want a drink, Bran? I'll go and check with Lucy and the kids.'

Paige dashed to the living room, where the doorway framed the beautiful picture of Lucy sitting on the floor with Susie in her lap, while Cayden showed her all the pictures in his new bug book. Paige was reluctant to interrupt, but Lucy looked up and saw her.

'Thank you for getting Cayden the book and magnifying glass. He's so happy.'

'That's OK, but it was my friend Taylor who got him the magnifying glass,' Paige responded.

'Well, we'll have to make sure we write a thank you note to Taylor, won't we, Cayden?' she asked.

'Did you know there are forty-six different types of ladybirds in this country?' he said, by way of response. Lucy smiled but it didn't quite reach her eyes.

'Would you like anything to drink, Lucy?' Paige asked.

'Tea would be great, if you have any.'

'Coming right up. I'll get these two some water, too.'

'Thanks, Paige,' Lucy said, before turning her attention back to the book that Cayden was now shoving under her face.

Later that night, after her family had left, Paige began the arduous task of cleaning up after the whirlwind that was her niece and nephew. The toys that she had carefully arranged in their rooms were spread all over the house, there were dirty handprints on seemingly every bit of glass, and she was sure there was something ground into the carpet by a tiny foot. But it had been so worth it. Spending time with them reminded her to try and see the world through optimistic eyes, seeing joy everywhere and always looking for opportunities for fun and for play.

She stripped the beds and put all the bedding on to wash before giving up for the night and sitting down in front of the television to unwind. It wasn't long before she realised that just television wasn't going to cut it, and she made herself a gin and tonic. Just as she sat back down again, her phone started ringing. It was Maya, but just a phone call rather than a video call this time.

'Hey Maya, what's up?' Paige said as she answered, closing her eyes.

'Hey, lovely, how're you?' Maya replied, avoiding the question.

'I'm OK. Tired. The kids have only just left.'

'How was their visit?'

'It was great, though I am looking forward to having

some time to myself. How was work?'

'Actually, lovely, that's why I'm calling. They've given me a moving date.'

'Oh?' Paige said, putting her glass down and sitting more upright on the sofa. 'When?'

'Two weeks tomorrow,' Maya said hesitantly.

'Two... two weeks?'

'I know, I know, it's soon, but they want to get the office up and running as quickly as possible, and it's such a great opportunity for me, I've got to do it. You understand?'

'I understand. It is a fantastic opportunity,' Paige forced out.

'Do you need to go do your pacing thing?'

'Please,' Paige said before abruptly hanging up. She picked up her drink again and downed it, before getting up to pour herself another one. This time she didn't sit back down, but instead started pacing back and forth in her living room, shaking her free hand as she walked. The kids had been a change, and Maya was really leaving, and she might be autistic, and novel-writing wasn't going well, and it was all too much. She unintentionally made her free hand into a fist and started thumping it against her chest, the slightly hollow sound reverberating up through her neck and down into her stomach. The regular beat of the thumping distracted her from the derailing train speeding through her head, bellowing as it did so. She put her drink back down on the table and used that hand to tap the side of her leg; a chaotic percussion performance that helped her regulate the pressure in her head.

Eventually she stopped pacing. She sat down in the corner of the sofa. She brought her knees to her chest and wrapped her arms around them. Her body still rocked slightly, but her head was slowing down. Sooty came waltzing into the room, stretching as he did so, and curled up next to her. When the expected stroking didn't come, he nuzzled into her, headbutting her until she paid him attention. The texture of his smooth fur under her fingertips helped ground her. She could feel his purring vibrating through her leg and was grateful for his company. She knew he would pretend it was pure coincidence he was sat with her, but he was always there when she got like this. His presence always helped calm her down, to the point where she often thought she related more to her cat that most humans.

It was nearly midnight by the time Paige eventually dragged herself up from the sofa. Her whole body ached like she had been mown down by a steamroller, and she had a headache that felt like an army of jackhammers was going off across her forehead. The physical toll of her emotions made her grateful that she didn't have to get up for anything in the morning, having pre-emptively taken a day off, knowing she'd be tired from having the kids over. She somehow made her feet move even though they felt like they had been turned to concrete, and she kept putting one heavy step in front of the other. Looking up the stairs felt like looking up a cliff face harder than she had ever climbed before. She used the handrail to help haul herself up the stairs to bed. Paige made herself brush her teeth even though her senses already felt like they were on fire, and the bristles on the toothbrush felt like needles. The sound they made felt like sandpaper grating against her skin and the smell and taste of the toothpaste burned. But still, she made herself do it.

Once in her room she simply took off her trousers and crawled into bed. She didn't have the energy to decide what pyjamas to wear, find them, and then get changed. She sent a quick text to Maya apologising and saying that she loved her, then turned her phone off. She pulled the duvet up tight around her neck, huddling under it even though she was quite warm. The streetlight forced its way through the blackout curtains. A cat yowled somewhere in the distance. Sooty jumped up on the bed with a thud, announcing his ungraceful arrival with a little chirp, before making his way up to where Paige's head poked out from under the duvet. Paige sleepily lifted her arms to allow Sooty under the cover, where he circled around a few times before settling down for the night, pressing himself against Paige's chest and stomach, his purr becoming a lullaby.

CHAPTER ELEVEN
Departures

That weekend Paige was at Maya's flat. Paige had cleared her schedule so she could spend Maya's last full weekend in the country with her, helping her pack. Maya was subletting her apartment while she was away, so she was putting all her belongings in storage. The flat had turned from a comfortable bachelorette pad into a city of boxes surrounded by mountains of empty furniture. There were lakes of bubble wrap here and there too, with packing tape boats sailing along their shores. Most of Maya's stuff would be going into storage for when she returned. She had two giant suitcases that she was taking with her on the plane, plus a large crate that had already been shipped out, and would arrive a week or so after she did. That evening the two women had ordered pizza, almost all the kitchenware having been packed already. The smell of fresh dough and melted cheese filled the flat. Maya collapsed dramatically into a particularly big bubble wrap lake and dragged her pizza box toward her.

'Remind me to never do this again!' she said to Paige, before folding a slice of pizza in half and shoving most of it into her mouth. Paige uncorked their second bottle of wine and poured two generous mugs - the only receptacle they still had to hand. Paige handed Maya her mug before sitting down on the floor next to her.

'Trust me, I wouldn't let you do this again,' Paige said, rubbing her lower back. The pair ate in silence, both of them too emotionally and physically tired to make idle conversation. Paige was looking aimlessly around the room when she spotted a card she recognised poking out from under one of the boxes. Reaching over, she dragged it out and smiled.

'I can't believe you kept this!' she exclaimed.

'Of course I did. It's not often your best friend puts it in writing that she's proud of you.'

'You'd just got your first graduate job, why wouldn't I have been proud of you?'

'I know, sweetie, it's just nice to have confirmation. You aren't always forthcoming with your emotions, good or bad.'

'I know. I'm working on it.'

'Is Taylor helping you work on it?' Maya teased. Paige shoved her friend, pushing her off her bubble wrap seat and onto the floor. Maya just giggled.

Once they had finished their pizza they forced

themselves to keep packing, the sound of unravelling parcel tape making Paige feel a bit ill. They didn't have a huge amount left to do; it was mainly the last fiddly bits that needed careful wrapping before being put into storage. Maya sighed as she taped up another box. When Paige had arrived Maya's flat had been in chaos; she had started packing very haphazardly with no idea what was in any of the boxes she had already packed. Paige had made her re-open the boxes, write down what was inside, and then carefully label every one before taping it back up. Maya complained, but complied. Organisational systems were definitely one of Paige's areas of expertise, so Maya had just let her take over. However, that meant they had been working non-stop for the best part of twelve hours.

Maya added her recently completed box to the pile, before turning to Paige. 'Shall we go out?'

'What?' Paige said, not really listening. She was in the middle of writing on one of the boxes.

'Let's go out, get plastered, and deal with the rest of this tomorrow.'

'Are you sure? There's still quite a lot to do,' Paige said, surveying the room.

'I know, but to be honest I'm done for the night, so it's either we go out or... I dunno... stare at the wall until we fall asleep.' Maya gestured around her, highlighting the lack of anything they could do in the flat. 'C'mon, Spence, one more night out, for the road?'

'Hmmm,' Paige said, thinking. Maya was looking at her with her best puppy dog expression. 'OK, fine. But you still have to get up in the morning to continue packing, OK?'

'Deal!' Maya said, grabbing her phone and looking around for her bag. 'Where did I -?'

'Here,' Paige said, handing Maya her bag, Paige had carefully placed it on a chair with the few other items that weren't being packed. She barely had time to register what was happening when Maya took her by the hand and dragged her out the front door. They were both giggling like misbehaving schoolchildren as they trotted down the stairs, too excited to wait for the lift. They burst through front door of the building, nearly colliding with a very surprised old lady wheeling her shopping bag along behind her.

'Where shall we go?' Paige asked, after they had apologised profusely to the startled old lady.

'Anywhere!' Maya said, waving down a taxi. The taxi pulled over and both women climbed into the back. Maya spoke to the driver.

'Take us wherever you would go if you were leaving the country for six months - and that doesn't have a dress code!' she said excitedly while looking herself and Paige up and down. 'We really should have planned this better. I mean, you're wearing trainers for Pete's sake. Planning is your department, so I reckon the first round is on you for this.'

'That's not fair!' Paige complained, doing up her seat belt. 'But I will buy the first round, as a leaving present to you.'

'Sweetie, you already got me several travel books for Japan,' Maya said, laughing.

'I know, but I figure you'd appreciate the drink more.'

The taxi pulled away, easing its way out into traffic. Paige could smell upholstery cleaner with an underlying tone of salt and vinegar. Out of the window the heart of the city rolled by. Students crawling from one bar to the next; indie rock venues with music so loud she could feel it, even in the taxi. Maya was also looking out of the window, smiling, but Paige could see her eyes shimmering in the streetlight. Maya noticed Paige watching her and, reaching over, took her hand. Paige squeezed her hand tightly and went back to watching out of her window.

Paige knew that this wasn't goodbye; Maya would be

on the other end of a phone or video call when their differing time zones allowed, and six months wasn't such a long time. But she still gripped her friend's hand tighter, like she was a child holding on to a helium balloon and one gust of wind would rip it away. Their earlier joviality had been replaced by silence as both women watched the world outside; watched other people continue their lives as if nothing in the world was wrong, when to Paige, it felt different. Like she was walking with a splinter in her foot she couldn't get out, yet she had no choice but to keep walking.

Eventually, they pulled up outside a quaint-looking pub and the taxi driver turned around.

'If I was leaving the country for a while, I'd want to spend my last night here with my friends, in a place I was actually able to hear them talk. The Fox and Hare is perfect for that,' he said, smiling gently at the sight of the two women holding hands.

'Thank you,' Maya said, reaching into her purse. The fare was only £5.50 but she gave him £10 and told him to keep the change. The friends got out of the taxi, Maya soon linking arms with Paige.

'Shall we?' Paige said, smiling at her friend.

Maya laughed and shook her head slightly before

leading them both inside.

The airport was bright white and silver, with splashes of bold advertising breaking up the monotony with its screams for attention. Hundreds of people were bustling around, rushing everywhere like ants on a scent trail. Most of the exposed walls were glass, allowing views out on to the tarmac where the planes jostled for position. Every now and again the announcement system would kick into life, an electronic polyglot informing people of gate numbers or expected delays. The shops and cafes that lined the concourse added a cacophony of noises to the melting pot, from hissing coffee machines to bleating checkout tills; the man-made jungle was awake. The ants rushing around didn't care if you were in their way; they just barged through you without a second glance, trailing their possessions behind them. The smell of cleaning fluid lingered in the air.

Maya stood with her parents; having checked in her hold luggage, she was spending every last precious minute with them before leaving. Paige was in the queue for coffee so as to give them time alone. The servers all hurried around behind the counter, barking orders at each other that could barely be heard over the din. A variety of travellers had queued up for a drink at this watering hole, most with heads bowed, staring at the phones in their hands. The queue shuffled forward. Eventually Paige made it to the front and a server demanded her order. She asked for a plain coffee, but the server's face looked like she was speaking a different language. He rattled off a variety of options, none of which registered properly in her brain. Looking around, she saw Maya was too far away to ask for help, so instead she just ducked out of the queue and sneaked across to the nearby toilets. The door swung open as another person exited and the sound of hand dryers screeching at her felt like someone was drilling directly into her skull. She turned on her heel and almost ran to the quietest-looking place she could see; a bookstore.

The sound felt dampened as soon as she turned the corner into the shop. There were still people, but not as many and not as loud. Paige walked slowly up and down the aisles, reading the titles and authors of each book. Occasionally she would take a book out and run her fingers along the pages, concentrating on how the many layers of paper felt under her fingers. She was on her third lap of the store when she noticed Maya standing on the boundary between the store and the rest of the airport, watching her.

'Hey,' Paige said quietly, making her way over to her

friend.

'Hey,' Maya responded softly.

'Is it time?'

'Yes, lovely. I have to go now.'

'OK,' Paige said, taking a big breath in and standing up a little straighter. 'I'm going to miss you so much.'

'I'm going to miss you too. You have to text me every day, OK? And I'll call when I can.'

Paige stepped forward and hugged her friend tightly, relishing in the last few seconds they had together for a while. Maya's arms wrapped around her like a shield, and Paige felt her squeeze as tightly as a vice. She was vaguely aware of people manoeuvring around them to get in or out of the bookstore, tutting, but she didn't care. Eventually the two women pulled apart, and Paige noticed Maya had tears falling down her cheeks.

'Why are you crying?' Paige asked.

'Because I'm sad to be leaving.'

'It's only for six months, it's not that long.'

'I know, lovely, but it still makes me sad, OK? Don't you feel sad?'

'I don't really know what to feel.'

'Feelings aren't a choice, Spence. You just have them,' Maya said, laughing slightly.

'Right. Yes. I knew that,' Paige said, joining in the mirth.

Paige and Maya's parents walked with Maya to the security gate, making the most of every last moment they had with her. Maya's dad insisted on carrying her hand luggage for her, even though it was just a rucksack. Her mum kept adjusting Maya's collar or trying to tame the same stray wisps of hair over and over. Paige just tried to be present.

'Right, you three need to leave now or I'm going to start crying properly. I can't have you stood there all forlorn, watching me queue to get through the metal detectors.'

Paige laughed before going in for one last hug.

'I love you, Maya, and I'll see you soon,' she said into her ear.

'I love you too, sweetie,' Maya whispered back with a small hitch in her voice.

Paige stepped back to allow Maya's parents to say their goodbyes.

'Now shoo! All of you!' Maya commanded once they were done, waving them away. Maya's dad took her mother's arm and started gently leading her away.

'Call me as soon as you land!' her mother shouted back

over her shoulder. Paige took one last look at her friend, gave a small wave, then took a deep breath and turned to walk away. Each step felt like it might make her shatter. But she kept walking, keeping her head held high and not looking back; she didn't want to make this any harder for Maya than it already was. She was proud of her friend and knew it was hard for her to leave, even if the promotion and extra responsibility were what she had been working towards for years.

Maya's parents tried to engage Paige in polite conversation as the three of them left the airport, but any words she could think of got stuck somewhere in her throat. She felt like she was choking. She gestured goodbye at Maya's parents and speed-walked in the other direction, with no idea where she was going or where her car was parked. It took a lot of self control to not run.

She eventually found a secluded part of the airport just beyond the drop-off zone, where everyone would be heading in the opposite direction, towards the airport main entrance. There was a low concrete wall and a solitary bin in the shadow of a large sign giving drivers directions. An empty crisp packet tumbled past as the wind whipped up, biting Paige's cheeks. She sat down on the grey wall and wrapped her arms around herself, shivering. She had left her coat in the car as she knew the airport would be warm. Breathing heavily, she did her best to hold back her tears. She did not understand why she was suddenly so emotional; the goodbye was done, and Maya would be back in no time. But a tear forced its way out. Then another. And before Paige knew it she was sobbing, her body jerking with the overwhelming emotion coursing through her.

An hour later, her phone vibrated in her pocket. She barely registered it. It vibrated a couple more times, not allowing itself to be ignored so easily. Paige gingerly unwrapped her arms from around herself; she had been holding herself so tense for so long that moving hurt. She dug her phone out her pocket and opened a series of messages from Taylor.

'*Hey, I was wondering if we could grab dinner together sometime this week? Not just as friends, as a date...*' the first text read, before, '*Sorry if you're not gay. I mean I think you might be but I'm not sure, maybe you're just nice to everyone.*' A third text read, '*Sorry if I ducked up our friendship.*' Paige squinted at the screen, not sure if her still watery eyes were obscuring her vision somehow, when a fourth text came through: '*Autocorrect knows that's not what I meant*'.

Paige smiled and wiped her eyes with her sleeve, before texting back, '*Dinner would be great. No duck though, please, I'm vegetarian.*'

CHAPTER TWELVE
The Date

TAYLOR

Taylor's bedroom looked like a tornado had formed in her wardrobe and gobbled up her clothes, then spat them out all over the bed, floor, and chest of drawers. Some had even made it as far as the landing. Almost all of her shoes had been dragged out from under her bed and were scattered around, only vaguely in pairs. Preparation for the date was not going well. Paige had only ever seen her in her climbing clothes or her work clothes, neither of which were chosen to make herself look more appealing. She had to be at the restaurant in under two hours, needed to shower and blow dry her hair, and there was the half hour's drive there as well. She quickly stripped off the red dress she had been trying on, deciding it was *too* formal. She didn't want to seem like she was trying too hard. The red dress was the latest addition to a pile of discarded clothes forlornly resting on the bed.

Taylor walked over to her chest of drawers and ripped one of the drawers open, digging through multiple pairs of very similar-looking jeans. She pulled them all out, one after another. She couldn't wear those ones, they had a hole in. This pair were too faded. That pair, the bottom of each leg had ripped where she had stood on the backs of them one too many times. The second to last pair of jeans stared up at her.

'Hmm. Maybe,' she said to no one.

The wardrobe doors were both mirrored, reflecting the chaos of the room back at her. She shimmied into the jeans and stood barefoot on the carpet in front of one of the mirrors, analysing her appearance from different angles. Finally satisfied, she removed the jeans and placed them carefully on top of the dresser. One piece of clothing down.

She had been so nervous sending that text to Paige. The last person she'd gone on a date with was Daniella, and after that fiasco she had given up on dating all together. But then Paige was thrust into her life, partly due to the endeavours of her brother, and here she was, trying on her fifteenth top of the evening.

Once she had finally made her outfit decisions, she checked the time and rushed into the shower. The warm water cascading down her body helped her muscles relax a little. The sound of the water droplets hitting the bathtub tapped away in her mind, reminding her of the passing of time and how she was probably already running late and what a bad impression that would give Paige. Turning off the water, she stepped out and wrapped herself in a huge fluffy towel, shivering slightly at the change in temperature.

Back at her dressing table she dried her hair and put some make-up on, quickly deciding it was too much, taking it all off, and reapplying it. She still wasn't happy with it when she stood up, but she didn't have enough time to do it again. She checked herself in the full-length mirror one more time. Her cream coloured blouse matched her cream coloured flat shoes, and the necklace she had chosen was a similar shade of blue to what was apparently the only smart pair of jeans she owned. It wasn't perfect, but it would have to do for now.

Just as she was getting in the car Dylan called, so she put him on speaker phone and set off.

'Hey, how're you feeling?' he asked, trying to hide the excitement in his voice and failing.

'Fine. OK, I guess. I don't know.' she responded, slightly distracted by the junction she was trying to pull out of.

'It'll be OK. You can always give me a call if you need

rescuing.'

'What, like my knight in shining armour?'

'Nah, more like your brother who can suddenly be taken ill and need you to come look after him.'

'Ha, thanks, I'll bear that in mind,' she said, pulling up at a set of red traffic lights. She looked at the car clock and willed the lights to change faster.

'Seriously though, Lor, how're you feeling?'

'Nervous, mainly. I'm a bit out of practice.'

'A bit?' he jibed.

'Not the time for jokes, Dyl,' Taylor said, just as a few paltry flakes of snow landed on her windscreen and slid gracefully down.

'You're right, I'm sorry. I'm sure you'll do great. You get on with her, and she obviously likes you or she wouldn't have said yes, so what have you got to lose?'

'I dunno, I might make a fool or myself, or freak out, or maybe she'll decide she just doesn't like me like that, and I'll have ruined our friendship.'

'Uh huh,' Dylan said, humouring her. 'Or, it could go really well and you'll both want a second date?'

'Yeah, that bit scares me too.'

'I know. But you've got this.'

'I know. Look, I've got to go; you know how bad I am

at multi-tasking, and I want to get there alive.'

'Roger that. Good luck!'

'Thanks,' she said before Dylan hung up.

Taylor pulled into the restaurant car park with a few minutes to spare. She looked around and couldn't see Paige's car anywhere, so she thought it would be safe to go in and order herself a drink, give herself a chance to acclimatise.

Inside the restaurant was a lot more formal than she had expected. It had been Paige's suggestion on account of the variety of vegetarian and vegan food they had, but she hadn't mentioned that it was rather upscale. Taylor turned slightly red as she made her way to the bar. Before she could get there, she was stopped by Paige calling out to her. She was already seated at the table, drink in hand. Taylor gave a shy wave and awkwardly changed direction.

'Hi,' Paige said, getting to her feet, and pulling Taylor's chair out for her. Paige had worn smart suit trousers that fitted her legs perfectly. The light blue shirt nicely framed her shoulders and flowed down her torso. She had worn her hair down, the first time Taylor had seen her do that. It almost glowed in the candlelight of the restaurant. She tried to respond to Paige's greeting but all she could manage was some kind of squeak. Taylor had hoped that she'd have a bit of time to settle herself before Paige got there; but here she was, staring at her with those beautiful brown eyes. Taylor shuddered slightly as she sat down.

'Did you find it OK?' Paige asked, taking a sip of her drink.

'Yes, thank you. I had a few wardrobe issues before leaving which is why I'm late, I'm sorry.'

'You're not late, and you look beautiful,' Paige said earnestly, her eyes twinkling and reflecting the candle's flame. Taylor swallowed hard. Paige must have noticed because she stopped a waiter and asked Taylor what she would have to drink.

'Just a lemonade, thank you,' she asked. The waiter nodded his head and floated away. Taylor shook her head slightly, trying to make her brain start working again.

'How're you? How was the airport?' Taylor asked. Paige had told her about seeing Maya off and how difficult it was over text, but Taylor wanted to check in person.

'It was… tough.' Paige said, taking another sip of her drink. 'The thought of not seeing Maya for so long is…' Her voice hitched slightly. Taylor instinctively reached out and took her hand. The instant sparks she felt electrified the butterflies in her stomach, and she blushed heavily; but she didn't let go. Paige smiled at her, though her eyes looked more like she wanted to run.

The waiter re-appeared, making them both jump and retract their hands simultaneously.

'Here is your drink, madam,' he said, lifting Taylor's lemonade off the tray he was holding and carefully placing it down in front of her. 'Are you ladies ready to order?' he asked, taking his tiny notepad and pencil out expectantly.

'Oh... right... yes' Paige said, picking up the menu. Taylor hadn't had a chance to even look at the different options, let alone decide what she wanted. She looked helplessly up at Paige, who was still focused on the menu in front of her. Taylor looked back down at her own menu, hoping something would jump out at her.

'Do you need more time?' the waiter asked, speaking directly to Taylor. She nodded, and the waiter floated away again.

'Sorry, I forgot,' Paige said, before explaining, 'I suck at decision making, so I always end up ordering the same thing. Most times I don't even look at the menu.'

'What do you normally have?' Taylor asked.

'I usually start with the melon or the soup, then have the roast or the halloumi.'

Taylor quickly scanned the text in front of her, locating

those items. She couldn't think straight, and every time she glanced up, she saw Paige watching her, one hand on the table while the other played with the stem of her wine glass. While still staring at the text in front of her, Taylor spoke.

'You make a habit of that, you know.'

'Of what?' Paige asked.

'Staring at people.'

'Do I? I'm sorry,' Paige said, looking down at the table. Taylor immediately wished she hadn't said anything, she hadn't wanted to make Paige feel uncomfortable.

The two women sat in silence until the waiter came back a few minutes later. Taylor still hadn't been able to make a decision so she just asked for the same as Paige, figuring it must be good if she ordered it nearly every time she came there. Taylor was trying to think of a way to reignite the conversation, but her brain felt like mush. Paige seemed to be actively avoiding making eye contact with her. But then, Taylor couldn't remember her making much eye contact any other time, either.

'How is work going?' Taylor asked, finally able to command her brain to form a coherent sentence.

'It's alright. My teaching schedule is pretty busy which doesn't leave me much time for any research projects.'

'What are you working on right now?' Taylor asked before taking a drink.

Paige launched into a long explanation of the novel she was writing, its relevance to the French Resistance, and how the women involved had been neglected in the annals of history. Taylor tried nodding and smiling in the right places, but she kept getting distracted by how Paige's face lit up when she was talking about her work. Her usually docile gestures became animated and excited, and Taylor could hear the passion in her voice as she spoke.

When their food arrived, Paige was forced to stop her monologue, allowing Taylor to ask some more questions. Taylor wanted to know everything she could about her, her hobbies, her family, her life before teaching, everything. Paige, however, had her own questions.

'How did you come to be working at the university?' she asked innocently. Taylor didn't know how to respond. This was their first real date, and it was way too soon to tell her about Daniella. But she didn't want to lie.

'An old professor contacted me about a research opportunity, and it was too good to pass up!' she said jovially, overcompensating for the dark clouds of memories attached to that point in her life. Taylor smiled and focused back on the meal in front of her. 'This is really good!' she said, loading another forkful of melon and attempting to gracefully put it in her mouth.

'It's one of my favourites,' Paige said, smiling.

'I can see why!' Taylor said from behind a polite hand covering her mouth.

'Why did you give up climbing for so many years?' Paige asked. No pre-amble; direct and to the point. Taylor knew the question was innocent enough, but it felt like Paige was homing in on all her weaknesses. Taylor normally controlled conversations by asking questions; people normally loved to talk about themselves, so it didn't take much to keep the conversation away from her personal life. But Paige wouldn't allow herself to be misdirected.

'Dylan had a few issues that meant he couldn't climb for a while,' Taylor said, trying to keep her voice steady as more unhappy memories threatened to fill her mind. 'It just didn't feel right without him, so I stopped.'

'I can understand that,' Paige said, giving her a comforting smile.

'You can?' Taylor said, amazed. Most people didn't understand why she gave up something she was good at, just because her brother stopped.

'Of course. It's just not the same, is it? Like you only

had half the pieces to the jigsaw,' Paige said, shrugging her shoulders slightly.

'Exactly,' Taylor said, beaming at her.

The waiter stealthily reappeared and cleared away their plates. Taylor didn't even realise she had left her hand on the table until Paige took it in her own, in what Taylor thought was supposed to be a reassuring way. Taylor immediately blushed again as the butterflies in her stomach became so erratic, she thought they might burst out.

'You make a habit of that, you know,' Paige said, jokingly echoing Taylor's earlier words. Taylor appreciated her attempt to put her at ease, but it only made her blush harder. She was so painfully aware of the burning in her cheeks that she did not need to ask what Paige meant.

They were broken apart by the waiter popping up next to them with their main course, and it wasn't long before they were talking again, the conversation slowly starting to flow more easily as they got past their nerves and actually began to enjoy themselves. Neither woman had room for dessert, and when the bill came Paige insisted on paying despite Taylor's protestations. Once outside the restaurant, neither woman was quite ready for the night to end, so Taylor suggested they walk to a nearby park.

PAIGE

Paige was grateful when Taylor suggested they go for a walk. She had been nervous for the entire day, so much so that she had arranged for the taxi to pick her up half an hour earlier than necessary. She'd smiled more that evening than she had the entire week since Maya left.

Despite wearing her thickest coat Paige was still shivering slightly as they walked. She hoped that Taylor would not hear her teeth chattering. The streets were fairly empty, most people having the sense to stay inside on a night where the temperatures threatened to dip below freezing. Lights shone out from behind different coloured curtains and blinds, like a multi-coloured mosaic lining the street. Paige could just make out the outline of large clouds, where the moonlight had forced its way through. There was a light breeze which made the scant trees whisper, gossiping about the two women walking down the street who were trying not to look at each other but edging ever closer.

They rounded the corner, and the park came into view. It was one of the smaller parks in the city; a small playground adjoining a larger patch of grass with criss-crossing paths. In the centre was an exuberant, intricately decorated fountain, with laughing cherubs holding up a large stone bowl. The fountain was silent now, hibernating, waiting for the spring and the warmer weather. Paige and Taylor started walking down one of the paths that ran around the outside of the park. Despite her best attempts, Paige couldn't mask the shiver that overcame her body, and she brought her hands up to her mouth to blow hot air into them, a minuscule respite from the cold.

'Are you OK?' Taylor asked, concerned.

'Yes, I'm fine, just a bit chilly,' Paige responded, ignoring the fact she could no longer feel her toes.

'Here,' Taylor said, taking off her scarf, gloves, and hat and handing them to Paige. 'Put these on.'

'What?! No, then you'll be cold!'

'I'll be fine. Please? You're practically turning blue in front of my eyes.' Taylor stopped walking and held the woollen items out towards Paige, staring at her, playfully daring her to try and decline again.

'Thank you,' Paige said demurely. The truth was as soon as she slipped her hands into the gloves, she understood why Taylor was so attached to them; her hands immediately began to warm and the headache she was starting to get abated.

They carried on walking, occasionally discussing the cold or climbing, but mainly in a comfortable silence. Taylor was walking so close next to her that she could see the individual eyelashes framing her eyes, and she had to resist the temptation to reach out and tuck some stray strands of hair, now free from their hat bonds, behind Taylor's ear. As if the weather had taken pity on her, large flakes of snow started falling from the sky, providing a welcome distraction. Taylor turned her face to the sky and laughed, sticking her tongue out to try and catch the snowflakes in her mouth. Paige just watched, in awe of her child-like joy.

'It's snowing! I wonder if it will stick?' Taylor said, grinning.

'The ground is probably cold enough for it to.'

'Isn't this great?' Taylor asked rhetorically, stepping out onto the grass and slowly spinning around with her arms out, her hair fluttering in the wind. She stopped suddenly and just looked at Paige thoughtfully. Paige didn't understand what was happening. Taylor held out her hand to Paige, inviting her to the side of childish fun. Paige hesitated briefly before extending her own, gloved hand and clasping the colder one that was offered. Immediately she was pulled forwards and Taylor began spinning her around like the nearby merry-go-round would, laughing the entire time. Paige couldn't help herself and she began laughing too, breaking away from Taylor's grip and spinning into a pirouette, finishing with a flourish. The two women couldn't stop grinning and stealing glances at each other, playing in the snow like they had when they were children. Eventually they were forced to stop due to dizziness, and they crunched their way back to the path, the frozen grass now littered with little white flecks of joy.

'We should probably head back soon, it's getting late,' Taylor said ruefully. She interlinked her arm with Paige's as if it was the most natural thing in the world. Paige, to her surprise, found she didn't mind.

'Where did you park?' Taylor asked

'I didn't, I got a taxi.'

'Ah, OK. If you call one now, it should be there by the time we get back to the restaurant?' Taylor suggested.

'Good idea.' Paige used an app on her phone to summon a taxi, having to remove the borrowed gloves to do so. 'I should probably give you these back now, before I forget,' she said, reluctantly removing the hat, scarf, and remaining glove. 'Thank you for letting me borrow them.'

'Not a problem,' Taylor said, seemingly trying to hide how grateful she was to be able to warm her hands up again.

They saw even fewer people on their walk back to the restaurant. There were less mosaic tiles of light, too, with many people having already turned in for the night. Paige shoved both her hands into her pockets, not wanting to give up the warmth she had managed to accumulate. Taylor re-linked their arms without need for an invitation.

There were only a few cars left at the restaurant by the time they got there, and they could see through the windows the last of the patrons finishing up their meals. Taylor stamped her feet a little, still recovering from her time sans woollens.

'I'll be OK if you want to go?' Paige offered gently. 'You look frozen.'

'I'm fine, and I'm not about to leave you on your own. What if that taxi doesn't show?'

'Then I'll call another one,' Paige stated

'*Fine*, Miss Practical, but I'm still not leaving you,' Taylor said, her lip now trembling slightly.

A few minutes later the taxi pulled into the restaurant car park, headlights picking up the snow as it danced its way to the ground.

'Thank you for tonight, I had a great time,' Paige said, smiling at Taylor. Taylor didn't respond, but instead went to her tiptoes and gave Paige a gentle kiss on the cheek. Paige was too stunned to respond straight away. She just stood there stiffly, and when Taylor withdrew, she was blushing heavily.

Paige tried speaking but was unsure what words if any she would be able to form. Her heart felt like it was doing a tap dance, while her brain felt like it had flat-lined, and her stomach was full of fireworks.

'Goodnight, then,' Taylor said grinning, as she opened the taxi door for Paige. It took a while for Paige to will her body to move; she felt like she had been cemented to the spot. Eventually she managed to force her uncooperative limbs into the taxi, and Taylor shut the door. The car window framed her date as she stood there, wanting to see the taxi off. She had the most beautiful smile spread across her face, whilst the snow spun around her like she was its choreographer. The taxi started pulling away and Taylor gave a slight wave, watching it the entire way out the car park.

'Where to, love?' the taxi driver asked, needing to know which way to turn. Paige gave him her street name and, finally, relaxed back into the seat. A small smile began to form on her face, and she wrapped her arms around herself. Her smile grew strong and wide, and she crossed her legs and began watching out the window. The street lamps they passed created their own stages, allowing the snow to be itself as it fell, dancing all the way.

CHAPTER THIRTEEN
Lost

Taylor was wrapped up warm in bed, two duvets tight around her like a cocoon. She was sleeping with a slight smile on her face, dreaming of the date she had with Paige, when the shrill sound of her phone woke her.

'Ungh,' she moaned, chastising herself for forgetting to turn her alarm off. It was Saturday and there was nothing specific to get up for. She fumbled for her phone with her eyes still closed, wanting to hold on to the last remnants of the dream, but it was no good. Reluctantly opening her eyes, she could see the bright blue light of her phone illuminating up her bedside table. The light seared her eyes as she held the phone in front of her face, trying to get her bleary eyes to clear enough to turn the alarm off. It took her a few seconds to realise what had woken her wasn't her alarm. Her parents were ringing her. At one in the morning.

She picked up, suddenly alert now, and pressed the phone to her ear.

'H-hello?' she stammered.

'Taylor, it's your brother,' her father said from the

other end of the phone. Taylor's eyes shot open and she immediately sat up in bed like a jack-in-the-box.

'Dylan?' she asked rhetorically. 'What's happened?' her voice trembled slightly as she braced herself for whatever was coming.

'He just called us. It sounded like her was in a club of some sort, we could barely hear him,' her father said quickly. 'Taylor, I don't think he was sober.'

'Shit,' Taylor said, already out of the warm confines of her bed and clumsily getting dressed one handed. 'Hang on, Dad, I'll put you on speaker,' she said, putting her phone down on her bedside table. 'OK.'

'Do you know where he might be?' her dad asked, pleadingly.

'No. He didn't mention going out. I have no idea.'

'It sounded very loud, so I'm pretty sure it was a club, but there must be loads of them near you.'

'Yeah...' Taylor shuddered. 'I'll find him though, Dad. I always do.'

'I know. I'm sorry to dump this on you... again. But we're just too far away now.'

'It's fine, Dad, honestly. The whole idea of him coming here was so I could keep an eye on him. I'd hoped I wouldn't need to...' she said as she shimmied into her jogging bottoms.

'We'll drive up first thing in the morning,' her dad said helplessly.

'You don't have to.'

'Taylor, we need to. We need to be able to do something,' he said authoritatively, before more quietly adding, 'You're going to need back up.'

'Yeah, I know. I need to go now, Dad, I'll text you when I find him.'

'OK. Thank you, sweetheart. We love you.'

'I love you too, Dad. Bye,' Taylor replied, then hung up. She was still only half dressed, trying to find some warmer layers to search the city in. It had snowed on and off for a few days, since her date with Paige, and she knew she would be no use to Dylan with hypothermia. She found her gloves and hat under a pile of dirty washing in the corner of her room, then pounded down the stairs and grabbed her scarf and winter coat off the hooks by the door. She violently shoved her feet into her snow boots and attempted to tie them up, only to keep dropping the loop or pulling them too tight and them coming undone.

'Damn it, Dylan!' she yelled at no one, ripping the offending shoe off and throwing it across the hallway, hitting the wall with a thud. Sat on the stairs, she buried her head in her hands and sobbed. It was one in the morning, she had only just woken up, and her brain was fighting to go back into that blissful dream state. Dylan had been attending all his classes and getting good marks, he had been going climbing regularly, and started making some real friends. It had all seemed to be going well. Nothing like the last time he had tried going to university, when he and Taylor left for separate universities at eighteen. Their grandad died, then their mother was diagnosed with cancer, all in Dylan's first year. He dropped out the summer between his first and second year. But everything was fine this time, which just made her more upset and angry.

Eventually she pulled herself together, retrieved her shoe, shoved it on her foot, and stood in front of the hallway mirror, steeling herself for the hunt she was about to go on. She had the advantage of knowing her prey quite well, but a drunk Dylan was an unpredictable Dylan.

Her first destination was his flat. She wouldn't normally entertain the idea of banging on someone's door in the small hours of the morning, but his flatmates might be able to point her in the right direction. She got into her car and brought up Dylan's number on her phone, hoping she could get through to him and wouldn't have to rudely awaken someone else. He didn't pick up any of the half a dozen times she called him on the way to his flat. She tried once more once she got there, praying for an answer, but nothing. She took a deep breath and dragged herself out of the car, through the always unlocked security gate, and up the three flights of stairs to his flat, ignoring the feeling of ratchet straps being tightened around her chest.

She steeled herself, raised her fist, and banged loudly on the door. She didn't expect a response the first time. She knew that if someone banged on her door at gone one in the morning she wouldn't be tempted to answer it, but she had to be persistent. Taylor paced back and forth a little, with every second she waited before knocking again feeling like an hour. Her willpower didn't last long and she banged on the door again, harder and with a higher tempo. She needed to get someone out of bed, if anyone was in there at all. She tried knocking a third time but still didn't get answer. Taylor sighed angrily before heading back to the stairs and bounding down them two at a time.

'Please, I just need to find my brother,' she pleaded with the bouncer. He didn't respond, unmoved by her plight. The queue for the club stretched out behind her and he clearly thought she was just trying to pull a fast one. She turned away from him, withheld tears burning her eyes. This was the sixth club she had tried; the other five had at least let her in to try and find him. She walked past the queue of people and shivered with empathy. Most of the boys were only wearing shirts and trousers and some of them were shivering. The girls were almost all wearing dresses that stopped above their knees, with nothing to keep their uncovered shoulders warm. The toes of their bare feet poked out of the end of their shoes, and some of them were definitely a little blue. Taylor took her phone out again, the screen lighting up the side of her face, and tried calling Dylan again. She must have called him over twenty times with no response, so she jumped a little when he actually picked up.

'Heellllllloooooooooooo,' he said drunkenly, laughing down the phone at her.

'Dylan, where are you?!' she almost screamed at him, the frustration of the night bubbling over.

'Whyyyy? Is the Taylornator out to get me?!' he said making fun of her.

'Dylan! I'm serious! Where are you?'

'Uhhh… I dunno.' He admitted. 'Hey, mate,' he said to someone else there, 'where are we?'. Taylor could hear a muffled response in the background.

'This fine gentleman says we are in King's Kebab House,' Dylan continued, slurring his words.

'OK. Stay there. I'm coming.'

'Are you joining us for some drinky-poos?' Dylan said excitedly.

'Yeah, something like that,' Taylor said angrily as she hung up. She quickly put the kebab place into the map app on her phone, and let out a frustrated screech. It was on the other side of town. She'd been looking in completely the wrong place. Shoving her phone back in her pocket, she walked back to her car trying to calm herself down, resisting the urge to run to the vehicle. She didn't need a speeding ticket, or worse, to put a bitter cherry on top of her night.

Back at her car, she took a long, deep breath before starting the engine. In the hour or so she'd been gone, the windscreen had partially frozen over, which hampered her departure. She started thinking of all the things she wanted to yell at her brother, about how he was selfish and how he'd thrown away years of sobriety over what? A few laughs? She gripped the steering wheel tighter and let out a frustrated growl as her knuckles turned white. Once the windscreen had cleared enough for her to drive, she set off, hoping that Dylan hadn't moved on from the kebab place.

Taylor kept thinking about all the other times she'd had to go out in the middle of the night to find her brother like this, but those memories were interspersed with others. Dylan talking her through her fear of heights when she first started climbing, when they were only eight. Dylan offering to beat up any boy who broke her heart, before she had told him she was gay. Dylan standing by her while her parents got used to that idea. Her anger began dissipating and she reminded herself that this wasn't him; addiction was an illness, and being angry at him wouldn't help him heal.

She pulled up outside King's Kebab House and her shoulders relaxed slightly; she could see him through the window. He stood next to one of his flatmates, talking to two women who clearly wished they were elsewhere. He stumbled a few times while gesticulating wildly, catching himself at the last second by grabbing onto a nearby table. Taylor turned off the car and went inside.

'Tayloooooooooooor in the house!' he shouted as soon as she walked through the door.

'Time to go, Dylan,' she said calmly, putting her hand on her brother's arm. He quickly shrugged it off.

'But the night is so young!' he said, throwing his arms out wide and looking up at the strip lights above him, blinking painfully and instantly regretting his decision.

'Please, Dyl?' Taylor said, barely above a whisper. 'Mum and Dad are worried.'

'Why? Did you call them to tell on me?' he said, still blinking the light out of his eyes.

'No, Dylan, *you* called them. From inside a club.'

Dylan's jovial smiled slipped.

'Oh.'

'Yeah, "oh",' she spat. 'I said I'd find you. They're driving up in the morning.'

'Why? I'm fiiiine. I've made some friends! See?' he said, standing next to one of the women and throwing his arm around her shoulder. The unsuspecting woman quickly removed it, as if it was something disgusting she had found on the bottom of her shoe. Dylan's smile faltered again. Taylor knew that somewhere in there he understood the gravity of what had happened.

'Who're you to spoil the party?' his flatmate said, stepping into her personal space and squaring up to her.

'I'm his sister, as you well know,' she said with as much bravado as she could manage; Dylan's flatmate was several inches taller than her and clearly frequented the gym often.

Dylan snapped, forced himself in between his sister and

the flatmate and pushed the flatmate hard in the chest. 'Don't speak to her like that,' he yelled, still struggling to keep himself upright. The flatmate quickly surveyed the kebab house and seemed to register the number of other people there, and more importantly, the cameras.

'Whatever,' he said, pushing past them and walking out.

'Yeah, you better leave!' Dylan said drunkenly, once his flatmate was out of earshot. The guy was several inches taller than him, too. The two women had also disappeared off into the street, leaving just Dylan and Taylor standing by the doorway.

'C'mon,' Taylor said gently, holding his arm and guiding him out of the kebab shop. She just about managed to open the passenger door while keeping him upright, before he tumbled in, hitting his head on door frame as he did so.

'Karma,' Taylor muttered under her breath, before slamming the passenger door and heading to the driver's side. She shot off a quick text to her dad before getting in, letting him know that she'd got Dylan and was taking him back to hers. She climbed into the car and started putting on her seatbelt before starting the engine. Dylan half leaned, half fell over, his head landing on her shoulder.

'I love you,' he laughed giddily.

'Uh huh' she responded, pushing him back into the upright position. 'Put your seatbelt on.'

Once they got home Taylor had to awkwardly manoeuvre her brother into the house, his arm over her shoulders and her hanging on tightly as he teetered everywhere. His control over his limbs seemed limited and his attempts to co-operate only seemed to slow progress down. She still hadn't set up the spare bedroom so she deposited him on the sofa, the springs groaning under the sudden weight.

'Stay here,' she commanded as she disappeared off into the kitchen. Dylan saluted her in response, giggling. Taylor let the tap run, checking the temperature of the water with her fingers before filling up a two-litre plastic bottle for her brother. She took that back into the living room and put it in his hands without saying a word, not trusting herself to keep her temper in check. She left again, this time on the search for the painkillers he would inevitably need in the morning when his hangover hit. He hadn't drunk in so long, part of her hoped that meant the hangover would be worse than ever, maybe bad enough to put him off. After she found the painkillers she went back into the living room only to find Dylan lying on his side, his feet still half on the floor, cuddling the water bottle and just beginning to snore. She put the painkillers down on the table in front of him and got several blankets to cover him with. He didn't seem to mind not having a pillow so she didn't bother trying to find one. Once he was sorted she retrieved her own duvet and pillow, laying them out on the other sofa, and attempted to settle down. She didn't want him to choke on his own vomit in his sleep. She realised she hadn't got him a bucket yet, so she reluctantly got back up off the sofa to get one from the utility room. It didn't take her long to find; she picked it up and turned to go back to the living room, but found she couldn't make her feet move. Instead tears started rolling silently down her cheeks and muffled sobs began to shake her entire body, her stomach full of stabbing pains from the effort it was taking to hold her crying in as much as possible. She dug her phone out of her pocket and thought about texting her parents, but she didn't want to worry them any more than they already were. She would see them in a few hours anyway. Instead, she leant back against the wall and slowly slid down until she was sat on the floor. She kicked the door closed and let her weeping overcome her, crying loudly and punching her small fists into the tiled floor. It wasn't fair that this was happening, again.

Eventually the crying stopped and was replaced by pure numbness; partially from being sat on the cold floor for so long but mainly due to not having any more emotions to give. She eased herself to her feet, the cramping in her legs quickly changing to pins and needles to the point where she had to steady herself on the washing machine for a few minutes. Taking a few deep breaths, she wiped her eyes and tried to make herself look unfazed, just in case Dylan was awake when she went back to give him the bucket. However, it turned out he was still fast asleep, snoring his head off with drool dripping out of his mouth and onto the sofa. She'd make him clean it tomorrow.

She put the bucket down by the sofa, the same end as his head, and then headed toward her makeshift bed. The lumpy cushions did not promise a comfortable night's sleep but it was better than lying awake upstairs, worrying. She wrapped the duvet around her as tightly as she could, trying to emulate the feelings she'd had before her parents had woken her a few short hours ago. She willed the nice dreams to come, of her and Paige playing in the snow or her and Paige climbing, but her brain seemed to always find a way to tie it back to Dylan and her relationship with him. Even dancing in the snow reminded her of their youth, when they were both building snowmen in the yard, so carefree.

She checked the time on her phone. It was nearly five a.m. now. Her parents would probably be setting off on the three-hour drive soon. She didn't want to think about the state her mother would be in when they arrived, and her dad's stoic face kept popping into her mind; a mask that tried to hide the hurt of the situation. She drifted off to sleep not knowing what tomorrow would bring. Would Dylan be repentant, or would he claim innocence, or that it was 'just one drink' so it wasn't a problem? Would he accept help, or fight it like he had done so many times before? Her mind flew back to the last time he had gotten this drunk, the time that finally had brought him to his senses.

The nightmare had started with flashes of blue light coming through her bedroom window, bright enough that they woke her up before the call of the doorbell did. Her pitch-black bedroom intermittently illuminated by blue allowed her to pick her way across the debris of the floor; the recent upheaval from living with her ex had not given her time to unpack. A door on the landing creaked open and her bleary-eyed father met her gaze. The doorbell rang again. Without saying a word her father signalled that she should remain upstairs and that he would go to the door.

Taylor followed him as far as the top of the stairs, out of curiosity and fear. There were gentle but gruff voices at the door, with words like 'your son' and 'hospital' and 'drowned' floating up the staircase. Her father's head dropped, chin to chest, as he took in the news. Taylor was joined by her mother at the top of the stairs. Her mother put an arm around her and Taylor could feel her shaking. The cold air blew the rain through the open front door, speckling her father's pyjamas with water.

With a flash the nightmare changed. The family were at the hospital, surrounding the bed of a forlorn figure wrapped in warming blankets. The doctors said they didn't know how long he had been in the water, or how long he had been without oxygen. The sun slowly rose and tried to crawl its way into the side room. Nurses bustled in and out, but the family did not move; frozen by the coldness of their brother and son's body.

A doctor tapped her father on the shoulder. The person who had jumped in to pull him out of the frigid dock was asking for an update, and they needed the family's permission to share information with him. Her father nodded silently, tears rolling down his cheeks. There was a knock at the side room door, but it didn't open. The knock got louder and more insistent, before Taylor woke with a start.

She peeled her eyes open, blinking into the light that was now filling her living room. The lumpy shape on the sofa indicated that Dylan was still there, sound asleep. Her weary body reluctantly complied with her commands to get up and open the door. The outline of her parents was visible through the frosted glass as she fumbled trying to get the keys into the lock to let them in.

'Oh, Taylor!' her mother said as soon as she opened the door. She caught sight of her reflection over her mother's shoulder as she was enveloped in a hug. Her eyes were bloodshot with heavy bags underneath them. Her skin was very pale, and her hair was all over the place. Her father quickly joined them in the hug, before raising his eyebrows questioningly.

'In the living room,' Taylor said in response, and her father slipped past them to investigate.

'Let's make you a cup of tea,' her mother said, fussing with the hem of Taylor's pyjamas.

'I don't drink tea, Mum,' Taylor said gently.

'I know, but I still don't know how to make coffee the way you like it,' her mother said, placing her hand on the small of her daughter's back and guiding her towards the kitchen.

The kitchen felt cold under the early morning winter sun. It beamed through the windows, highlighting all the hard edges that existed in the tiled room. Taylor's mum filled the kettle up and put it on, then began rummaging for mugs. She also started filling the sink with hot water and dropping the few dirty dishes around into the soapy bowl.

'Mum, you don't need -' Taylor began.

'I might as well while I'm here,' her mum responded, cutting her off.

'Mum, it's OK -'

'Where do you keep your washing up liquid?' her mum asked, ignoring her.

'Mum, stop!' Taylor said, louder than she meant to. Her mum froze at the sound of her daughter's raised voice and braced herself on the counter, hands either side of the sink.

'Mum, it's OK,' Taylor said more gently, getting up off the chair and walking over to her mother, turning her around and hugging her. Her mother hugged her back tightly and began crying.

'Shhhhh, It's OK.' Taylor said, stroking her hair. 'It's going to be OK.'

CHAPTER FOURTEEN
Found

Dylan woke up not long after his parents arrived. He avoided making eye contact with anyone and instead slipped away to take a shower. Taylor tided up all the bedding while her mum made everyone more hot drinks, then the three of them sat in near silence waiting for Dylan to return. The ticking of the living room clock echoed around the room and the sound of the shower running drifted through the ceiling. The sun climbed a little higher in the sky and more cold light flooded into the room. Taylor took a sip of her tepid tea. Her father was staring straight ahead, gripping his still-full mug with white knuckles. Her mother kept fidgeting, first with the cushions, then with the books on the table, finally getting up and putting them back on the bookshelf. Taylor didn't have the heart or energy to tell her that that wasn't where they lived.

The pipes clunked as the shower was shut off, making Taylor and her mum jump. All her father did was set his tea down on the table. Dylan eventually came down the stairs and walked straight through the living room into the kitchen, without saying a word. Their father clenched his fists until his nails dug into his palm. The smell of toast drifted into the room, as did the sound of the kettle boiling and clicking off. A chair scraped on the tiled floor as Dylan sat at the kitchen table to eat his breakfast. Their father moved as if to stand up, but their mother put her hand out and touched his thigh, with a slight shake of the head; that wasn't how to hunt, you had to let the prey come to you.

Eventually Dylan appeared in the doorway, staring at the floor. He opened his mouth a few times as if to speak, but quickly closed it again and swallowed hard. Unable to take the tension anymore, Taylor spoke.

'What happened?' she asked, trying to keep her voice calm.

'I... I don't know' Dylan answered.

'What do you mean, "you don't know"?' their father said, his nostrils flaring.

'I went out for lunch with Mark and the rest of my flatmates. That's all. That's all it was supposed to be,' he cried silently, his tears trickling down his face.

'How did lunch turn into getting so drunk you could barely stand up straight?' their father demanded.

'I don't know!' Dylan screamed before storming off

upstairs.

'That went well,' Taylor bit sarcastically, taking another sip of her now cold tea. Her mother got up and resumed straightening things around the room, whilst her dad just ran his knuckles up and down his thighs.

'I'm going to call Mark,' Taylor said, getting up and heading into the hallway, careful to shut the living room door behind her. The last thing she wanted to do was speak to the brute from the kebab shop again, but she needed answers.

The phone rang for quite a while before Mark groggily answered. Taylor tried to be diplomatic and polite, shoving the memories of last night's confrontation out of her mind. They discussed yesterday's events in calm tones while she passed up and down the hallway, her fingers trailing across the wall. The facade of calmness was quickly shattered.

'You did WHAT?' Taylor yelled down the phone. The living room door flung open as her parents rushed into the hallway. Taylor and Mark exchanged a few more heated words before Taylor angrily hung up, throwing her phone to the floor, causing the screen to crack.

'Taylor?' her mother said, gently reaching out for her daughter, who aggressively shrugged her off. Her father stepped forward and put his hands on either side of her shoulders to force her to stop pacing. The rage boiled in her eyes.

'Mark spiked his drink,' she eventually managed to spit out. 'He thought Dylan was being "too uptight", so he ordered him real cocktails, instead of the mocktails he'd been drinking. I'm going to *KILL* him!' Taylor said, ripping out of her father's grasp and starting to pace again. Her father's features softened.

'I'll go and talk to him,' he said, turning to go upstairs.

'I need to get out of this house,' Taylor said, grabbing her shoes and coat and heading for the door, slamming it behind her.

The trees lining her street were almost completely bare now, the last few brown leaves clinging on as tightly as they could, fighting the inevitable. The wind picked up and blew some of their fallen fellows into her path, making a satisfying crunch every time she put her foot down. Taylor zipped her coat up tighter, so it covered her mouth, and shoved her hands deep into her coat pockets; in her haste she hadn't grabbed her hat, scarf, or gloves. She started walking faster to try and keep warm.

There were some children playing in the street up ahead, kicking a football between them and laughing as one nutmegged the other. The cars parked on either side almost looked like they were wincing every time the ball came near them. The sound of the children faded as Taylor moved further away, marching forward despite her heart pulling her back with memories of her brother, interlaced with the hopelessness etched across his face that morning.

It had taken months of rehab and therapy for him to get sober. And before that her parents were on first-name terms with the local police officers due to the number of times they had brought him home for his own safety. But Dylan had worked so hard to stop drinking. He had cut ties with all his unsupportive friends, which didn't leave him with many. He started using exercise as a way to escape, first at the gym in the rehab facility and then he'd finally got back into climbing. At the same time, he worked hard with a therapist to be more open with his emotions instead of burying them, which is what had led him to start drinking excessively in the first place. All of that could be lost due to the actions of one vindictive person, spiking Dylan's drink for his own amusement. Taylor could feel the anger rising up inside her again. It wasn't fair.

Back at the house, Dylan had come back downstairs and sat on the sofa. He was quietly crying while his mother comforted him, making shushing noises and holding him tight. Taylor found her dad in the kitchen in the middle of making more drinks.

'Hey, kiddo,' he said once he noticed Taylor's presence.

'How is he?' she asked.

'Hurt. Scared. He feels betrayed by someone he thought he could trust and he's scared it's taken him back to square one with his recovery.'

Taylor put a comforting hand on her dad's back and started the kettle boiling again.

'What are we going to do, Lor?' he asked, his voice shaking and his eyes shimmering.

'We move him in here,' Taylor said matter-of-factly. Her father didn't respond straight away, but stood up straighter and looked at his daughter, almost as if he was sizing her up for the challenge she was about to take on.

'Are you sure?' he asked, trying to keep the hopeful tone out of his voice and failing.

'I'm sure. I believe he didn't mean for this to happen. And the best way for it to not happen again is to get him out of that flat. I can keep an eye on him better if he's here.'

Her dad reached out and put his hands on her shoulders again, gently pulling her towards him and kissing her forehead, before slipping away to the living room where, Taylor assumed, he was telling her mum and brother the plan. Taylor made herself a strong black coffee and took a large gulp. This was not going to be easy.

She pulled her phone out of her pocket and sent a quick email off to her supervisor, asking for a week of emergency leave, citing family issues. She knew she was just being polite; there was no way she was going into work that week. She downed the rest of her coffee and went back into the living room where her family were huddled together on the sofa. Dylan's eyes were dry now, but they were still crimson.

'Dad, can you help me sort the spare room? And Dyl,' she said, speaking to her brother for the first time since last night. He couldn't meet her gaze. 'Make a list of everything you need from your flat for the next few days, stuff we can grab quickly. We'll move the bigger stuff once we've sorted out a van; I don't really want to do multiple trips with Mark around.'

Dylan nodded and immediately retrieved a notebook and pen from the side table, putting his head together with their mother as they discussed what he might need.

Taylor and her father made their way upstairs and into the spare room, surveying the towers of boxes.

'Where do you want to start?' her father asked.

Taylor shrugged before ripping open the nearest box. Her dad imitated her and soon the sound of packing tape ripping and cardboard crunching filled the room. The sun lazily peaked in the sky before beginning its descent towards the horizon. They kept working, Taylor directing her dad to the appropriate room with every new discovery. They had placed a 'to donate' box by the door and it was quickly filling up as they worked their way through the room, bulldozing the towers that had stood there for so long. Taylor's father started on the top box in the last tower and suddenly froze, pulling out a china doll Taylor had had since her childhood. Or what was left of it. Inside the plastic container the separate pieces of the doll had been carefully wrapped in bubble wrap. Taylor had her back to her father so had no idea what he had found.

'Lor, what happened?' he asked, softly, holding out the box of broken doll bits.

'It's nothing, she got broken, that's all.'

'Taylor,' her dad said sternly. She didn't meet his gaze.

'Daniella broke it. On purpose.'

'I'm sorry, sweetheart. I'm so sorry,' he said, putting the box down and wrapping his daughter in a hug. Taylor allowed herself to be consoled for a few seconds, nostalgic for a softer time when a hug from her father could fix all the world's problems. She didn't indulge herself for long. There were only a handful of boxes left now; she could see the floor in this room for the first time in years. A distinct layer of dust adorned the carpet in the few spaces where there hadn't been boxes, or where there had been gaps. It created a haphazard maze; one that disintegrated if you touched it. The maze was bordered by another layer of dust running the entire way around the edge of the room on the skirting board, framing it. This was going to take a lot of cleaning.

'Dad, can you take Dylan to get his things? Take Mum as well. He can sleep on the sofa again tonight and we'll go furniture shopping tomorrow.'

'Of course, sweetheart,' he responded, kissing her gently on the head before leaving the room. A few minutes later Taylor heard the front door click shut as her family departed. Silence filled the house for the first time in what felt like months. The sun slipped lower in the sky as dusk began to fall, and Taylor flinched as she turned on the bright ceiling lights. Having cleared the last box, and taken the donation box downstairs, she went to get the vacuum cleaner and some rags to dust with. But she couldn't find the vacuum cleaner attachments.

'Perfect,' she said, turning the utility room upside down looking for them. Her mind flashed back to last night, when in this same room the dam had broken and she'd begun almost wailing with the pain of not being able to protect her brother. Her eyes started filling again, the flood threatening to break through the levees. She took a deep breath and mentally shook herself.

'Right, come on!'

That night the smell of greasy pizza and garlic bread filled the living room. The only sounds were the occasional movement of a pizza box or the opening of a pop bottle. It was completely dark outside, the moon just about visible through the clouds. A large navy-blue duffel bag now leant against the side of the sofa, its seams groaning under the tension. Taylor and Dylan were sat at opposite ends of one sofa, whilst their parents sat side by side on the other, their father's right hand resting gently on their mother's left. In the soft light of the living room her parents looked younger than their years, and from the outside they could be any happy couple just enjoying being in each other's presence. But Taylor could see the worry lines on her mother's face had gotten that little bit deeper, and the warmth that normally glowed in her father's eyes had all but disappeared. They'd been here before. Each battle leaving them a little bit more weary, taking another little piece of them that they had no way of getting back.

Taylor put her half-full pizza box on the table, picked up the television remote, and dragged one of the blankets over herself, wanting to fight off the evening chill.

'Shall we watch something?' she asked, her voice slicing into the silence. Dylan didn't give any indication that he had heard her, and her mum gave a forced sweet smile but didn't say anything. Her father however stretched his legs slightly and moved his and his wife's shared pizza box to the floor.

'I think we should probably head off soon, it's getting late,' he said, getting to his feet. Her mum stood up, still silent. 'It was good to see you, kiddo,' her father said, walking the few steps over to his daughter and hugging her tightly. 'Call us if you need anything, OK?' he whispered into her ear, so quiet that only she could hear. Dylan stood up from the sofa to say goodbye to his parents, and his father offered him his hand to shake. Dylan hesitated, before eventually taking it. They shook a few times before his father pulled him forwards and into a hug, and Taylor could see Dylan's eyes begin to fill with tears. When they broke apart again Dylan coughed and muttered about having something in his eye.

Taylor's mother now stood in front of her, having patiently waited her turn with her kids. Her father and brother had already started making their way to the door so were out of earshot. Her mother grabbed both her hands and squeezed them tightly.

'Make sure you take care of yourself too, OK?' she said, her eyes pleading.

'I always do, Mum, don't worry.'

'No… you don't,' her mother said enigmatically, with a hitch in her voice. Taylor didn't understand what she was on about. 'Just make sure you keep doing whatever you were doing before he moved in. We'll find him a programme here, then his sobriety will become their responsibility, not yours, OK? You don't have to babysit him.'

'Have you tried babysitting Dylan? He'd drive me up the wall!' Taylor chuckled.

'Well, yes, that's what all the childminders you had when you were kids said. But what I mean is, don't sacrifice your life for his. His happiness isn't any more important than yours, and I think you forget that sometimes.'

'Mmm-hmm,' Taylor said, not really believing her.

'Promise me, Taylor, please? Or I'll just end up worrying about the both of you.'

'OK, Mum, I promise' Taylor said, retrieving her hands from her mother's grasp and embracing her.

'I love you.'

'I love you too.'

Taylor and Dylan stood by the open front door to wave their parents off. Their mother tried waving back with a smile but even from that distance Taylor could see it was forced. She hoped Dylan couldn't.

The door shut with a gentle click and the house quickly fell silent again. It was the first time the siblings had been alone together since the night before.

'Taylor, I'm s -' Dylan began almost as soon as they were back in the living room.

'Don't, Dylan,' Taylor responded.

'But -'

'No. You don't apologise. This wasn't your fault,' Taylor said sternly. Dylan beating himself up over this was not going to help him stay sober. Taylor watched as the tension in her brother's shoulders eased slightly and the tears threatened to fall once more. 'You're a different person when you're drunk, and you shouldn't have to apologise for that other person, especially when Mark is the one who unleashed him.'

'Taylor, I'm scared,' Dylan whispered, his voice trembling. 'I can't go back there. I don't think I'd survive it again.'

'We won't let you slide down that slope. We're all here for you, we've got your back, we're going to help you through this.'

'You saw Mum and Dad. How much this hurt them. I'm not sure they can take any more.'

'So don't make them. Stay sober. We'll find a group or something for you to join on Monday. As for now, let's just worry about eating the rest of our pizzas and finding furniture for your room.'

'I already finished mine...' Dylan said, a half smile creeping across his face.

'Of course you have,' Taylor said, rolling her eyes and laughing at him. 'Well, *I'll* finish my pizza while you look at furniture, then,' she said, flopping back down on the sofa and pulling her pizza box toward her again.

CHAPTER FIFTEEN
Bedding and Beginnings

The next day the twins were slowly wandering around IKEA, trying to pick out items for Dylan's new room. He had to be quite restrained in his choices, such as opting for a single bed rather than a double, so he at least still had floor space in the small room. The store was buzzing with the sound of couples chatting, and families yelling at each other from the other side of the room about something-or-other they'd just found that the other person *had* to see. Each 'room' within the store had been tastefully decorated, but the contrasting colours so close together was quite jarring, and the bright lights were giving Taylor a headache. About halfway around the store the twins decided to stop and grab a drink in the café. They sat down and Dylan started running through his list, identifying anything they'd missed and would have to go back and find. Taylor slowly sipped her drink, squinting every now and again as pain radiated around her head.

'Are we missing anything?' she asked, as her brother folded his list back up and put it in his pocket.

'Just a duvet set and some coat hangers,' he said,

getting ready to stand up again.

'Wait,' Taylor said, holding her hand out. 'Five more minutes? My head's killing me.'

'Do you want to go wait in the car? I can get this stuff myself,' Dylan offered.

'If I go wait in the car, you'll come out with that giant stuffed giraffe that is twice as tall as you.'

Dylan smirked and settled back down.

'Have you spoken to Mum and Dad today?' Taylor asked, rubbing her eyes with her hands.

'Mum texted this morning saying she loved me. Nothing from Dad.' Dylan started playing with the spoon in his cup, slowly scraping it around the inside, while tapping his foot.

'They do love you, you know,' Taylor said gently, reaching out for his hand, partly to comfort him and partly to stop the unpleasant noise.

'I know. That makes it worse,' he said, sighing sadly. 'You're not supposed to hurt the ones you love.'

'But you didn't do it on purpose!' Taylor said, grasping his hand in both of hers. 'It was Mark, he's the -'

'I knew! Alright?' Dylan said, snapping and pulling his hands away as if burnt. 'I knew he'd put alcohol in it. I could taste it on the very first sip. But everyone was having such a good time and I thought it had been so long that it'd be OK, that I could be normal about it all.'

Dylan picked up his mug and squeezed it until his knuckles turned white. Taylor didn't know how to respond. She had convinced herself that this wasn't his fault. She had been prepared to dedicate her whole self into helping him stay on track, and move past this 'accident'. But deep down she'd known, too. It was just easier to believe the sugar-coated version of the truth. Having blind faith in him allowed her to shove her fears into a small box, lock it, and bury it somewhere, never to see the light of day; because this wasn't his fault. Except it was.

'Lor?' Dylan said quietly. It had been several minutes and she still hadn't spoken.

'Come on,' she said, getting quickly to her feet. 'We still need to find bedding and coat hangers.' She picked up her bag and charged off, leaving him in her wake. He scrambled to his feet and jogged after her.

'Lor, can we -'

'No, Dylan.'

'But -'

'No. We're going to carry on shopping, get your things, get in the car, and go home and spend the rest of the day putting flat pack furniture together. How about these?' she said, pulling a bedding set out at random and shoving them in front of his face.

'They... they have unicorns on, Lor,' he said quietly, glancing down at the bedding and then back to her.

'Oh. Right. So they do,' she said, properly looking at them for the first time, before handing them to him like she had been burned. 'OK, you pick the bedding. I'll go find coat hangers.' She turned on her heel and marched off. Dylan just stood there staring after her, holding a unicorn-covered pink duvet cover with matching pillowcases.

Taylor made it as far as next room before her eyes started stinging with tears. She took a deep breath to steady herself. Not here. Not now. She stopped a passing staff member to ask where the coat hangers were, her voice still a little shaky. The obviously confused staff member pointed her in the right direction, and she marched off again, still taking slow, deep breaths.

The coat hangers were next to some light blue fabric storage boxes, and even as she reached up to grab the hangers she couldn't help but stare at them. They were almost the exact same colour as Paige's shirt had been. Despite all the emotions she had bubbling under the surface, a small smile crept across her face as she remembered that evening in the restaurant, and how she hadn't laughed like that in so long. The memory helped calm her as she carefully retrieved the coat hangers and made her way back to her brother.

'Here,' she said, dumping the hangers in his arms. 'That's everything?' she asked. He nodded in response, trying to juggle the hangers as they started to slide from his grasp. They walked in silence to the section of the store where they had to collect the bigger items on their list. The cavernous space was packed floor to ceiling with nondescript cardboard boxes. Taylor snorted. She'd spend most of yesterday getting rid of boxes and here she was, surrounded by them, inviting them into her house. Dylan grabbed a nearby trolley and started scanning the aisles for the correct product code. Taylor aimlessly wandered off in the other direction, looking at the few un-boxed products littering the aisles. She used the opportunity to pull out her phone and text Paige; but, when she opened the text screen, she found she didn't know what to say. *'Hi, how're you? My brother's an alcoholic and just fell off the wagon'* didn't seem to cut it somehow. Taylor stared at the flashing line on the screen, awaiting her input. Eventually she settled on just a simple *'Hi, how're you today? x'*. Her finger hovered over the send button, before she went back and removed the *'x'* from the text. Satisfied, she returned her phone to her pocket and went off in search of Dylan among the walls and walls of boxes.

Back at the house they sat on the floor of what was now Dylan's bedroom, pouring over the scant instructions for the bed they had just bought. There were no words, only diagrams, and the pieces in them weren't all that easy to identify. Every now and again Dylan would pick up one element and try it with another one, the way someone would if they were checking if a jigsaw piece fit.

'No, that's not right,' Taylor scolded, pointing at the instructions. 'That big bit has to go into these two smaller bits, see?'

'Right,' he said tersely.

Taylor's phone vibrated on the floor beside her. She snatched it up quickly, not wanting to give Dylan the chance to tease her. Paige had replied to her text, saying she was well and asking if Taylor wanted to meet for lunch later in the week. Taylor's insides cringed as she had to ask if they could postpone until the week after, telling a little white lie about a busy work schedule. Once she put her phone down, she let a small smile drift on to her face and her eyes started to twinkle a little, a re-ignition of the spark that had been so violently put out on Friday night. She quickly shook herself, not wanting Dylan to see and ask questions, and re-focused on building the bed.

'I've found a group that meets every evening. I've signed us up for Monday,' Taylor said, paying particularly close attention to the screw she was inserting into the bed frame.

'Us?' Dylan questioned.

'It's hard to get to by bus,' Taylor offered by way of explanation. She left out the part where she didn't yet trust him to leave the house unattended.

'It doesn't work like that, Lor,' he said gently.

'What do you mean?'

'I need to be able to be completely open and honest in the group,' he said, looking away from his sister. 'I can't do that if you're there.'

'Oh,' Taylor said, stinging with the rejection.

'And I'll get a taxi. There is no reason you should have to give up all your evenings.'

'I don't mind,' Taylor lied.

'Yes, you do. And even if you don't, you should,' Dylan said, slotting one of the wooden pieces into the other. 'I'll be OK. I'm a big boy now' he added sarcastically.

'I know,' Taylor's voice quivered. 'I'm just trying to

help.'

'That's the problem,' Dylan said, tossing aside the piece he was holding. 'I don't want to need help, yours or anyone else's. It makes me feel weak, like I'm less of a man.'

'There's nothing wrong with needing help, Dyl. Remember when I left Daniella? Mum and Dad had to basically scrape me off the floor.'

'That's different. You didn't do it to yourself.'

'Didn't I? I pretended like everything was fine, but I knew what she was doing to me was wrong. Deep down I knew, and I still stayed.'

'It's not the same.'

'If you say so.'

'It's not. You were a victim in that situation,' Dylan said quietly.

'And you're not?' Taylor asked, making him go still. 'You can be a victim of something, as well as of someone. You're a victim of addiction, and it's OK to ask for help.'

Dylan didn't move but his eyes started filling up. He tried his best to stifle the tears and sniffed a few times.

'And it's OK to cry, you dingus,' Taylor said, gently shoving her brother on the arm. 'We all do it. Put a sad film on and I can't turn the waterworks off!' she said, making him laugh.

'Thanks, Taylor,' he said quietly, going back to working on the bed.

'Any time,' Taylor said, smiling at him.

They worked together to finish assembling the bed, deciding that the wardrobe and desk could wait until tomorrow. Taylor threw Dylan's new bedding at him, telling him that he could do that particular job himself. She went downstairs and put two frozen meals in the microwave, then checked her emails while she was waiting. Her supervisor had thankfully approved her emergency leave, meaning she could concentrate solely on Dylan this week without stressing as much about work. She brought up the alcoholics support group website on her phone and re-read the 'about' section, taking comfort in the success stories they shared there. They met at seven p.m., meaning the traffic shouldn't be too bad. She wondered if they chose that time as the likely time people with nine-to-five jobs would end up in pubs.

The siblings watched a random reality television show with their dinner, laughing with and at the people on the screen and forgetting their own lives for an hour. Dylan's jaw seemed less tense, and his forehead was no longer furrowed. Their parents called to check in on them and wish them good night, and Dylan seemed excited to tell them about the furniture they had bought for his new room. Taylor had insisted on paying, joking that it would be just like letting a fully furnished flat, only much smaller. Whilst the television show was on, she started making lists of possible man-and-van companies she could ring to move the rest of Dylan's stuff out from his old flat. She knew they could probably fit most of it in her car but she didn't feel safe coming face to face with Mark again. Even if Dylan had known the drink was alcoholic as soon as he tasted it, Mark had still spiked it in the first place, and then tried to intimidate her.

Once she was happy with the list she checked her bank balance, only to find her parents had transferred her some money with the note '*for Dylan x*' attached to it. Her insides felt all fuzzy and warm as a result, combined with a little guilt… and was it shame? Her cheeks had flushed red at least. It was a reminder that she wasn't alone with this, and she knew Dylan really was sorry and she believed him when she said he was determined to stay sober. But looking across at him as he was laughing at the television, she couldn't help flashing back to Friday night, when a very different laugh had passed his lips. It quickly cooled the warmth that had settled nicely in her body, as if she had been dunked in an ice bath straight from the comfort of her bed. She knew he had a long road ahead of him.

The alcoholics support group met in a draughty church hall on the outskirts of the city. The faded wood flooring reminded Taylor of their secondary school sports hall, complete with mystery stains and an immeasurable number of chips and scratches. A table off to the side supported a large silver coffee urn that was spluttering to life, threatening to spill its contents over the white cloth it rested on. At the far end of the hall the musty-looking red curtains had been pulled back to reveal stacks of chairs and some soft play equipment. In the centre of the room, under a single, low-hanging light, was a circle of chairs with black metal frames and burgundy cushions that looked lumpy and faded. A few of the seats were occupied; the people using them either looking at their phones or staring at their hands, almost as though they were praying to be somewhere else. Around the outside of the circle there were a few pairs and groups of people, talking in low voices. To Taylor it seemed like a twisted form of the childhood game 'duck, duck, goose', where at any moment someone might just get up and run.

Taylor and Dylan stood in the arched doorway, on the

boundary between inside and out, between cold and… well, slightly less cold. Dylan was fidgeting with his feet, unable to stand still or keep his hands by his side. Instead, he kept pulling out his phone or his keys and passing them from one hand to the other, distracting himself from the scene in front of him.

Seemingly out of nowhere a portly bearded gentleman popped up next to them and offered his hand.

'Hi, I'm Andy,' he said, shaking their hands quite vigorously. 'First time here?' Dylan just nodded in response. 'It's OK! We were all new once. Come in, get a tea or coffee and grab a seat. You'll get to know everyone soon enough.' Dylan took one last begging look at his sister before being led away by the jolly Andy, whose braces outlined his large stomach like a picture frame.

Taylor waited a little while until Dylan joined the rest of the group in the circle, then slipped back out of the front door. The cold air immediately bit at her fingers as a breeze swirled around her. She thought she might freeze to death if she just sat in her car for the next two hours.

The door of the coffee shop chimed as she walked in, not that anyone seemed to notice. It was a warmly decorated, quiet place, with a few patrons splattered about here and there. The coffee menu was in simple English without all the added extras that would sometimes be found in the bigger chains. 'Perfect,' she thought as she made her way to the counter and ordered her drink. The woman behind the till looked old enough to be her grandmother, and she pottered slowly around as she made the coffee, humming to herself the entire time.

'Here you go, dear,' the old woman said as she handed Taylor her coffee. Her voice was sweet and frail, her hands trembling slightly as she handed the coffee over, causing the spoon to rattle on the saucer. Taylor chose a comfy-looking seat at the back of the coffee shop and settled in for the next couple of hours. She rummaged around in her bag for the book she had been meaning to read for months, but never had the time. Before she delved into its pages, she checked her work emails by force of habit. One hundred and fifty-four unread emails stared back up at her, and a knot started forming in her stomach. One of the emails near the top of the list had a small red exclamation mark next to it, indicating the sender had thought it was important. Against her better judgement she opened it and scanned the text.

'Please find attached next term's teaching schedule for your perusal,' she read, before opening the attachment.

The knot in her stomach got tighter, as if it was in the middle of a tug of war rope. They were asking her to take on even *more* teaching hours, all while her PhD supervisor was on her back about how far she was falling behind. She started feeling a little sick.

'Are you OK, dear? You've gone awfully white,' the old woman said as she bustled around, wiping down tables.

'What?' Taylor said, tearing her eyes away from her phone. 'Oh, yes, sorry. I'm fine, thank you. Just work stuff.'

'Sweetheart, work shouldn't make you white as a sheet,' the old woman said unsolicited. 'Maybe it's time for a career change?' She continued picking up the used cups that were dotted around the cafe. There were only a couple of other people there now and no one at the counter. Once she had taken the now full tray of cups over to the counter, she came back and sat down sideways on a nearby chair, resting an elbow on the table.

'Take this job. I could have retired years ago but I just love it. It gives me a reason to get up in the morning, I meet new people every day, and it keeps me active. Can you say the same for your job?'

Taylor stammered slightly, not knowing how to respond to the sudden onslaught of philosophical wisdom from a septuagenarian, 'Well, no, not right now. But to get to where I want to be, I have to get through this... less pleasant stage.'

'Do you, though? Or could there be another way?' the old lady said, getting back to her feet. Then, with a sudden change of tack, she said, 'We close at eight, just so you know,' before shuffling away, not giving Taylor a chance to respond. Taylor wrapped both her hands around her coffee mug, allowing the heat to radiate into her cold palms, and mulled over what the old woman had said. Was there another way? When she had signed her contract with the university there was only a minimal teaching requirement, and she'd spent the first few months of this new career falling in love with this research project. Now she had been forced to focus elsewhere, she didn't feel that same excitement and joy every morning she got up for work. While she enjoyed teaching, the real reason she'd left industry was for the research; she wanted to make a difference in the world, and maybe she was naive, but she really believed her research project could. She took a sip of her coffee, letting the warm liquid flow into her stomach and begin to loosen the knot.

At five minutes to eight she put her book back in her bag and took her now empty mug to the counter.

'Thank you, dear,' the old woman said warmly.

'No problem,' Taylor responded. 'And thank you... for the coffee,' she said pointedly, causing the old woman to wink at her.

Taylor made her way slowly back to the church hall, the ends of her scarf flapping around in the wind like a bird trying to take off. Her attention turned back to her brother with trepidation. How had the meeting gone? Had he been honest? Had it been helpful? She would find out soon enough.

Once back at her car she fumbled with the keys, trying to unlock it with cold hands. Even inside the car her breath misted in front of her, and she was glad she had put so many layers on before leaving the house. It didn't take long for the windscreen and windows to steam up, creating a misty layer protecting her from the outside world. She dug her book back out, ready to delve back between its pages, hoping to drift away into another time and place, so she could forget about the cold.

Nearly an hour later, the sudden opening of the passenger door made her jump.

'You must be frozen!' her brother said as he dived into the car, blowing heat into his hands.

'How was it?' Taylor asked, immediately putting her

book away.

'It was OK. I'm going to come back tomorrow. Andy said to go every evening this week and see which group I was happiest being a part of and to stick with that one. Each group meets twice a week, but you can always drop in on other groups if you need it.'

'That sounds really positive,' Taylor said, starting the engine.

'Yeah, it was,' Dylan said with a slight sense of surprise in his voice. Taylor started driving them home through the criss-crossing streets.

'I really appreciate you driving me -' Dylan started

'It's not a problem,' Taylor said, checking it was safe to pull out of a junction.

'- but I'll find my own way from now on,' he finished in a stubborn tone. 'I meant what I said. You need to have a life that doesn't revolve around me.'

'But I honestly don't mind!'

'I know you don't, but as I said, you should. Keep going climbing, go hook up with your hot secret agent...'

Taylor took one hand off the steering wheel and shoved him lightly in the arm.

'Hey!' he said in mock offence, rubbing his arm. 'No fair! I can't hit you back when you're driving!'

'Yup!' Taylor said with a grin.

They drove home mostly in silence, Taylor letting Dylan control any conversation; it sounded like the group had been quite intense. She wasn't surprised that, once home, he went straight upstairs to his room. Taylor wasn't far behind him; the earlier hit of caffeine having already worn off. Once she'd climbed the stairs she paused outside his bedroom door, the knot in her stomach threatening to tighten once again. She was glad Dylan's group had gone well, but this was only day two of being sober and she worried about the toll recovery was going to take on him. He was already beating himself up so much for slipping up in the first place, leaving him more vulnerable than she'd seen him in a long time.

Taylor sighed, went to her room, and began to get ready for bed. It would be difficult, but she was determined to be there for him every step of the way.

CHAPTER SIXTEEN
Reaction and Action

PAIGE

Paige had been a little disappointed when Taylor had asked if they could postpone their lunch date for a week. Like the happy balloon that had been inflating inside her had got a puncture. She had kept herself busy with work, having sporadic text conversations with Taylor as the days went on. But it was finally date day, and Paige was at her desk, unable to keep her dancing feet still. There was a large wall of text on the screen with lots of floating red comment boxes, strike-throughs, and replacement text. It was the first draft of the first few chapters of her novel, which she had sent to Maya for her opinion; Maya hadn't held back. The overarching feedback she had given was to focus less on facts and dates and more on the person and dramatising the story. Paige had felt a little disheartened when she had opened the file and seen all that red.

Rain started spattering the window, gently tapping the glass. Paige closed the text document and instead opened her emails, thinking she could use the time before the date to sort through her inbox and reply to anything urgent. She opened a random email and started trying to read it, but her mind wandered, and she ended up re-reading the same sentence again and again, until she gave up and closed that window, too. Eventually she gave up trying to work, gathered her things, and decided to walk to the cafe where she was meeting Taylor. A slight detour would eat up the time between now and the date, and it would take her along her favourite part of the river. Before leaving her office, she wrapped up in a woollen hat and scarf, and put on a matching pair of gloves. She did her coat up so high that only her eyes were really visible, the zip finishing just under her nose, and made her way downstairs.

Across the foyer, ascending the stairs from the basement, she spotted Dylan and gave him a brief wave. He nodded his head in acknowledgement and adjusted the bag on his shoulder. Paige thought he looked a little thinner than last time she saw him, and like his skin hadn't seen the sun in a while. No sooner had she decided to go and check in on him, though, than he had disappeared into the throng of students making their way to the cafe, their next class, or home. Paige sighed. She hadn't seen him at climbing in a while. She made a mental note to ask Taylor if he was OK.

The path along the river had a dusting of frost on it, with the odd patch of ice that hadn't been touched by the sun yet. Paige kept her eyes peeled for any of her usual wildlife companions but even the ducks seemed to be avoiding her, and she couldn't hear the usual chorus of birds in the trees. She wrapped her arms around herself tightly. Without the distraction of nature, her mind wandered back to her work, back to the meeting she was having in a few days. Her autistic masters student had booked a tutorial for the end of the week. He was progressing well with his studies but struggling to settle; he had moved from the other side of the country to be here, away from his support networks and familiar environment. It had obviously had a jarring affect on him.

Images of her niece and nephew sprang into her mind. Their smiling faces as they roasted marshmallows on the fire in her living room, Cayden's bug book becoming increasingly tattered and dog-eared every time she saw them. Susie's brunette fringe getting in her eyes and Brandon saying she was still refusing to get a haircut.

A crow let out a loud squawk from above her head, jolting her out of her thoughts, and making her realise she had missed the path that would take her towards the cafe, requiring her to double back on herself. The ground made small crunching noises with every step she took on the sheltered path. The bare bushes lining it were interlaced with a few evergreen trees and shrubs, breaking up the monotony of the brown. The water pelted down the river with a roar, the recent rains had almost made it flood a few days ago. There was even a felled tree wedged behind some rocks off to one side, its branches tickling the water as it slowly receded.

Paige finally made it to the correct path and forced her way through the slightly overgrown bushes on either side. She called it a path, but it was really a muddy track worn into the ground by countless people clambering through it to get to the pavement on the other side. One of the branches caught her scarf, a twig jabbing through one of the loosely knitted holes and trying to rip it from her neck.

'Damn it,' Paige said, seeing the now wider hole in her new scarf, and trying to smooth it out with her fingers. She managed to fix it a little, but that part of the scarf still looked uneven and misshapen. She sighed as she carried on walking, the small smile on her face returning as she edged closer to the cafe.

Even from outside the cafe looked warm and cosy. The yellow wall lights perfectly balanced the mismatched chandeliers in this eccentric establishment. The bottom halves of the walls were covered in dark wood panelling and the table and chair sets had been stained to match. Once inside Paige could hear the radio playing quietly in the background, harmonising with the murmurs of the other guests. At one end of the counter there was a glass display cabinet housing a variety of indulgent-looking cakes, from strawberry cheesecake to rich chocolate fudge cakes; Paige's mouth began to water. She weaved through the tables to a more secluded one in the back right-hand corner of the cafe, where the lighting was slightly dimmer and where it was less likely that people would be walking past. Shedding her hat, scarf, gloves, and coat and piling them onto one of the chairs, she rolled up her sleeves and joined the queue at the counter. Paige didn't want to occupy an empty table without at least purchasing a drink while she waited for Taylor. The queue slowly crawled forward, and by the time Paige got to the front she still hadn't decided on what to order.

'What herbal tea would you recommend?' she said to the woman behind the counter, while still staring at the menu above her head.

'I'm quite fond of the liquorice one, if you wanted to try that?'

'Sure, thank you.' Paige got her wallet out and rummaged through it for any loose change she could get rid of, handed over the money, and took her tea back to her table. The steam rose off it rapidly. Paige tried to occupy herself with her phone, or by looking around the cafe, or fiddling with the napkin they had given her with her tea, but she couldn't help looking at the door every few seconds just in case. Her arms involuntarily wrapped around her midriff, and she subconsciously hugged herself, smiling.

The door opened again and this time when Paige looked up, Taylor was there in the doorway, wrapped up in so many layers she looked like she'd worn her entire wardrobe.

'Hi, sorry I'm late!' she said, slowly peeling off some of the layers. Her face was red with the cold and she was shivering slightly.

'You're not late, I was early,' Paige said, finally taking a sip of her drink. She had to fight the impulse to spit it out, it was vile. Instead, she grimaced and swallowed before setting it down beside her, vowing to never touch anything liquorice-flavoured every again.

'What would you like to eat?' Taylor asked, getting her purse out.

'A jacket potato would be great, with cheese and beans, please,' she said, also digging her wallet out.

'No, no,' Taylor said, waving her away. 'You paid for dinner the other week, I can certainly pay for this. Another tea?'

'Yes, please. The regular kind, not... this,' she said, crinkling her nose up at the offending drink.

'Gotcha,' Taylor said, laughing, and taking the liquorice tea back to the counter.

Paige watched her go, her low-cut jeans accentuating her curves and her T-shirt swaying slightly with her movements. While queuing, Taylor kept glancing back at Paige and smiling. Paige remembered what she had said about staring and tried to make sure she looked away. Taylor quickly placed their order and carried two mugs back to the table, the smell of tea and coffee intertwining in the air between them.

'She said it'll be about five minutes,' Taylor said as she sat down.

'Great' Paige said, smiling. 'So how are you?' she said, leaning forward slightly.

'Umm... I'm fine' Taylor replied, picking up a napkin and starting to tear it into tiny pieces. 'You?'

'OK, busy with work and stuff. I saw Dylan earlier,'

Paige continued, and as soon as she mentioned his name Taylor visibly tensed up. 'Is he OK? He looked quite thin and pale.'

'Yes, he's fine,' Taylor said, dark clouds moving behind her eyes.

'So you're both fine?' Paige said, mistrustful.

'Just had a hard couple of weeks, that's all. But I don't want to talk about it. Tell me about your week, what's been happening? What have you got coming up?'

'Um... well...' Paige stuttered, trying to adjust to the sudden change in topic, 'work has been busy as usual, and I've got a meeting with one of my masters students on Friday. He's not settling in so well here.'

'Oh?'

'He's autistic and I think he is struggling to cope with the change.'

'That makes sense.'

'I think I might be autistic,' Paige blurted out before quickly taking a sip of her drink.

'What?'

'I mean, it's been suggested, and I think people have a point.'

'You don't look autistic,' Taylor said with a sudden twang of bitterness in her voice.

'Autistic people… don't have a look?' Paige said, confused.

'You're a successful academic, why are you diagnosing yourself with a problem?' Taylor continued, slamming her mug down on the table a little too hard.

'I'm not diagnosing myself. I'm just saying it is a possibility -'

'So?' Taylor interrupted. 'It clearly doesn't affect your life in any way, so what does it matter?' she said, her face turning red and her eyes starting to flame.

'I… I…' Paige stammered. She recognised that Taylor was getting angry, but she had no idea why, or what she had done wrong, or what to say to fix it. Taylor suddenly stood up.

'You know what? Some people have real problems in this world, like real disabilities or addictions. I'm not here to be part of a pity party,' she said, gathering all her things back up.

'I wasn't asking you -'

'I know how this goes. Suddenly you've got this label and I have to put my life on hold as a result. I won't do that, not again,' Taylor said, taking one last look at a very shocked Paige before storming out of the cafe. Paige felt frozen to her seat and her mind went completely blank.

The rest of the patrons in the cafe had turned around to watch, and Paige could feel all their eyes burning into her.

A waitress came out the kitchen with their order, oblivious to what had just happened.

'There you go,' the waitress said, putting the meals down on the table. 'Is your friend coming back, or...?' she asked. Paige didn't respond, but just carried on staring forwards.

'O-kay then,' the waitress said, rolling her eyes and walking away. Paige felt like every muscle in her body was tense, as if holding up the weight of the building she was in. Her mind was both blank and going a hundred miles an hour at the same time. The lights felt like too much. The sound of crockery on the counter felt like she was being slapped in the face. The sound of people around her talking felt like rising flood waters when she was anchored to the floor. She had to get out. As if coming out of a trance she was suddenly back in the room.

'Can I have these to take away?' she said, clumsily putting the plates back on the counter.

'Of course. Is everything alright?' the lady behind the counter said.

'Yes, *fine*,' Paige said sarcastically.

Paige unintentionally snapped the polystyrene

containers out of the woman's hands and rushed out the door, leaving a few confused faces in her wake. A few minutes into her walk back to her university building she spotted a homeless man cowering from the cold in the doorway, and handed him the meals. She started walking away, but only made a few steps before turning back, wallet out, and handing him all the cash she had on her - around thirty pounds in total.

'It's not much -' she began, stuttering.

'Thank you!' he said, not believing his eyes. Paige smiled weakly at him and headed back to the university, back to her car. She didn't walk by the river this time but took the most direct route, emailing her department head as she did so.

'*I won't be in for the rest of the day due to suddenly feeling ill,*' she wrote with no preamble. Her department head was used to her to-the-point emails, so she had no qualms about sending it.

Once back at her car she threw her bag and coat onto the back seat, then herself into the driver's seat. The engine roared into life, and she started backing out of her parking space, causing a passing cyclist to swerve to avoid her. She hit the steering wheel in frustration. She felt like someone was inflating all her muscles and the only way the pressure could escape would be by her brain exploding. She concentrated on her breathing, counting the seconds, but there was a quiver in every inhalation and exhalation. The texture of the steering wheel felt coarse under her fingertips as she ran them over the fake leather. Out of the corner of her eye she saw a car waiting to take her space. She closed her eyes and let out one long breath, before opening them, placing both hands on the steering wheel, and putting the car into reverse.

The drive home seemed to be over in a few seconds; Paige was on auto pilot and hardly noticed what she was doing. It was around half past three by the time she put the handbrake on in her driveway. She didn't get out of the car immediately. Instead, she just sat there, not really noticing as the car got colder around her. It was gone four o'clock by the time she wearily got out of the car, her limbs having stiffened from being in the same position for so long. Zombie-like she unlocked the door, dropped her bag in the hallway, and made her way into the living room. Sooty picked his head up with a chirp, not expecting her home so early. She collapsed on the sofa next to him and he lazily stretched before moving to her lap. She absentmindedly stroked him, his smooth fur providing enough sensory input to start bringing her back to reality.

Paige looked at her phone, hoping to see some kind of communication from Taylor. That it was all a mistake, some big misunderstanding, and that they could be friends again. But there was nothing. So she texted her, apologising, though she wasn't sure what she was apologising for. Then she rang Maya.

The phone rang for a long time before Maya groggily answered.

'Hello?' she said sleepily.

'Hi, Maya. It's me.'

'Spence? It's one in the morning, why are you ringing me?'

'Oh,' Paige said, internally swearing. 'Sorry, Maya, I forgot.'

'You forgot I'm in Japan?'

'I forgot there was a time difference.'

'Right... if it's OK with you I'm gonna go back -'

'Taylor and I had a fight. A big one. I don't really know what happened,' Paige said, desperately wishing her best friend wasn't on the other side of the world right now.

'What happened?' Maya said, sounding more alert.

'I don't know.'

'What were you talking about?'

'Her brother, work, one of my masters students, autism.'

'Autism?'

'Yes, I mentioned that I might have it. Then she started yelling.'

'Oh, sweetie.'

'What?'

'It sounds like she didn't react well to you identifying as autistic.'

'I didn't *identify* as autistic, I said it was a possibility that I am.'

'Right. And what did she say?'

'That me having a label would mean she had to put her life on hold.'

'Hmmm.'

The two women sat in silence for a while. Every now and again Paige could her the muffled rustling of a duvet.

'Honestly, lovely, I don't know why she reacted like that either. Maybe she's got something else going on. But the point is, if you are autistic, then it's part of you; it's intrinsic to who you are. If she can't accept that part of you then it's her loss.'

'But -'

'No buts. You are a wonderful human being, "quirks"

and all.'

'Thanks, Maya,' Paige said, tears welling up in her eyes. It had been a long, emotional day and her ability to cope with any emotions, even nice ones, was limited.

'Now if it's OK with you, I'm going to go back to sleep. I'll call you this evening, OK? This evening *my* time, that is.'

'OK.'

'Love you.

'Love you too.'

Paige hung up the phone and leant back on the sofa, melting into the cushions. Sooty got up, made a few lazy circles on her lap, and settled back down. Paige smiled and began stroking him, his purrs reverberating into her thighs and stomach. At least he was predictable. As long as he was fed and had somewhere to sleep, he would love you no matter what. Paige wished people were that easy.

Paige began looking up information about autism on her phone, such as how to get a diagnosis and what a diagnosis would mean. There were many accounts online of adults, some in their fifties and sixties, getting a diagnosis and it changing their lives. Some of them were able to stop blaming themselves for social faux pas they had committed as children or teenagers, that they now knew were due to being autistic. Others found it opened the door to a new community of friends and felt they had finally, after decades, found where they belonged in this world. Paige thought about where she belonged and couldn't come up with an answer. There was here, with Sooty. She knew she was part of the group at work, but only on a professional basis; she didn't get invited to any social events that weren't official and run by the department. She belonged with Maya, but how much of that was due to Maya accommodating her 'quirks' and idiosyncrasies? Most of the stories mentioned how the person had gone to their doctor about getting a diagnosis only to be turned away or told it was unnecessary. But they had kept fighting and eventually been referred and subsequently diagnosed. Paige didn't know if she had the strength for that.

The sun had disappeared behind the horizon and the living room was now pitch black. Paige hadn't turned the light on when she got in and wasn't about to disturb Sooty to do so. The boiler kicked into life and the heating came on at the time Paige was usually home, making the radiators gurgle and groan. Slowly, the house warmed up; Sooty even moved off Paige's warm lap and back to the other end of the sofa. Paige finally got up and put the lights on, the warm glow flooding the room, her eyes taking a while to adjust.

As the kettle was boiling to make a cup of tea, Paige booked a doctor's appointment via the surgery website. It felt like it was now or never. She wasn't ashamed of who she was, however her brain was wired.

By the time she settled back on the sofa she was shaking, despite now being warm. It had been a long day.

CHAPTER SEVENTEEN
Appointments

The doctors' surgery was chilly, and most of the patients still had their coats on. Mismatched chairs lined the wall, circling the wonky table littered with out-of-date magazines that sat in the centre of the room. The clock on the wall ticked away with the occasional cough or snivel interrupting its monotonous sound. Parents spoke in low voices to their children, willing them to be calm and quiet, handing them their own mobile phones to keep them entertained. Sticky fingers belonging to little people who barely knew how to talk happily scrolled through apps to find their games, or through videos to find a particular one. Rain splashed onto the window before trickling down and pooling slightly on the windowsill. The woman on the reception desk was busily clicking away at the computer screen, deliberately ignoring the queue of people lining up to check in. Only the ringing phone seemed to be able to get her attention.

Paige checked the time again. Her appointment had been ten minutes ago, and she couldn't understand how they were already running late this early in the morning.

She had planned to be in by ten, but that was looking less and less likely. An announcement and name crackled over the tannoy and an older gentleman unsteadily got to his feat before shuffling towards the consulting rooms. Paige uncrossed and re-crossed her legs, adjusting her posture to try and alleviate the discomfort from the old, lumpy chairs.

'Paige Spencer to room four' was suddenly ejected from the speakers, and Paige jumped to her feet. She knocked before entering the doctor's office, just as her mother had taught her to do, and was greeted by a mumbled 'Come in' from the other side of the wooden door.

The slightly overweight, grey-haired doctor sat at his desk, squinting at the computer screen as he scrolled with his mouse. Various posters and office memos decorated the notice board above the computer screen, some of them with dates from over two years ago. The blinds were pulled across but not fully closed, allowing some privacy while also letting light into the room. An antiseptic smell mixed with must floated around in the air.

Page sat down on the chair placed parallel with the desk and waited for the doctor to finish what he was doing.

'Hello, how can I help you today?' he said, turning in his swivel chair to look at Paige, his moustache brushing the top of his lip as he spoke.

'I would like to be referred to be assessed for autism.'

'Mmm-hmm, he said, bringing his hands to his lips, holding them like a person would when praying. 'And why do you want that?'

'Because I think I'm autistic,' she said bluntly.

'Ah-ha, yes.' He smirked. 'I mean, why do you think you have autism? You seem a nice, well-spoken young lady.' He smiled a patronising smile and Paige half expected him to finish with a 'run along now' or offer her a lollipop.

'It has been suggested by colleagues, my niece and nephew are probably autistic, and I know there is a genetic element -'

'Ah, been consulting Dr Google, have we?'

'That's not... I mean... wouldn't you research it?

'And why else do you think you have autism?'

'A lot of the characteristics fit. Ever since I was a child I've needed routine, I've never been able to tolerate loud noises, I don't like being touched -'

'Do you work?' he interrupted.

'Yes...'

'As what?'

'I teach at a university.'

The doctor slapped his legs as if he had just made a great scientific discovery.

'So you are a fully functional member of society! Even if you do have autism, which I think is unlikely, you would be considered high-functioning and have no need for a diagnosis!' He swivelled back to the desk and started writing up notes from their appointment.

'Anything else I can help -' he began. This time it was Paige's turn to interrupt.

'I would still like to be referred. Many autistic adults have jobs, that doesn't mean they're not autistic. Functioning labels seem to just be used to deny people support or deny autonomy.'

'I mean… it's true people with autism sometimes have jobs,' he said, glossing over Paige's thoughts, 'but you don't just have a job, you have a career! One that involves social interaction!'

'So autistic people can't have careers?'

'That's not what… I didn't mean…' he said, becoming flustered.

'So you are prejudiced against autistic people?'

'No! Of course not!'

'So having a career is not an excuse for you not to refer me. I have many of the "symptoms", if this was a medical problem we wouldn't be having this discussion,' Paige said sternly.

'*Fine*, I will refer you. But I must warn you the waiting times are on average around twelve months, as children going for assessment are given the priority - they are the ones that can be helped,' he finished, slamming his index fingers onto the keyboard keys. Paige felt her anger swell inside her, but she bit her tongue; she didn't want to give him an excuse to change his mind.

'Thank you,' she said through gritted teeth as she got up to leave. She heard the doctor sigh as she left the room, and could almost feel his eyes rolling, but she forced herself to keep walking so she did not say something she regretted.

Once outside the surgery the cool fresh air helped her calm down. She thought it was ridiculous that someone in the medical profession could say and believe such things.

Paige walked back to her car and tried not to think about the old doctor and his patronising words. Instead, she thought about the woman in her book; how she had thought differently and how it had made a positive difference to the world.

The car park was full and there were people waiting for a space. Paige gestured at the driver at the front of a queue that she was leaving, so he could have her spot, and he gave her the thumbs up in thanks and slowly followed her to her car. It took her a while to unlock the door as her hands were so cold, and even longer to get the key into the ignition, but she finally was able to back out. The other driver flashed his headlights, thanking her again, and swung his car in.

Paige made her way to work, hoping that she hadn't annoyed anyone with her lateness. At least she was on time for her eleven a.m. appointment with her masters student.

Paige's masters student was already waiting outside her office when she got there. Headphones in, head bowed, his dark clothes almost made him blend into the background. His personal assistant stood there awkwardly rocking backwards and forwards from his heel to the ball of his foot, smiling at everyone.

'Hi, Jacob, come in,' Paige said as she unlocked her door. Jacob responded by looking up slightly and taking his headphones out. At Jacob's request, the assistant always waited outside.

The first dry weather in a while meant the sun was shining from an almost clear sky, so her office was fairly brightly lit for a winter's day. There were no longer papers piled around a beanbag in the corner; instead, they had been neatly filed into a much more transportable binder. She had started writing in different environments, her favourites being cafés or coffee shops. It allowed her to people watch and get inspiration for the characters without being disturbed.

'Have a seat,' she said, noticing Jacob still standing awkwardly by her desk. He sat and retrieved his tablet from his bag, setting it on his lap, before folding his hands in front of him and playing with one of the many different fidget toys she had seen him use. She'd mentioned how easily distracted she could get by sound once, and he'd only brought silent fidget toys to their meetings since. She looked across her desk at the dark-haired man. In his late twenties, he had long black hair and almost exclusively wore superhero T-shirts, seamless trousers, and trainers. Paige wished she could be that nonchalant about the judging eyes of others.

'So how are you, Jacob?' Paige asked gently.

Jacob spoke through the tablet, typing his response before having the tablet read it out loud. 'I am OK, thank you.'

'In your email you said you were a bit lonely and struggling to get used to the city, is that still the case?'

'Yes.'

'Can I do anything to help?'

'No.'

'OK. Have you joined any clubs or societies since you got here? Either within the university or just the city in general?'

'No. I'm scared,' his electronic voice responded with its pronounced English accent, which was jarring, as she knew Jacob was Welsh.

'What about joining an autistic group? Do they exist?' Paige asked, turning to Google to try and find out. Jacob didn't respond immediately but looked down at the floor in thought.

'Maybe,' the voice said monotonously.

'OK, well there is one group in the city I can send you a link to it. Will you try?'

'Yes.'

'Good. OK, now down to business. I've read your research thus far and, honestly, you've done a fantastic job. There are a few tweaks I'd like to run through with you, but I think we could potentially publish this as a paper, if you were willing to put the work in?'

A smile slowly spread across Jacob's face and his eyes sparkled. His fingers frantically tapped on his tablet like they couldn't keep up with his brain.

'Really? That would be amazing. That would show them,' his electronic voice said blandly, failing to communicate his excitement.

'Yes, it would,' Paige said, smiling. Jacob had struggled in school, where his needs as an autistic person weren't met; the school had just focused on trying to make him appear 'normal'. They ignored his non-verbal communication to try and 'encourage' him to speak with his mouth. His parents withdrew him from school, helped him learn how to type into an electronic device that could speak for him, and started home-schooling him. All the while his social worker tried to paint Jacob's parents as neglectful by taking him out of school, saying he'd never succeed without their help.

Paige brought her chair round to the other side of her desk to sit next to Jacob and go through his work, turning her computer monitor around so he could see. Paige tried to focus on the screen so she wouldn't read what he was typing before he was ready to 'speak'; she wouldn't like it if people constantly tried to finish her sentences. They worked for about an hour, discussing the finer points of academic writing and the research he had done on nineteenth-century politics. When it was time for their meeting to be over, Paige scooted away in her chair back to the other side of her desk, and booked in their next meeting.

'Would the sixteenth January at the same time suit you?' she asked. Jacob checked the calendar on his phone and nodded.

'Great, see you then,' Paige said, turning back to her computer to write up their meeting notes. Jacob left, making sure that the door didn't slam loudly behind him.

It only took a few minutes to type up the notes and email them across to Jacob, after which Paige gathered her things and her binder and made her way downstairs. She had booked the afternoon off to work on her book, so was heading to her favourite café. On the way there she kept thinking about her meeting with Jacob and the doctor's words floated into her head: 'I don't think it's likely'. Taylor's voice intruded not long after, screaming that she didn't look autistic. Paige started walking faster, and playing with the buttons on her coat. Many cars sped past her as she walked, belching metallic fumes. Stopping at a pedestrian crossing she watched as they flew past as multi-coloured blurs. The beep beep beep of the crossing signal scratched at her throat and the studded paving slabs made her feel like she was falling.

Paige took a slightly longer route through a park to get away from all the different sensory inputs, only for the park to bring back memories of her date with Taylor and cause her even more input, this time from her own emotions. There was a couple sitting holding hands on one of the benches, the woman resting her head on the man's shoulder. Paige hurried past them. A robin started singing from one of the trees, its little red breast swelling with the tune. Paige tried to concentrate on the song, and her breathing, and slowed her pace, not wanting to startle the little bird. He looked at her with his dewy eye and continued his melody. Paige stopped to listen. After the robin had finished, he flew away, off to serenade someone else. Paige took a deep breath and carried on toward the coffee shop, strolling slowly. So what if she didn't have many similarities with Jacob; people are inherently different, it's the natural human state. She smiled, thinking of how each robin sang a similar, but different song.

The coffee shop had its windows decorated with stencils and fake snow. Fluffy white fabric adorned the windowsills on the inside, and local children had made reindeer out of paper plates, which had been hung behind the glass. New flavours of coffee had appeared on the menu, such as gingerbread and black cherry, and

Christmas songs played on a loop in the background. Christmas had definitely landed.

Paige pushed open the heavy front door and made her way inside, the warmth hitting her immediately. She removed her coat and tucked it under her arm while she waited in the queue to order. Someone had gone to a lot of trouble to draw holly and Christmas trees on the chalkboards behind the counter, and there was tinsel wrapped around the till, slightly hindering the opening of the cash drawer.

Paige ordered a luxurious-sounding hot chocolate and a chocolate croissant. The server recognised her and smiled as she said she'd bring it over. Paige turned away from the counter and hesitated; her usual corner was taken by an old man. He sat perched on the edge of the seat, sipping his drink and squinting at the newspaper in front of him. The hiss of the coffee machine startled her into action, and she sat down in the nearest seat she could find pulling out her laptop. There was no plug at her current table, and she was immediately anxious that the battery would die before the older gentleman left.

The server brought over her drink and croissant, the delicious smells mingling in the air. The warm pastry almost melted on her tongue, satisfying her sweet tooth before she started work.

She was about halfway through writing the book, and her character was at a crux. Historical records were vague at this point, so Paige would have to make a creative decision; something that she was not used to doing. Did the young woman try and find shelter in a local farmhouse, and risk being caught, or did she keep walking and hope to get to her destination alive, despite the cruel winter biting at her heels? Paige took a sip of her chocolate and felt a pang of shame. This wasn't some fictional character; she had been a real woman, resisting the Nazis. Despite how much Taylor's words still stung, they were just words; they didn't compare. A tidal wave of guilt from the self-pity she had been wallowing in washed over her.

CHAPTER EIGHTEEN
Gifts and Gratitude

TAYLOR

It was late evening on the twenty-third of December when Taylor and Dylan set off on the drive to their parents' house, loudly singing along to the Christmas songs on the radio. The roads were packed with cars, people going home for the holidays or going somewhere just to get away from the Christmas spirit. The twins were in full song, competitively warbling to keep themselves amused on the car journey. Most of the houses they passed on the way to the motorway had decorations in the windows. There were tasteful baubles and metal Christmas trees, religious mangers, and inflatable jolly Santas looking like they could float away any minute. Some people even had blow-up snowmen and snow globes in their garden, tethered tightly to the ground.

Dylan had finished his classes for the holidays a couple of weeks ago, but had stayed in town so the siblings could travel home together; it was a long drive and Taylor had been working so hard, Dylan had joked he didn't trust her to keep her eyes open. Taylor was grateful. She hadn't been sleeping properly since her fight with Paige. Every time she thought about it her stomach twisted itself into knots and she started feeling a bit sick. They hadn't spoken since that afternoon, abruptly breaking their pattern of texting nearly every day.

Dylan reached forward and turned the radio down, catching Taylor out, who was singing at full volume. For a brief second just her loud, out-of-tune voice filled the car.

'Hey!' she said, briefly glaring at him. 'No fair!' Dylan could hardly breathe for laughing.

'Yeah, don't give up your day job, sis,' he said through the tears.

'That was a good one as well,' Taylor said grumpily.

'I know.'

'So why'd you turn it down?' she said, reaching for the volume dial. Dylan stretched out his hand and stopped her.

'Because...' he said, directing her hand back toward the steering wheel, 'you still haven't told me what happened between you and Paige.'

'Not this again,' she said, her smile quickly fading and her eyes staring forward.

'Yes, this.' Dylan said, half turning in his seat to talk to her. 'I know something happened; you're miserable.'

'Am not.'

'You are.'

'No, I'm not.'

'You -' Dylan took a deep breath, refusing to get drawn into the back and forth. 'Look, I know you've been worried about... other things,' he said, 'but that doesn't mean you can't talk to me. I want to help.'

'I don't think you can,' she said, deflated.

'Why not?'

'Because I screwed up.'

'How? Can't you just apologise?'

'I don't think an apology is going to cut it.'

Taylor relayed most of the argument to her brother word for word, and even from her peripheral vision she could see him wince when he heard what she had said.

Rain started pouring down just as they hit the motorway, with the huge number of cars chucking up lots of spray. Taylor put the wipers on full and they squeaked every time they ran awkwardly over the glass. She had composed an apology text about a hundred times, before deciding not to send it and deleting the whole thing. Paige's own apology text made her feel even more guilty, considering Paige hadn't done even the slightest thing wrong. She wasn't sure Paige would pick up the phone if she tried calling, but a text just seemed like she was wimping out. Dylan was right, she was miserable. Despite being utterly exhausted these days, every time her head hit the pillow her brain started replaying the argument as if it was a film, with Taylor cast as the villain. It had affected her sleep more than any horror movie she and Dylan had watched together ever had.

The longer they drove, the worse the rain got. The extreme vigilance needed to drive in the awful conditions took its toll, and it wasn't long before they were pulling into a service station. They didn't get out of the car right away, hoping the rain would abate slightly and they could make a run for it. Instead, it carried on hammering the car, making the metal echo and water trail down the glass like tears.

Eventually they exited the car and ran inside, coats held over their heads, the people already inside hastily moving out of the way as they accidentally flicked water everywhere. They went to their respective toilets before meeting back up in a fast-food queue. Taylor groaned at how many people were already waiting; a coach must have gotten in before them. Dylan stretched his arms high above his head, clicking his wrists and knuckles before cricking his neck. Taylor shuddered.

'I wish you wouldn't do that!' she said.

'What, this?' Dylan moved his hand close to her ear and made his wrist click repeatedly. Taylor ducked out of the way and scowled at him.

'Have you tried apologising to her?' he asked, after she made him promise not to click any more joints.

'I dunno how.'

'Sure you do, it's just five little letters.'

'It's not that simple and you know it.'

'Yeah,' Dylan admitted with a sigh. 'But it's got to be worth a try, right?'

'What if I make it worse?'

'Isn't she worth the risk?'

Images of Paige's smiling face flashed across her mind. Her freckles framing her warm smile. How she had selflessly given her so much help with her climbing technique, despite having better and more competent climbers to pair up with. The way her brain worked, how fast she could think and how much she knew. How she always took things literally. And then there was that spark, that electric shock that jolted through her whole body, when she'd kissed Paige's cheek after their dinner date…

Yes, of course she was worth it. Taylor felt her face go red and turned slightly away from her brother. If he noticed, he had the tact not to say anything.

Back at the car, coffee in cup holders, they pulled out of the services and onto the motorway. Their half-hour pit stop had allowed the traffic to clear a little, and the rain had eased off, so Taylor turned the music up and put her foot down. The bass flowed through her like a river pounding the rocks in its path. Dylan dramatically acted along with all of the songs, making Taylor laugh and her shoulders relax a little.

Dylan's phone started ringing, so he waved his hand in Taylor's line of sight, indicating the call and that he was going to turn the music down.

'Hi, Mum!' he answered. Taylor could hear the muffled sounds of their mother speaking to him, but was concentrating too much on driving to hear the words.

'Yes, we're about an hour away now, I think. There was some traffic in the city so it's taken a little longer than we thought.'

Taylor pulled out to overtake a lorry.

'Yes, Mum, Taylor's fine. Taylor, tell Mum you're fine,' Dylan said, holding the phone up to her ear.

'I'm fine, Mum!' she said smiling. Dylan took the phone back.

'OK, we'll see you in a bit then, Mum… love you too.'

He hung up. 'Mum sends her love,' he said to Taylor, putting his phone back in his pocket.

'Was she checking up on us?' Taylor asked, already knowing the answer.

'Yeah, isn't she always?' Dylan said, before adding, 'Now, where were we?' and cranking the volume all the way back up.

Taylor knew their mum was checking up because she had rung nearly every day since Dylan's slip-up, un-subtly probing Taylor for information, and offering to come back down. Taylor had to convince her to stay put, and that Dylan knew she cared but he needed space to sort himself out. She understood her mum's impulse, though; Taylor worried every time he left the house. She worried when he was more than five minutes late getting home. She worried when he was at his group. She just worried.

Taylor glanced across at her brother, gesticulating wildly as he sang along to the song. She knew he was genuinely happy now, but he was also quite adept at pretending to be happy, of masking his true fears and feelings, and that's what she worried about the most.

It was quiet at their parents' house on Christmas morning. There was no background hum of traffic, no drunken revellers in the street. Even the sun wasn't up yet. Their parents' house backed on to some fields that during the warmer months were filled with sheep, their bleats drifting through any open windows, but for now the fields were silent. Taylor found it strange waking up in her childhood bed, even though she had done it thousands of times before; it was always different as an adult. Her parents had barely touched her and her brother's old rooms, keeping them as shrines to their children. Her dad came in to clean every now and again, but they were quite content leaving the soft toys sitting on the shelf, and the barely played-with dolls on top of the chest of drawers. Taylor lay there for a while, soaking in the silence and the calmness of the house. Slowly, as the sun sleepily crawled over the horizon, the room filled with a glorious golden glow, almost making the walls change colour. The light-yellow paint matched the flowery curtains and bedspread, and a few carefully placed pictures and pieces of furniture hid childish accidents and wall graffiti.

Taylor heard the floorboards creak outside her room as one of her parents walked past on their way downstairs. Taylor slowly swung herself out of bed, sliding her feet into the comfy new slippers her parents had given her the night before. It was a family tradition, new pyjamas and new slippers every Christmas Eve, because if you managed to catch Santa in the act you wanted to look your best. Even though the twins had stopped believing in Santa long ago, the tradition continued. Taylor crept out of her room, not wanting to wake anyone else still sleeping. She danced down the hallway, tiptoeing around the squeaky floorboards as part of a well-practiced routine. She took care to miss the bottom step of the stairs, not wanting its creak to echo back up to the rooms above.

She padded towards the kitchen, rubbing her eyes and yawning widely. Opening the door she saw her mother bustling about with the kettle boiling in the background. She was humming Christmas carols to herself and hadn't noticed Taylor walk in. She turned around and jumped, clutching her hand to her chest.

'Jesus Christ, Taylor, don't creep up on me like that!' her mother said, still breathing heavily.

'And a happy Christmas to you too,' Taylor said, trying not to laugh.

'Of course, dear, Happy Christmas,' she said, hugging her daughter tightly. Even though Taylor was taller than her mum, she still found that embrace protective, like an impenetrable shield.

'Did you sleep OK?' her mum asked while retrieving a

second mug from the cupboard.

'Not too bad, but I've not been sleeping much anyway.' Taylor stifled another yawn; her body was trying to betray her.

'Yes, I heard,' her mum said, putting slices of bread in the toaster.

'You heard?' Taylor said confused. 'Dylan?'

'Yes, who else?' her mum said, turning towards her. 'I can never get a straight answer out of either of you if I ask you directly.'

'Sneaky,' Taylor said, smiling.

'Sometimes a mother has to be.'

A few minutes later the toast popped up and her mum began buttering it before Taylor had even had a chance to move. She put jam on only one slice, just like Taylor had liked as a child, cut them up, and handed her daughter the plate.

'Are you up to helping Dad with the dinner today?' her mum asked, starting to pull baking trays and knives out of cupboards and drawers.

'I help every year, Mum.'

'I know, but you know he won't ask for help.'

Paige rolled her eyes. Her father didn't need to ask for help; it was a given.

It wasn't long before they heard the telltale creak above them as Taylor's father crept across the landing, not quite as adept as Taylor at missing the squeaky floorboards in his older age.

'Ah, how are my two favourite girls?' he said, embracing them both in turn. 'Merry Christmas!'

'And you, Dad!' Taylor said, squeezing him tightly.

'Right, let's get this show on the road!' he said excitedly, retrieving a humongous bag of potatoes from the pantry.

'You're got time for breakfast first, haven't you, dear?' Taylor's mum said, pulling out his usual cereal and handing it to him.

'I can multi-task,' he said, winking at his daughter, causing her to giggle.

It wasn't long before there was a mountain of vegetable peelings and offcuts on the kitchen table, with Taylor and her dad sat at opposite ends, hard at work. Dylan, and their mother, would be banished to the living room when he came down. There was a giant pot of water on the stove, ready to pre-boil the potatoes, and a rogue Brussels sprout had fallen to the floor and rolled under the fridge. The pork, which had been in the slow cooker overnight, was filling the air with a delicious salty smell; every year it tested Taylor's vegetarian resolve. Her alternative was still hiding in the freezer, ready to be put in the oven at the last minute. The radio played Christmas carols loudly and Taylor's father hummed along, occasionally forgetting he had company and singing in his low, dulcet tone, before going red and stopping. Taylor didn't understand why, he had a lovely voice.

Through the window they could see snow on the mountain tops, their own version of festive hats. The garden had only been graced with a light frost, which had wrapped itself around every blade of grass and had coated the fish pond with a thin layer of ice. A lone robin hopped around, pecking hopelessly at the cold ground, unable to get to the worms beneath; denied its own tasty Christmas dinner.

'I must remember to fill the bird feeder,' her dad said, pausing what he was doing and watching the little robin through the window. Not even the smallest creatures should go hungry at Christmas.

Taylor carefully tipped all their peeled potatoes into the pot of water and turned on the stove. It wasn't long before the soft bubbling was harmonising with the radio, and the slowly warming oven.

A 'thud, thud, thud, thud', followed by the creaking of

the upstairs bathroom door, indicated that Dylan had risen from his prolonged slumber. Their mum quickly appeared at the bottom of the staircase, waiting to greet her son. She didn't even let him make it down the last step before comically hugging him around the middle; he was nearly a foot taller than his mother, and the added height of the step made her head about his elbow level.

'Morning a-a-a-a-ll' he said, yawning. 'Happy Christmas!' He greeted his sister by rubbing his knuckles on her head, making her duck out of the way quickly.

'Hey!' she shouted, throwing some carrot peel at him.

'Now, now, you two, none of that on Christmas Day,' their father tried to say sternly, but his cheeky smile gave him away as he put bubbles from the washing-up bowl on his son's head.

'I guess I deserved that,' Dylan said, scraping them off in resignation.

'Right, presents!' their mum said joyfully, grabbing Taylor by the sleeve and dragging her into the living room.

The sizable Christmas tree engulfed one end of the room, the top slightly bent as a tall person would bend their neck walking through a low doorway. Many ornaments weighed down its spindly branches, including a plethora of brightly coloured clay and card ones the twins had made as children. It was too bright to appreciate them at that moment, but the three separate sets of Christmas lights would illuminate the individual needles on the tree, creating a mini light show in their lounge.

Underneath the tree were piles and piles of presents, all wrapped in brightly coloured festive paper, all tied with extravagantly garish gold ribbon. Taylor knew that all but maybe two of those presents were for her and her brother.

'Mum, you know you don't have to do all this!' Taylor protested meekly, as she did every year. 'We love Christmas because we love spending time with you.'

'Oh, I know, but it's a mother's prerogative to spoil her children, and what better excuse than Christmas?'

Taylor rolled her eyes, but inside she was warm and smiling. It wasn't the gifts themselves that made her so content, but the amount of time and effort she knew her mum would have put into them.

Dylan bounded back upstairs, two steps at a time, to retrieve the bag of presents the twins had brought with them. By the time he got back downstairs, all of his presents had been piled next to an empty space on the sofa by the deft hands of his mother. She was perched on the edge of a chair, ignoring the two presents her husband had put on its arm, and her eyes were shining with the excitement of watching her children unwrap their gifts.

Dylan dutifully dished out the packages from his and Taylor's bag, and they all began to rip open the wrapping paper, their mum begrudgingly so, after much prompting from her family.

Dylan had got Taylor the new climbing harness she had been eyeing up for several months, which gave her a twinge of guilt in the pit of her stomach. She hadn't been climbing since she and Paige had fallen out, and she couldn't face seeing her after how she had acted, so she wasn't sure when she would get a chance to use it. Dylan had noticed her discomfort and subtly squeezed her arm. Taylor smiled back at him and placed her hand over his, so genuinely grateful and touched that he had been paying enough attention to get her the exact harness she wanted.

'Open that one next, Dyl,' she said, pointing to a unimposing-looking box wrapped in brown paper that had come out of their shared present bag. He looked at her quizzically before dragging the box towards him, and carefully peeling back the sticky tape.

'A lot of pretend snakes aren't going to jump out at me, are they?'

'Just open it!' she said, practically bouncing in her seat.

'OK, OK, just be warned I will get you back if it's -'

He stopped mid-sentence as he slid the box out of its wrapping. It was a new, very expensive, games console that had only been on the market a few months. Dylan had said that for every month he stayed sober he would put twenty pounds towards it, and it would have still taken him about two years to save up for it.

'Now you can put your money towards buying new games,' Taylor said quietly. Dylan didn't respond verbally but instead threw his arms around his sister and squeezed so tight she could barely breathe.

The dining table looked like it might bow under the weight of all the food on it. Her dad, as usual, had cooked enough to feed the whole village instead of just their small family. A dome of crispy roast potatoes occupied the centre of the table along with the slow-cooked pork. Taylor's vegetarian roast had been put next to her place setting, and garnished with a piece of parsley, just like the meat. There was also stuffing, gravy, apple sauce, and every vegetable that Taylor's dad could think of. She also knew that there were a couple of desserts defrosting on a side and a third, an apple crumble, waiting to go in the oven.

'Crackers!' her mum said loudly.

'We know you are,' Dylan replied, instantly, causing

his mum to laugh and tap him over the head with the cracker she was holding.

'Ready? Pull!' she instructed, and four tiny bangs went off, one after the other.

Their dad immediately donned his hat, and made everyone read out their awful cracker jokes. They laughed, and ate, and laughed some more during the course of the meal. Their belt loops and trouser buttons strained under the extra pressure, each belly laugh threatening to make them pop at any minute.

Their mum cleared the table, with their dad 'helping' – in other words, making sure she stacked the dishwasher just so. Taylor and Dylan took their coffees into the living room and stretched out at opposite ends of the sofa, the only light now coming from the brightly coloured lights wrapped around the Christmas tree. The curtains were drawn, making the room feel even more cosy, with the electric fire keeping them warm. There were a couple of recycling bags in the corner, stuffed full of the wrapping paper they had ripped off their presents just a few hours ago. Taylor sipped her coffee contentedly.

'Thank you for the console,' Dylan said quietly.

'Thank you for the harness,' Taylor said, smiling.

'No, I mean, thank you. For believing I can do this.'

'I've always got your back, Dyl,' she said, putting a hand on his stray ankle.

'I know you do. But that doesn't mean you have to miss out, you know.'

'What do you mean?' she said, turning to face him.

'Dad's going to come in here in a few minutes and offer you a sherry, and even though sherry makes you all nostalgic, you're going to decline. Because of me.'

'Maybe I've just gone off sherry,' Taylor said, taking another sip of her coffee.

'And wine? And gin? Just because I don't drink doesn't mean you can't.'

'But -'

'Look, I appreciate you not having alcohol in the house. I'm not saying open a bar in the living room. Just… don't forget to have fun, OK? We're still in our early thirties, start acting like it!' he said, throwing a pillow at her.

'Hey!'

'Payback,' he said, grinning.

The family spent the remainder of the day watching their traditional television shows. Their dad's head slowly dropped to his chest and his quiet snores started growing louder, making their mum tap him awake and send him off to bed, saying she wouldn't be far behind him. She hugged each of the children goodnight and went upstairs. The twins stayed up a little longer, watching another show. Taylor pulled her phone out and just stared at it for a while, before putting it back in her pocket. She repeated this a few more times until Dylan couldn't keep quiet anymore.

'Just text her,' he said, the fifth time Taylor had taken her phone out.

'What? she said, turning red.

'Just text her. Get it over with. Rip the plaster off.'

'What would I say?'

'Errr, how about "Merry Christmas?"'

'Oh, right. Yeah.'

'Yeah,' he said mockingly.

Taylor left her phone on her lap, but didn't say anything else.

Their show finished and they headed up to bed. Dylan gave her a meaningful look before disappearing off into his room, and Taylor heavily made her way to her own.

Sinking into the mattress she pulled out her phone once more, the blue light dazzling her as the cursor blinked at her tauntingly. She typed and retyped a message a dozen or so times, before eventually deciding on a simple '*I'm sorry. I know I messed up. I hope you had a good Christmas'*, allowing it to send before turning her phone off. She knew if she didn't, she would just lie awake waiting for a response. She didn't want to give her brain another reason to keep her awake all night.

She lay there, staring up at her childhood bedroom ceiling, and the glow in the dark stars she had stuck there as a teenager. She hoped that, wherever Paige was, she had had a good day and that, maybe in the spirit of Christmas, she could find it in her heart to forgive her.

CHAPTER NINETEEN
Christmas at the Spencers'

PAIGE

Paige had also gone home to her parents' house for Christmas; but she travelled alone on Christmas Eve. Thomas still lived at home, and Brandon was travelling up on Christmas morning with Lucy and the kids. Jenna would be catching a tan in Hawaii.

Paige's Christmas morning started very differently. She was also up early, but instead of putting on warm fluffy slippers, she put on her running shoes and headed outside. The crisp morning air meant her warm-up took a lot longer than usual, and she cut her stretching time in half so as not to get cold again. She didn't know the routes around her parents' house very well - they had downsized many years ago, leaving behind the trails she used to run. Paige had run on Christmas morning for many years; she wasn't much help in the kitchen and she didn't like just sitting around doing nothing. Until Brandon got there with the kids there wasn't much opportunity to spend time with her family because her parents would be cooking and Thomas would be asleep for a few more hours, his artistic insomnia having thrown his sleep patterns out of whack since he was a child.

Paige chose to stick to the streets, not wanting to get lost in unfamiliar countryside. She had found solace by running more than usual the last couple of weeks, the pounding of her feet and her rhythmic breathing helping her to regulate her emotions. She ran on the sunny side of the road, not wanting to spend Christmas in Accident and Emergency having slipped on ice. Her breath rose up in a mist in front of her as she ran, making her look like she was chasing clouds down the street. The naked trees looked like they were shivering in the light breeze, while the evergreen shrubs looked like they were hoarding all the warmth. There were a few bird calls floating around in the air, cheering Paige on as she ran. Most of the houses she passed were still dark, waiting for the magic of Christmas to start. Paige could just imagine little kids bounding downstairs to see if Santa had been. As a child she had quickly worked out that Father Christmas was a ruse, and her five-year-old brain had run an experiment, to prove her theory, by asking for the most ridiculous presents she could think of. Her parents had sworn her to secrecy for the sake of her sister, who was just becoming aware of what Christmas was. Thomas hadn't been born then, but his arrival helped prolong the magic. Now that Brandon had children, her entire family got to pretend all over again, and live in that childish fantasy.

By the time Paige got back to the house it was clear someone was up, as the lights were on in the kitchen. She popped her head in to see her mother sitting at the kitchen table with a cup of tea, relishing the peace and quiet before the true hectic-ness of the day set in. Aunts, uncles, and cousins from both sides would all descend on the house at various points during the day. Whilst it was nice that most of their family lived locally, it did create a large amount of work for her mum, who wouldn't let anyone else in the kitchen while she cooked Christmas dinner.

'Hi, Mum, Merry Christmas,' Paige said around the edge of the door.

'Merry Christmas, Paige,' her mum said, smiling sweetly at her. 'Have you just got back from your run?'

'Yes, it was a chilly one. I'm just going to jump in the shower.'

'OK,' her mum smiled in response. She'd have a few more minutes of alone time.

Paige retracted herself from the door and made her way upstairs. The gleaming white bathroom was still cold, as the heating had only turned on a few minutes ago. Paige reluctantly disrobed while she waited for the shower to warm up, before gratefully stepping in. The hot water warmed her numb extremities while washing the sweat off the rest of her body, and she felt like she was washing away the bad memories of the last few weeks and starting anew.

Back downstairs after her shower, she found her dad sitting in the living room, reading a book and waiting. His self-appointed job at Christmas was to be the perfect host every time a family member dropped in. As soon as they walked through the door he would put the kettle on or pour them a glass of wine, depending on who it was; he had all their orders memorised. The kids always got hot chocolate, whether they really wanted it or not.

'Morning, Dad,' Paige said, sitting down in the living room with him.

'Morning, Paige. Did you sleep alright?'

'Yes, thanks.' Her parents' spare room had a luxurious double bed with a soft mattress and extra thick duvet. When Brandon and his family came to stay, they put air beds up for the kids. The money her parents had gained from downsizing had allowed them to do all the travelling they missed out on when raising four children.

Paige's dad put his book away and took off his reading glasses, giving Paige his full attention.

'You're looking skinny,' he said, furrowing his brow. 'Are you OK? Are you eating enough?'

'Yes, Dad, I'm fine. I've just been doing a bit more running than usual.'

'Hmmm,' he said, with his brows not changing. 'How is work going?'

'Well, you know how my research project got rejected again?' Her dad solemnly nodded once. She had given him her proposal to read and he had thought it was very good, hurting with her when it was rejected. 'Well, Maya had the idea that I should find another way to do the project. So I'm writing a book.'

Paige's dad sat up straighter in his chair and leant forward.

'A book?'

'Yes. A fictional book based on a real person and her life throughout the war,' Paige blurted out quickly.

'Well,' he said, leaning back again. 'That's something, isn't it?' he added, smiling. 'That's really something.'

Brandon and his family got there at around eleven. Their arrival was announced by the kids bursting through the door, Cayden shouting 'Merry Christmas!' at the top of his lungs, and Susie taking a running jump onto her grandad's lap, her little feet so fast he hadn't even had the chance to put down his half-full coffee mug. Lucy came in not far after them, carrying coats and the kids' tablets that had kept them entertained on the car journey. Brandon then came waddling in, two big bags on his back and several carrier bags in each hand. For the last few years the kids had opened their presents from their parents at their own house, but they always brought Santa's presents with them, so their grandparents could enjoy the spectacle. Brandon dropped all the bags in the hallway with a thud, before picking up the ones with the presents in and taking them into the living room. Kneeling down by the Christmas tree he artfully arranged them underneath, along with the decent-sized pile already there. As Cayden and Susie were the only grandchildren, they always got spoilt at Christmas, with even the aloof Thomas not being able to resist buying them adorable, and sometimes loud, toys.

Thomas appeared in the living room doorway just then, wrapped in a navy-blue dressing gown. He nodded a greeting at his brother, who was still on the floor by the tree. Thomas scratched the black stubble on his jaw as he yawned by way of greeting everyone else. Just then,

Cayden ran into the room, joining his sister on his grandad's lap.

'And here is my favourite nephew, who announced Christmas so loudly a few minutes ago,' Thomas said, offering Cayden a high five.

'Did you know that most insects' life cycles are so short that they don't survive the winter?' he said, by way of season's greetings.

'…Right' Thomas said, before heading into the kitchen to get some much-needed coffee.

'Story!' Susie demanded from her grandad's lap.

'Oh… well… I suppose,' he said, as if it was some big chore, and that he didn't have a stack of children's books by his chair, waiting for their arrival.

Brandon brought himself slowly up from the floor, several of his joints cracking as his did so.

'Hey, Paige,' he said, hugging his sister, able to greet her properly now.

'How was the drive?' she asked, as they separated.

'It was fine. The roads were pretty much empty, so it took just over an hour. You?'

'Same, it was quiet, but I did leave quite late in the day. How're things with you?'

'Oh, fine…' he said, scratching the back of his head.

Paige raised her eyebrows at him, but just as she was about to ask what was wrong, the doorbell rang, announcing the arrival of some cousins.

'Can somebody get that, please!' yelled a distant voice from the kitchen. Brandon didn't quite meet his sister's eye before heading to the door to let in the horde.

Traditionally the family waited until they were all sated from dinner to open presents, so that their mum could sit down and enjoy it with them, leaving a pile of washing up in the kitchen for the kids to do later. All of the adults, except Brandon, were sat on the sofas. Brandon was sat by the tree, and both his children were stood next to him, bouncing up and down excitedly, Susie clapping her hands and Cayden flapping his.

'Can you give this to Grandma please, Cayden?' he said, handing him a present. Cayden took his responsibilities very seriously, and carefully transferred the package to his grandmother before dashing back to his father's side.

'Suse, can you give this to Uncle Thomas?' Susie took the present off her dad hesitatingly, under the jealous watch of her brother, and shuffled over to Thomas.

'Thaaaaaank you,' he said, plucking the present from

her little hands, and she grinned before dashing back.

'Aaaaaaaaaand... I wonder who these could be for?' Brandon said, theatrically, holding up two presents that were clearly labelled in big letters. 'Susie, I'm struggling to read this, can you help me?' he said softly.

'That one says Cayden and that one says Susie!' Cayden interrupted before reaching out for his present. Brandon relented and handed the presents over to his children, who immediately sat on the floor and began tearing off the paper. He then deftly threw Paige's present over to her, and slid his mum's present across the carpet.

'Is that everyone?' he asked, but no one could really hear him, he was drowned out by the squeals of his daughter, who had just opened a 'My First Pony' set, which included a soft toy pony with a real mane, brushes, and a saddle.

'I think it's safe to say that went down well!' Lucy said, before turning to Susie. 'What do you say, Susie? Grandad and Grandma bought you that, so what do you say?' Susie didn't even look up from her gift, she just gently held the box in her hands, as if it was fragile as glass.

'Susie?' her dad said, touching her leg. Finally she looked up. 'Say thank you to Grandad and Grandma.' Susie, still clinging on to her present, went over to her grandparents and gave them the best hug she could, given she still had a large box under her arm. Paige saw Brandon's smile falter.

'Wow, thanks, Mum and Dad!' Thomas said, holding up a box containing camera film; something that was quite hard to get hold of now everything had gone digital. Thomas was experimenting with film cameras, and his supply was running dangerously low. Paige opened her gift next, which contained a new chalk bag and climbing shoes. She knew about the shoes as her parents had called to ask her what size and brand she wanted, but the chalk bag was a nice and thoughtful surprise.

'The nice man in the shop said you would be able to use the bag,' her mum explained.

'Thank you,' Paige said, smiling. Her old chalk bag was looking pretty tatty.

The rest of the presents were opened gleefully, mainly by the children, and soon the living room looked like there had been an explosion in a wrapping paper factory. At around seven Brandon and Lucy started getting the kids ready for bed; they'd be taking over the spare room once Paige left. Cayden shook hands with everybody, as he'd seen a scientist in his insect documentaries do, and Susie refused to let go of her grandad's hand. Paige helped

Brandon take the several bags of recycling outside. The stars shone brightly through a clear sky as they put the bags down the side of the house.

'So... how are you really?' Paige said, after checking no one had followed them out.

'Ha,' Brandon smiled wryly. His sister was always seeing through his lies, even when they were children. 'How did you know I wasn't being honest?'

'You always scratch the back of your head when you're hiding something,' Paige said, folding her arms and staring at him.

'I really am fine, it's just the kids... they got assessed in school before the Christmas break. The educational psychologist says he's going to give them a diagnosis.'

'So? Isn't that a good thing? They'll get extra help?'

'I guess...'

'But?'

'But it kind of makes it final, doesn't it? Once it's written down, it's... real'

'Brandon, it's always been real. Autism doesn't just turn up overnight, it's always been a part of your lives; it's who they are.'

'You're right, I guess. I haven't told Mum and Dad yet, I'm not sure how they'll react, after...'

'I'm sure they'll be OK with it. They love the kids.'

'I know, but it takes them a while to get used to anything different'

'Ha, maybe they're autistic too,' Paige said, only half joking. Brandon smiled and made as if to walk back to the house, to help his wife shepherd the kids up to bed.

'Brandon, wait -' Paige said, grabbing him buy the arm. He stopped and looked at her. 'I've asked to be referred to be assessed too. I just thought you should know.'

'You have?' he said quietly.

'Yes. They said it could take up to a year to get an appointment but... well, I'll worry about it when it happens.'

'I'm proud of you, Paige, that can't have been easy.'

'It wasn't - the doctor really didn't want to refer me.'

'I'm glad he did, I wouldn't have wanted to go all big brother on his ass.' Paige rolled her eyes, but laughed.

Back in the house, the family were saying their goodbyes and goodnights. Susie had been picked up by her grandad so he could come to the door to see Paige off, rather than be restrained to the chair where Susie wanted him to stay. Her head was lolling on his shoulder as she fought sleep; the excitement of the day having worn her out. Even Cayden was tired; his factual monologues had been replaced with silence and hand gestures and him struggling to make his little limbs move.

Paige could have stayed longer, but her early start and the sheer volume of people and noise had worn her out. Once she got home she dragged herself up the stairs to bed, even though it wasn't even nine o'clock yet.

Paige woke up early on Boxing Day morning to a text from Taylor, sent the night before. She wasn't entirely sure how to respond so she simply put her earphones in, her running shoes on and left.

CHAPTER TWENTY
Spring

The chilly frosts of winter soon gave way to a wet and wonderful spring. By March, the bulbs were in full bloom, a carpet of purples, yellows, whites, and oranges filling the woods behind Paige's house. The once bare trees now had leaves that were unfurling, though always when no one was watching.

With the warmer weather came the prospect of climbing outside. Paige enjoyed climbing at the centre, pushing herself to her limits there, but nothing could compare to making it to the top of a real rock face, conquering and respecting nature at the same time. The club often did informal outdoor climbs, organised a few days or a few hours in advance. But in the summer they also arranged a formal trip to France, with sometimes up to thirty members coming along, bringing their families with them. Paige was grateful to not be organising it this year.

In addition to the climbing, Maya was now over four months into her six-month stint in Japan, and Paige was counting down the days to her return. They video called regularly, and texted even more often, but nothing could compare to being able to hug your best friend in person, instead of typing it or sending a GIF.

Paige had also made more progress on her book; she was about three-quarters of the way through writing the first draft, and her stomach filled with jumping grasshoppers every time she thought about finishing it. She had waited so long to tell the stories of these women, and she hoped this would be the first stepping-stone across a wide river, with recognition of their contribution on the other side.

Overall, Paige was happy. She was optimistic for the coming months. Even Jacob, who she had been worried about, was flourishing. He had found a group of friends, via an autistic social club, and was happily settling into life in the city. Everything was going well, but Paige couldn't shake the nagging feeling of something being missing.

At the climbing club one evening, she was practising on the triple overhang. Someone else had lead climbed it already and left the rope up for her, to give her some time on the wall before attempting the lead herself. She desperately wanted to crack it before the summer trip to France. She was happy with her technique to get around the first overhang, but the second was proving more of a challenge. No matter which way she contorted her body, she always ended up falling off and dangling there helplessly, until lowered back to the ground.

After her ninth time being lowered back to the floor, having fallen off yet again, she told the person she was climbing with that she was going to take a break, and untied the rope from her harness, offering the rope to them, but they declined, deciding to go home instead. Paige thanked them, grabbed her wallet from her bag, and headed to the cafe.

There were a few people sitting scattered around their tables. She knew most of them so greeted them with a smile or a wave as she went up to the counter to order her tea. One of the groups closest to the till invited her to join them, which she duly did.

'So I told him that if he made it to the top of the 6c on his first go, I'd go on a date with him,' one woman said, continuing her story.

'Honestly, guys, I've never climbed so well in my life. Before or since,' the man said, making everyone around the table laugh.

'And after that, well... he just kind of stuck around.'

'If by stuck around you mean I bought you a helluva ring!'

'Yes, that's true,' the woman said, pulling her fiancé in for a kiss.

'Congratulations, I didn't realise you had got engaged!' Paige said as she caught up with the conversation.

'Yes, last week,' the woman explained, offering Paige the ring to see.

'Very nice,' Paige said, smiling, before pouring out her tea.

Everyone sat around the table seemed to be partnered up with someone, or had someone waiting for them at home, as they re-told their own stories of how they and their current partner got together. Paige sat there quietly, sipping her tea, and wishing she had made just one more attempt at the triple overhang. Eventually the conversation naturally petered out, and they started instead discussing where they might go for the France trip this year.

'Has anyone seen Dylan climbing recently? Or... Taylor?' Paige asked in a natural lull in the conversation.

'Who?' one person asked.

'You know, the lanky guy that always races up the walls, falls off them even faster.'

'Oh, him. No, I haven't seen him for a while now.'

'I've seen him a couple of times when I've climbed during the day,' one of the women said; she was also a student so had a bit more flexibility with her schedule.

'That'd explain it, I only climb in the evenings,' someone else chimed in.

Paige didn't respond, instead leaning back in her chair and taking another sip of her tea. She was glad to hear that Dylan was still climbing - he really hadn't looked well the last time she had seen him. But if people didn't even know who Taylor was, she probably hadn't been in months, probably not since their ill-fated lunch at the cafe.

Slowly the people around the table filtered out, either going back to climbing or going home, until Paige was the last one left. She pulled her phone out and scrolled down her messages to the text Taylor had sent so many months ago. Her fingers hovered over the keyboard as she considered messaging back, but eventually she shook her head and put her phone back in her pocket. Taking her mug back to the counter, she made her way back into the climbing wall, milling around for a while before deciding to use the auto-belay instead of trying to pair up with someone. She deftly tied in, picked the easiest route on the wall, and started with that one; the cold cafe had chilled her muscles. She made light work of that route, and had soon worked her way up to the hardest route on the wall, rapidly climbing it until she got to one difficult move she just couldn't get past. Someone belaying on a nearby route shouted over to her to try a different approach, to try looking at the problem in a different way. Paige thanked him and stared back up at the wall. It was worth a try. She re-chalked her hands using her new chalk bag, clipped to the back of her harness, and began climbing again. This time, when she got to the problem, she placed her other foot on the hold, which actually gave her that little bit more leverage to extend up to a better hand hold. And just like that, she was past the problem and at the top of the wall. She lifted her eyes to the ceiling in celebration as she topped out, giving thanks to the climbing gods, before the auto-belay lowered her to the ground. The whirring sound it made always made her feel like she was falling much faster than she actually was, but even so, the floor always came as a bit of a surprise, and she ended up sitting on it rather than stood up. The person who had advised her gave her a thumbs up with her free hand, before concentrating back on her climber. Paige got to her feet, elated, and made her way over to her bag to change out of her climbing shoes and start adding more layers. It might have been spring now, but it still wasn't that warm outside.

Puddles from recent rain dotted the car park, and her brain flashed back to her night of climbing with Taylor, when they had run to her car together. Paige could still feel the intensity of her gaze, even though she was alone amongst the remaining cars. Her elation faded, and she quickly got into her car and drove away.

Unlocking the front door, Paige heard the draught excluder catch on a pile of post waiting for her. She had gone climbing straight from work, so this was her first chance to check her mail. Dumping her bag in the hallway, she took off her coat and hung it up on the hooks, before picking up the letters and rifling through them for anything interesting. Most of it was junk mail; one of the disadvantages of living in a city. There was a postcard from her sister, who was currently in India on holiday, and there was a brown envelope with one of those see-through windows on the front, with her address typed in it. She flipped the envelope over and saw a hospital address on the back. Furrowing her brows slightly, she put the junk mail in the bin she kept by the door, took the letter into the living room, and slumped down on the sofa. Sooty sleepily raised his head, wondering what the commotion was. He gave her a look saying 'Oh, it's just you' before going back to sleep. Paige ripped it open and unfolded the white paper, scanning the text, her brain barely processing what it was reading. The only words that really sank in were 'appointment', 'assessment', and 'November'. She re-read the letter, made harder by the fact her hands were trembling, making the words jump around in front of her. She had put the potential autism assessment out of her mind. The doctor had said it would take around a year, so she mentally packed it up into a little box and put it away into storage, so she could concentrate her mental energy on other things. But here the letter was, violently tugging the box, causing a whole lot of others to come tumbling around with it. She didn't recognise the name of the hospital; she only knew where the local minor injury unit and accident and emergency were, she had never heard of 'Blue Forest Centre'. She took a deep breath and started playing with the hem of her shirt sleeve. At least she would have time to plan a route, probably organise to take a day off work, and work out what she was going to do afterwards when she expected to be mentally drained.

Putting the letter down on the coffee table, she got up from the sofa. Sooty stretched and followed, meowing loudly, demanding to be fed.

'I know, I know,' she told him as she got his food out of the cupboard. 'You're staaaaarving,' she said, as he circled around his food bowl expectantly. In his eagerness to fill his stomach, Sooty immediately started eating as soon as the first bit of wet food fell out of the pouch, which mean that the next, bigger bit landed squarely on his head before slipping off to the side. He didn't even seem to notice. Paige chuckled at him, then set about making her own meal for the evening.

Paige took her own meal back to the sofa; a batch-cooked meal from the freezer. She had just enough time to eat it before Maya was due to call, before her workday started. Paige turned the television on and zoned out as she ate, vaguely listening to the weather report. The forecaster was talking about some incoming storms with a likelihood of flooding, as well as thunder and lightning, followed by some warmer weather. Paige missed the sun. The short days of winter had made her feel enclosed and claustrophobic, and she longed for the freedom of summer and climbing outdoors, and warm evening runs through the woods where the trail wasn't a river of mud. Paige changed the channel to try and find something more uplifting, but it was all soaps, drama, and the news, which was the worst of them all. Maya rang then, rescuing her from the doom and gloom of the television.

'Hi, Maya,' Paige said, tucking the phone between her neck and ear as she moved her plate to the table. 'How're you?'

'I'm good, lovely, really good. How're you?'

'I'm OK. Work is going OK, and it's getting warmer and sunnier here so that's nice.'

'Anything on the Taylor front?'

'No. No one has seen her at the climbing club. I think Dylan's gone during the day a few times but that's about it.'

'Has she tried to contact you again?'

'No.'

'Hmmm. As your loyal best friend, I will always have your back, and be there to beat people up if needed. But maybe, this once, you should reach out to her?'

'Maya, you couldn't beat up a flea. You have no upper body strength. And I wouldn't know what to say.'

'How about just asking how she is?'

'I would feel too awkward doing that after nearly four months of silence.'

'OK, lovely, I won't push it. I just thought she was good for you. Aside from the whole cafe freak out thing.'

'How is business?' Paige asked casually.

'Yeah, about that. It's been going really well, too well... they want me to stay out here for a bit longer.' Maya said hesitantly.

'For how much longer?' Paige asked, her voice shaking slightly.

'Another six months.'

'Another...' Paige started, but couldn't finish. She swallowed hard, bewildered by the whole situation.

'Paige?' Maya said gently after a few minutes of silence.

'I'm... OK. I'm OK, Maya.' Paige said, measuring her breathing and maintaining her composure. 'I'm so glad it's going well, I'm so proud of you.'

'I'm proud of me, too. I can't believe they want me to stay. They've promised me a big promotion when I come back if I stay, with the freedom to basically choose where I work and how much I will earn,' Maya said quickly, the words tumbling over one another in her excitement.

'That's amazing!' Paige said, genuinely happy for her friend.

They talked a little while longer, mainly about Maya's next set of responsibilities out in Japan, and a little bit about Paige's book, before Maya had to leave for work. After she hung up, Paige just stared at the home screen of her phone, Maya's words having not quite sunk in. But this wasn't like last time. Paige had coped this far with Maya being so far away, she'd coped with Taylor, she'd coped with taking her research in a whole new direction, so she knew she could cope with this. Yet that didn't mean she didn't feel vulnerable.

She took her plate and empty wine glass out to the kitchen, then went upstairs and ran herself a bath. She poured a liberal amount of bubble bath in. The water quickly foamed up, creating a mountain of white fluffy clouds floating around on the surface. She lit some candles, and the smell of lavender and melting wax filled the small room. Paige ran the water as hot as she could stand it, and it enveloped her as she lowered herself in, almost burning her skin, but making her sore, aching muscles relax with every inch she slid down the tub. Closing her eyes, she leant her head back and let out a deep breath, focusing on the warmth of the water wrapping around her, and the quiet sound of the bubbles popping, the smell of the candles. She thought about how nice it would be to see Maya when she got back, even if it was going to be later than she expected. She smiled to herself, so proud of her friend she could almost burst. Paige wondered if maybe Maya was right about contacting Taylor; maybe it would be a good thing to extend an olive branch…

Paige awoke with a start. She had slipped down the bath, the tepid water jolting her awake. Her fingertips resembled prunes. She clambered out, turned on the light, and blew out the dangerously low candles, chastising herself for falling asleep. She must have been much more tired than she realised.

CHAPTER TWENTY-ONE
Brotherly Intervention

TAYLOR

When the second university term started in January, Taylor had, with support of her director of studies, arranged a meeting with her the person who scheduled her teaching hours. They had been completely unaware about how much she was struggling. They had assumed that, as she had agreed to everything he had asked her to do, that everything was OK, completely ignorant of the power inequality in their situation. With the help of her director of studies, they worked out a new and better teaching schedule that would actually allow Taylor time to work on her PhD. She was supposed to start writing her thesis come September and there was no way that was going to happen, so they also organised an extension, both members of staff reassuring her that it was OK and perfectly normal. That cold January morning meeting turned into a February of re-invigorated research and then a March of falling back in love with her project. If anything, she was now spending more time at university than she did last term, but out of choice and the pure enjoyment of it, rather than because teaching required her to do so.

Dylan was still living with her, and more importantly, still sober. He had achieved good grades in his January exams, and was happily knuckling down to study in the small bedroom he occupied at Taylor's house. He was also counting down the days to buy the next game for his new console; the ones he had already bought sat proudly on a shelf above his desk. Dylan had been nagging Taylor to go climbing with him again, but she always used the excuse of being too busy with her research, and it being his thing more than hers now. But they both knew the truth: that she didn't want to risk bumping into Paige. It had been nearly four months since they had spoken, and the hopeful text Taylor had sent on Christmas Day had gone unanswered. Taylor had thought about trying again, but she wasn't sure she could handle the sting of rejection a second time. Instead, she settled for throwing herself vigorously into her work and trying to forget about the beautiful secret agent.

One evening near the end of the first week in March, Dylan dramatically flopped down onto the sofa opposite his sister, having just been dropped off from a climbing session with one of the members of the student climbing club.

'I nearly managed it today, Lor.'

'Hello to you too,' Taylor said, barely looking up from her laptop. She had been planning to turn her spare room into a study for herself, but now that her brother occupied it, she used her laptop to work wherever the mood took her.

'The triple overhang. I nearly got it!'

'Yeah?' Taylor said, still typing away, not really listening.

'Yeah, but then I got distracted because Paige was climbing next to me, naked, so...'

'Very funny,' Taylor said, pressing the save button on her project and closing her laptop. 'I *can* multi-task, you know.'

'I was just checking,' Dylan said innocently. Taylor threw a pillow at him.

'I managed the first two overhangs but lost my grip on the third. It'd taken me all night to get past the second, so I was pooped.'

'Progress though?' Taylor said, watching a little bit of chalk fall off his gesticulating hands and onto her sofa. He had been mimicking his hand position on the last hold.

'Yeah. Paige really was there though.'

'Not naked, I assume,' Taylor said, opening her laptop

back up again and pretending to scrutinise the work she had just completed. But her eyes remained statically staring at the screen.

'No, not naked. Still hot though.'

'Mmm-hmm,' Taylor said, not wanting to get drawn into the conversation.

'She asked after you,' Dylan said quietly.

Taylor's eyes snapped up and stared at him, not entirely trusting that she heard him correctly.

'She asked if you'd given up climbing.'

'What did you tell her?'

'I told her that you were hiding from her.'

'Dylan!' Taylor said, her face flushing red with anger.

'Joking! Just joking, T, sorry.'

'Not funny, Dyl.'

'I told her you were busy with work.'

'OK…' Taylor said, looking at him distrustfully.

'Pizza?' Dylan said, noticing his sister's discomfort.

'Only if you shower first. You stink.'

'C'mon, I can't smell that b -' he said, lifting up his arm and taking a whiff. 'No,' he said, gasping for clean air, 'I stand corrected.' He spluttered a little, before getting up from the sofa. 'Order the usual? I should be out of the shower by the time it gets here.'

'Oh, I see, I'm paying, am I?'

'I'll pay you back!' he shouted, his voice fading away as he bounded up the stairs. Taylor rolled her eyes and brought up the website of their favourite pizza place. She had expected Dylan moving in to be more jarring, upsetting her routine and disturbing her personal space; after all, they hadn't lived together for over ten years, not since they both left for university the first time around. But they'd fallen into an easy routine, living together more harmoniously than they ever did as teenagers.

It didn't take long for the pizza to arrive. Dylan sat on the sofa in a towelling dressing gown, stuffing slices into his mouth like he hadn't eaten in days. The smell of tomato and melted cheese drifted around, accompanying the sound of the television and the rain hitting the windows. Dylan stuffed his last slice of pizza into his mouth, while Taylor was only about halfway through hers. Dylan threw the pizza box on the table triumphantly, stretched, and patted his stomach contently before letting out a loud belch.

'Ew!' Taylor said, wrinkling her nose and leaning away from him.

'Sorry,' he said, picking up his drink and settling back into the sofa.

'I forgot how gross you could be sometimes,' Taylor said, closing her pizza box and putting in on the table. 'And don't you dare snack on my leftovers while I'm at work tomorrow,' she threatened, pointing her finger at him and raising an eyebrow.

'I wouldn't dare,' he said, pulling what he evidently felt was an innocent face.

'Uh-huh...'

They watched television in silence for a while. Dylan kept glancing over at his sister, opening his mouth slightly and then focusing back on the TV. After about the fifth or sixth time this happened, Taylor called him out.

'Spit it out, Dylan,' she said, exasperated.

'What?!' he said, trying to act innocent.

'Whatever you're thinking about saying, just say it, so we can go back to watching the telly.'

'I just... I was wondering if maybe you should try talking to Paige again,' he said gently.

'Again with this?'

'She asked after you! Clearly the door isn't all the way closed.'

'I said some terrible things, Dylan.'

'I mean, yeah, but she'll forgive you! If you give her the chance to, I'm sure she'll forgive you.'

'I doubt it.'

'Why not?'

'I may have also told her that her problems were nothing compared to dealing with alcoholism…' Taylor said, her face burning red. Dylan went quiet, which was unusual for him. Eventually he spoke, in barely a whisper.

'Do you really think that?' he asked

'What I actually think is the two aren't comparable. Like apples and oranges. But I didn't think, did I? I just lashed out, and now…'

'And now you spend your evenings sat on a sofa, working, or hanging out with your brother,' he said pointedly.

'Yeah,' Taylor said with a sigh. 'I want to tell her, to explain about you, and Daniella. But I just don't think I can face her,' she said in resignation.

'Sounds like you two need your heads knocked together. I genuinely think she misses you.'

'I guess we'll never know,' Taylor finished, shutting down the conversation.

They carried on watching television before Taylor turned in for the night, citing work in the morning. Despite being overly tired from working well into the evening, sleep did not come easily for her. Her brain kept re-playing the argument with Paige, like it had so many times before, creating an ache inside of her that hurt like nothing she had felt before. She had never thought of herself as a bad person, but with this film strip on repeat in her head there wasn't really any other conclusion she could come to. She knew her reaction had been due to fear stemming from her last relationship, ignorance of what Paige was trying to tell her, and the stress of what was going on with Dylan, but it was no excuse. A good person would never have said those things.

'Well, I can fix one of those things at least,' she thought to herself, deciding that if she wasn't going to be able to sleep she might as well do something productive, and she started researching autism on her phone.

PAIGE

Paige was at university that morning, searching the library shelves for a specific book on World War Two garments and nutrition, to add to the large pile of books she had already placed onto a nearby desk ready to check out. She was repeating the Dewey Decimal Number over and over in her head as she scanned the volumes, having finally narrowed down her search to one shelf. Normally she searched for things by shape and colour, matching it to the image her search revealed in the database, but she had no idea what this book looked like. Her eyes flicked over it the first time she saw it, barely registering the thin spine and tiny numbers, but something made her go back and check. She gratefully pulled the small book off the shelves and added it to the pile, thankful not to be adding much more weight as she heaved the books into her arms.

After scanning the books out, Paige made her way to the lift, awkwardly leaning around the book stack and pressing the button with a barely extended index finger, to call the lift down from the third floor. She was only one floor down, but her arms were already aching from the additional weight, so she wasn't going to even attempt the stairs. The lift was empty when it arrived and Paige gratefully stepped in, only just managing to negotiate the small corner where the control panel was to press the button for the third floor.

Paige was relieved when she got to the final corner before turning onto the corridor leading to her office. However, stood in front of her office door was a lone figure, seemingly peering through the window. It wasn't a History student or staff member that she recognised, and she immediately tensed up, taking a few more steps forward. The strange person had just turned to leave when Paige called out to them, prepared to challenge them if they weren't supposed to be here.

'Can I help you?' Paige shouted from her end of the corridor. Her stomach twisted as the strange man turned around; she hated confrontation. But now the man was facing her, she recognised him straight away.

'Oh, hi, Dylan! I didn't recognise you, not in climbing gear!' she said with a smile as she continued walking down the corridor, relieved it was someone she knew.

'Hi, Paige, how are you?' he asked, a slight nervousness in his voice.

'I'm good, and yourself?' she said, finally reaching the office door and awkwardly fumbling with her keys. The stack of books she now had precariously balanced in one arm was restricting her movement and visions.

'Err... need a hand?' Dylan asked, awkwardly, offering to take the books off her.

'Thanks,' she said, dumping the heavy books in his arms. He stumbled slightly at the weight; clearly not expecting them to be that heavy.

'Do you want to come in?' she said, holding the door open for him. He mumbled an answer, before staggering into the room and dumping the books on her desk with a thud that made the frames on the walls quiver.

'Is this a social call, or are you looking to switch degree programs?' Paige said, offering him the chair her students usually sat in, while she started putting the stack of books away onto what looked like a new set of shelves.

'Err... social,' Dylan said awkwardly. 'Kind of.'

'Kind of?'

'It's about Taylor,' he said. Paige froze briefly, book mid-air, at the sound of her name. She quickly regained her composure and continued putting the books away.

'How is your sister?' Paige asked, still with her back to Dylan.

'She's OK, I mean, she's happier now her research is going well, but...' he trailed off. Paige carried on stacking her books. 'She's very sorry. And I think she misses you.'

Paige suddenly dropped the book she was holding. She scrambled to the floor and snatched it back up, clearing her throat as she did so.

'Did she tell you why she was sorry?' she asked, trying to keep her voice steady.

'She told me you two fought. Or, rather, that she completely over-reacted, yelled, and in general messed up, but hasn't stopped beating herself up about it since.'

Paige kept her back to him, not wanting him to be able to read the many expressions that must have been appearing on her face. He seemed to take her silence as encouragement to continue.

'She told me what she said. And, more importantly, what she didn't say. She hasn't told you about Daniella, has she? Or... or me?'

'You?' Paige said, finally turning around.

'Yeah. See, I'm an alcoholic. I've put her through hell. And your lunch date with her was a few days after I had fallen off the wagon. The first drink I'd had in years.'

'Oh,' Paige said, sitting down. She still wasn't able to look at Dylan. He hesitated a little before continuing.

'Also, her ex, Daniella, used to fake illnesses and use it to manipulate her. I mean real, serious illnesses, life-threatening ones. She used her apparent illness to stop Taylor leaving the house, seeing her friends or family, and she was constantly having to take time off work to look after her which meant she was passed over for promotion...'

'That sounds awful,' Paige said, still not looking up.

'It broke her, when she finally learnt the truth. She had built this whole life with someone, and it turned out to be one manipulative lie after another. She hasn't dated anyone since, well, not until -' He stopped himself.

'Until me.'

'Yeah.'

The two sat in silence for a while, neither really knowing what to say. The clock on the wall ticked away loudly, and Paige's computer fans occasionally whirred into life.

'She really is sorry,' Dylan said eventually. 'And so am I, for my part in this.' Paige smiled weakly but didn't respond. 'Would you... would you see her again? Give her a chance to apologise in person?'

Paige lifted her gaze to him. Not really seeing him, but his sister.

'I think so,' she said eventually. 'Would she... want to meet up with me?'

'I don't know. She's so ashamed. I was hoping we could arrange for you two to... bump into one another.'

'Right. Just like at climbing,' Paige said with a smile. 'Taylor told me you'd engineered that.'

'I don't know what you're talking about,' Dylan said sarcastically, feigning innocence. 'So you'll do it?'

'Yes,' she said after a pause, sounding more confident. 'I have missed her, too.' She spoke quietly this time, more to herself than to Dylan.

'Great!' Dylan said, jumping to his feet. 'I'll arrange to meet her at the coffee shop at a time that works for you, and hopefully she'll have the sense not to run away.'

'I imagine it will be more a "deer in the headlights" kind of scenario,' Paige said, laughing as she also stood up.

'Great, well, I'll see you at climbing sometime?' Dylan said awkwardly.

'Yes,' Paige answered. 'Dylan... thank you,' she said, offering him her hand to shake. He laughed slightly but took it anyway, and she squeezed his hand tightly. 'Thank you.'

Dylan smiled at her and then darted out the door, seemingly wanting to get as far away from her office and their conversation as possible. Paige watched the door slowly shut behind him and sighed, not entirely sure what she had just gotten herself into.

CHAPTER TWENTY-TWO
The Meet Up

PAIGE

Paige didn't know what to expect as she made her way to the coffee shop that blustery March morning. It was a Saturday, and Dylan had arranged to meet Taylor there but sent Paige instead. Paige wasn't sure how on board she was with the mild deceit, but she trusted Dylan's judgement when it came to his sister. Going against her normal standards, Paige had deliberately aimed to be on time, rather than early as usual. She didn't want to spook Taylor by getting there before her. She wasn't entirely sure why she was being so considerate of someone who had hurt her feelings so badly; when Dylan told her about his sister's history, she had felt the pain in empathy, which probably had something to do with it. The wind picked up slightly, blowing some rubbish around in circles, making it skip away.

Paige paused outside the glass coffee shop doors. She could see Taylor sat with her back to the door in the middle of the coffee shop, working on something on her laptop. The coffee shop was fairly busy, with shoppers taking a mid-morning break or late risers getting their caffeine hit before perusing the local stores. Paige took a deep breath before pushing on the heavy glass door, the noise of the wind dying away as soon as she crossed the threshold. She hesitated at the end of the shop counter, hovering somewhere between ordering a drink, sitting straight down, and simply running away. Taylor was too engrossed in her laptop to have noticed her come in, so she settled on getting a drink. It gave her a chance to run through what she was going to say, and what she needed Taylor to say to be comfortable with forgiving her.

'The usual?' the barista said when she got to the front of the queue. Paige just nodded, paid, and resumed fiddling with the hem of her jumper. The closer the barista got to finishing making her drink, the more Paige felt like her stomach had been replaced by a hollow void. She picked up the tray with her pot of tea, cup, and saucer and made her way over the table where Taylor sat. Her hands were shaking so badly the teacup rattled on the plate. Paige was sure the rest of the coffee shop was being deafened by it. A large family occupied one corner; three generations in one space, smiling and laughing. Paige could hear each of the individual noises each person was making just by existing.

Within a few more steps she had made it as far as Taylor's table. She stood opposite her, holding her tray, waiting. Taylor had earphones in and was deftly tapping away on her keyboard, oblivious to her observer. Paige just stood there, not quite sure how to proceed. Taylor looked up from her screen, deep in thought, and saw Paige standing in front of her. She jumped, before violently ripping the earphones out of her ears, adding the tinny sound to the cacophony of other sounds bombarding Paige's senses at that moment.

'H... hi' Taylor stammered, staring open-mouthed at Paige.

'Hello,' Paige said, still standing like a statue.

'Are you... would you like to sit?' Taylor asked hesitantly. 'I'm meeting Dylan but I'm sure -' she began, before her brain caught up to the situation. 'Did he -?'

'Yes, and yes. Dylan set this up.'

'He's done it again, the git. When will I learn?' Taylor said, placing the palm of her hand against her forehead. 'I'm sorry, don't feel you have to stay because you thought you were meeting Dylan,' Taylor continued, before starting to pack up her stuff. 'In fact, I'll leave, you can have this table - it seems pretty packed in here anyway.' She rushed the words out in her effort to escape the situation as fast as possible.

'Sorry, I should have explained,' Paige said calmly, 'Dylan *and I* set this up. I knew I was meeting you. He didn't think you'd come if you were likewise informed.'

'Oh...' Taylor said, ceasing her packing and slumping in her chair. 'Wait, you agreed to this? I didn't think you'd ever want to see me again,' she continued, sitting up slightly straighter and tucking her hair behind her ears, before nervously adjusting the hoodie she was wearing. Paige, seeing that Taylor had decided to stay, placed her tray on the table and sat down, removing her coat and putting her bag on the floor.

'So... er... how are you?' Taylor said awkwardly.

'I am well, thank you. I haven't fallen down any hills recently, anyway.' Paige responded, smiling, trying to put a clearly uncomfortable Taylor at ease.

'Haha...' Taylor laughed awkwardly.

'Dylan told me about his alcoholism and about Daniella,' Paige said, cutting straight to the point. Taylor's eyes immediately widened, and she went very pale, before turning red.

'I... I...' she stammered.

'He also told me you were sorry and were beating yourself up over what you said.'

'I... I *am* sorry. I am so sorry. I should never have said any of the things I said. You didn't deserve that. You really didn't deserve that.'

'I know, but you don't deserve to beat yourself up over it either. You're not a bad person,' Paige said, trying to put on an air of calmness, but her hands were still trembling as she lifted her teacup to her lips. They sat in silence for a few minutes, neither woman wanting to make eye contact with the other. Paige was once again unsure how to proceed.

'Can I... What can I do to fix this?' Taylor said carefully.

'You've apologised, and you seem to have meant it -'

'I do!' Taylor nearly shouted, taking Paige aback.

'So I will accept your apology,' Paige continued deliberately, 'and maybe we can be friends?' she finished hopefully.

'Really?'

'Yes, really. I enjoy spending time with you,' Paige said in an awkward, formal manner.

'I would like that,' Taylor said, a laugh twitching at her lips. They lapsed back into silence. The coffee shop started to quieten down as the shoppers ended their breaks and braved the outside world once more. This meant the coffee machines were also quieter, and there was no one yelling orders; just little old ladies nattering quietly and lonely-looking older gents squinting at their newspapers. Paige sipped her tea, the warm liquid spilling down her throat, providing a familiar comfort. Taylor seemed to still not know where to look, and seemed to have taken particular interested in some of the paintings on the coffee shop wall.

'What are you working on?' Paige asked, aware that she had interrupted something studious.

'Oh, just my research project. I've finally got some actual time to work on it, but I've got a lot of catching up to do.'

'How far have you got?' Paige asked, choosing a topic of discussion she knew Taylor would be more comfortable talking about. It greased the wheels of the conversation, and it wasn't long before they were almost at the speed they had been at back in December. Paige updated Taylor on her own research, empathising with the frustration of not having as much time to work on the research project as she would like. She even managed to make Taylor laugh a few times. She had missed that smile. But she could still feel that her walls and barriers were very much still up, unsure what kind of bulldozer would be needed to knock them down. As it stood, she was happy to speak to Taylor again, but was still keeping her at a safe distance. She knew Maya would tell her she was just isolating herself once more, but she didn't think she could take being hurt like that again.

'Right, well, I have to go now. I'm going to the climbing centre,' Paige said when their conversation had hit a natural lull.

'Oh, OK,' Taylor said, visibly disappointed. 'Well, it was lovely to see you,' she added, her eyes sparkling. Paige stood up and offered Taylor her hand to shake, just had she had done in the pub all those months ago. Taylor took it, gripping it tighter than she had back in autumn. Paige matched her force.

'Will you come climbing again soon?' she asked, trying to phrase it as a question, but the words that left her mouth definitely sounded more like a request.

'Umm, yeah, maybe,' Taylor said, caught off guard.

'Good. Bye, then.'

Paige strode out of the coffee shop, feeling able to hold her head high. She had done something that terrified her, and it had paid off, it sounded like she had her friend back. But at the same time she had shown herself respect by creating boundaries. A good day, all in all. Now to take on that triple overhang.

TAYLOR

Taylor watched Paige leave, almost going as far as twisting all the way around in her seat to do so. She closed her laptop suddenly, her eyes roving around the room, her brain having no idea how it was feeling. The heavy weight she had been carrying in the pit of her stomach for the last few months had all but disappeared. Her neck felt less tense, and there was a swelling inside her chest that vaguely resembled... joy? Triumph? Was that what she was feeling? Either way, she couldn't tolerate just sitting there and dwelling on whatever the feelings were. Once she was sure enough time had passed since Paige left, she packed up her things and exited the coffee shop, with no idea where she was going. She passed many people in the streets, either moving with purpose or dawdling the day away. Some of them were couples holding hands, cherishing that physical connection. Others had headphones on, eyes to the ground, shunning the world around them. Taylor took it all in and none of it at the same time.

Eventually she found herself by the river; a section of the city she had barely explored. Here there was a hydroelectric weir and its housing. A few people were wandering around, reading the placards or looking at the giant turbines spinning slowly, sloshing the water around. Taylor went up to the railings and leant on them, breathing deeply in what felt like the first time in months. A few ducks floated past, oblivious of her or the giant whirring turbines a little further down. She felt like a helium balloon barely tethered to the ground.

A cloud slowly drifted in front of the sun, blocking out the light to the river. What if Paige would only ever want to be 'just friends' now? What if their relationship could never be repaired enough to cross over that thin line? Taylor shivered slightly. She'd still take friendship over silence any day.

She hitched her bag back up on her shoulder and pushed off from the railings, heading back to her car. She'd walked much further than she'd realised so it was going to take her a while to get home, and she wanted to be there when Dylan got back from climbing; she had a bone to pick with him.

Later that evening Taylor was sitting in her living room, the space lit only by the flickering light of the television. Dylan should have been home a couple of hours ago, but she wasn't worried; she knew he was avoiding her. Eventually she heard the quiet clink of a key in the lock, and the slow depression of the handle as someone tried to enter unheard. Taylor turned off the television, the room now bathed in darkness. She heard Dylan kick off his shoes in the hallway and gently put his bag down. The carpet made the tiniest of rustling sounds with every step he took, crossing the living room to get to the kitchen. When Taylor thought he was about halfway across, in line with where she was on the sofa, she quickly illuminated her face with her phone torch and shouted, 'Hello, traitor!' loudly, before falling over sideways laughing. Dylan had jumped so much that he had thrown himself backwards and landed sideways on the other sofa, making the whole thing tip dangerously backwards, before gravity took pity on him and brought him back to earth.

'Taylor! Jesus - what?!' he stammered clutching his chest, struggling to get the words out.

'That's payback, Dyl!'

'Payback for what?' he said, before realisation dawned on his face. 'Oh,' he said sheepishly.

'Yeah, "oh",' she responded. 'You set me up! Again!'

'Did it work?' he asked quietly, making her throw a pillow at him. 'What? A man can be curious if his devious plan worked, can't he?'

'It kind of worked,' she said, relenting.

'Kind of?'

'She wants to be friends.'

'That's good!' he said excitedly, finally arranging his limbs to sit properly on the sofa, just as Taylor put the side lamp on.

'Yeah, but, *just* friends…' she said, trailing off.

'Oh' he said, the deflation in his voice obvious. 'That's still better than nothing, right? And I mean, who knows what might happen in the future?'

'Don't get my hopes up, Dyl,' she said curtly. 'I can't risk it, hurting her again.'

'What's life without a little risk?'

'A safe one. One where you don't lose friends because you pushed them too far.

'Yeah, there is that,' he said, shrugging his shoulders. 'What's for tea?'

Taylor threw another pillow at him.

'I swear, whoever invented scatter cushions has a lot to answer for!' he said, standing up, scooping the pillow up from the floor, and throwing it back at her in one swift motion.

'Be grateful they did, or I would have found something

harder to throw instead!'

'Good point.'

Dylan disappeared off into the kitchen and started rummaging through the freezer for something to eat, the sound of crunching ice echoing through into the living room. Taylor retrieved her laptop from the coffee table and opened it up, the blue light harsh on her eyes. She decided to read over what she had written that day, having completely lost the thread when Paige had popped up in front of her at the coffee shop.

Dylan's head appeared around the corner of the kitchen door. 'Want anything?'

'Sure, as long as there's some kind of vegetable on the plate.'

'You're no fun.' His head disappeared again, to be replaced by a lot of clattering and Dylan whistling away to himself. Her phone buzzed on the table, making it dance perilously close to the edge. Taylor picked it up and was surprised to see Paige's name flash up on the screen. She was equal parts excited and terrified to open the message - what if Paige had changed her mind about being friends? Taylor put the phone down on the sofa next to her, resolving to look at it later once she had done some more work on her research. She lasted about five seconds before picking her phone up again.

'*Would you like to go climbing at the centre on Thursday?*' the text read, making Taylor's heart skip a beat. She quickly texted back in the affirmative, having to correct her message multiple times, the eagerness of her brain not matched by the speed of her fingers, leading to many typos. By the time Dylan came back into the room carrying his dinner and a glass of squash, Taylor's cheeks hurt from grinning so much.

'Tea's ready,' he said, plopping down on the sofa and looking around for the television remote. Taylor picked it up and tossed it over to him before practically floating out into the kitchen.

'What's got you so happy?' Dylan shouted to her as she retrieved her food.

'Paige wants to go climbing,' she said once she was back in the living room.

Dylan just grinned in response.

'Don't you look so pleased with yourself!' Taylor tried to chastise him, but she couldn't stop the smile creeping across her face.

CHAPTER TWENTY-THREE

A Change of Plans

PAIGE

It was nearing the end of May when Paige finally finished editing the first draft of her book. She had decided to stretch her legs by the river, her reward after being cramped up in her office for so long. Spring was getting ready to transform into a glorious summer. Young birds who had hatched only a few short weeks ago, danced around the sky, stretching their wings and learning how to sing. The river was calm and tranquil. It gurgled softly as it drifted by, not worrying about its destination, just enjoying the ride. The river banks were alive with activity, with small mammals visiting the water's edge to drink and butterflies fluttering between the wild flowers. Bees buzzing as they travelled between petals, their humming providing the sweet rhythm for the rest of the world to thrive. The sun gazed down, gently warming everything its light tendrils touched. A heron perching on a high branch waiting, expanded his large wings and took flight at the sound of cyclists coming down the path, his shadow flickering across the water as he flew. Paige moved over to the side of the path to let the cyclists past. They slowed down and gave her a curt nod, before zooming off into the distance, the whirring of their wheels fading away. Paige arrived at one of her favourite spots by the river. There was a small clearing in the trees and bushes that allowed for amazing views across the water. At some point the river had deposited a felled tree trunk which provided the perfect place to sit. The old trunk's bark was flaking and gnarled, but you could still make out a few places where young lovers had carved their initials into its soft shell.

Paige sat down and closed her eyes, letting the dappled sunlight warm her face. She stretched her neck side to side, easing out the muscular kinks that had formed after working at her desk for so long. She tried to maintain good posture while working, but it was easier said than done. The latest cohort of History students were all but done for the year. There were a few more exams Paige would have to mark, but most of her teaching commitments were over until September. A few ducks floated past the riverside nook, their quacks almost sounding like laughter. Somewhere nearby someone was having an afternoon barbecue, the smoky smells intermingling with the smell of freshly cut grass from one of the fields on the other side of the river. Paige stretched her arms out wide and tried to convince herself that she couldn't stay here all day.

She felt her phone start vibrating in her pocket and debated not answering it, not wanting to be dragged back to reality. This feeling was compounded when she pulled the phone out and saw it was a blocked number. It was probably some scheme ringing about an accident that wasn't her fault. She sighed and answered, deciding that nothing could dampen her current spirits.

'Hello?' she drawled, smiling at a duck cleaning itself on the water.

'Hello, is that Miss Spencer?' came a sickly-sweet voice on the phone.

'This is Doctor Spencer? Who is this?'

'Right, sorry. *Doctor* Spencer, my name is Amanda, I am a receptionist here at the Blue Forest Centre. I believe you are due for an autism assessment in November?'

'Yes, that's right,' Paige said, sitting up a little straighter, her muscles beginning to tense. She wasn't sure if she was hoping they weren't ringing to cancel, or that they were. She hadn't given her assessment much thought since she'd had the initial letter.

'Right, well, we've had a last-minute cancellation and we were wondering if you would like an appointment sooner?'

'Err - yes, maybe,' Paige stammered. 'When?'

'Tomorrow, at one.'

'Tomorrow?' Paige asked, her face draining of all colour, despite the warm sun.

'Yes,' the woman said, sounding marginally frustrated.

'Oh, um, I don't know -'

'Miss Spencer, there is every chance your appointment in November could get moved if we have more urgent cases come up.'

'What? But -'

'So I would suggest you take this one.'

'Oh, right. Errr - OK then?'

'Great!' the woman said, her tone changing back to sickly-sweet. 'I'll book you in for one p.m. Please bring a family member if you can, or a friend if no family member is available.'

'What?!'

'For the assessment. The psychologist needs to ask someone who knows you some questions.'

'Why?'

'It's part of the assessment,' the woman said unhelpfully.

'Err, I'll... try?' Paige said helplessly. None of her

family lived close enough or were likely to be free at such short notice. And Maya was still in Japan so she didn't know what she was going to do.

'Great! See you then!'

'Err, OK. Bye,' Paige said, and the receptionist promptly hung up. She sat staring at her phone for a few minutes, not entirely sure what just happened. Eventually she slowly got to her feet, her previously relaxed muscles all tense and twitchy. Her formerly light legs now felt like they were made of lead as she struggled to put one foot in front of the other on her walk back to the university. The previously pleasant sound of the birds singing now felt loud and intrusive, a crow's call particularly grating her insides. She resisted the temptation to cover her ears, having been told repeatedly by her family that it made her look weird or mentally unstable. The university seemed like such a long way away. She decided to distract herself by texting Maya, concentrating carefully on each letter as she typed it, relaying the news about the appointment. Originally they had planned that Maya would go with her to the assessment as moral support, but that wasn't going to be possible now. Maya wasn't even going to be awake when it happened, like she wasn't awake now to respond to Paige's text. Paige roughly shoved her phone back in her pocket and kept walking, not really knowing to do with her hands. She alternated between putting them in her pocket, clicking her fingers, and holding the hem of her jumper.

Finally making it back inside her university building, she pressed the lift button and waited. Normally she would take the stairs, but this would be quicker and require less contact with other people. The lift doors opened and were blissfully empty, and she had never been more grateful that the university hadn't decided on having lift music. She was on her office floor in a matter of seconds, her legs co-operating more fully now, allowing her to quickly make her way to her office. She slipped in and locked the door behind her, leaning back against it, the cool wood soothing her back.

Her office was still glowing with the afternoon light, the multiple stacks of books on the floor looking like flowers reaching up to it. Paige had been looking up various publishing houses before she left for her walk, trying to decide which, if any, she should approach with the manuscript. A notebook still lay open on the desk in front of the sleeping computer screen, half-written notes scrawled across its pages. An empty glass of water sat off to the side. There was a new photograph on her desk, its purple frame standing out, as it did not match the wooden frames that contained photographs of her family. It was a photograph that Taylor had given her, taken on one of the group excursions to a local climbing spot. In the photograph Paige and Taylor stood next to each other, Taylor with her arm around Paige's shoulders. Paige picked the photo up and a light bulb went on in her head. She quickly scrambled to get her climbing gear from under her desk, shut her computer down properly, and made sure the window was closed and locked. After locking her office door, she pulled out her phone, wanting to check if Taylor was climbing this evening. She replied quickly that she was, and Paige almost ran down the corridor towards the stairs.

A few members of the climbing club had chosen a local spot for their excursion this evening. It was a low rock face where presumably, at some point millennia ago, some kind of tectonic shift had sheared one slab of rock away from another. The resultant rock face varied in height, between about three and five metres, and was a well-loved local bouldering spot. To reach the rock face climbers had to park their cars about a mile away and carry all their equipment, the most cumbersome being the heavy crash mats they used to break their falls.

Paige pulled into the remote car park at around six o'clock. There were many other cars already there; other climbers, ramblers, even the odd kayaker or two exploring the local river. Paige nodded and smiled politely at anyone she recognised as she grabbed her kit from her car. As she had not been expecting to climb tonight, she didn't have her crash mat with her, but she knew that didn't matter, someone was always willing to share. Finally she set off towards the rock face. The many birds in the nearby trees sang to her as she walked, their voices once again sounding beautiful rather than overwhelming. As she neared the wall she could see specks of bright colours; other climbers already scaling the rocky surface. Jumping over a small stream she could hear the water trickling past, duetting with the laughter of the climbers as they chatted at the base of the wall, waiting their turn.

'Hey,' Paige said as she walked up to Taylor, standing next to her. Taylor was watching another climber, arms folded in front of her, trying to analyse how that person was moving.

'Hey yourself,' Taylor said, glancing sideways at Paige before focusing back on the wall. 'I didn't think you were coming tonight?'

'I wasn't, originally.'

'Change of plans?'

'Kind of,' Paige said, cryptically. The climber reached the top of the wall and shouted down to the person spotting for them that they were about to jump down. The person stood underneath them had had their arms stretched to the heavens the entire time, waiting to guide the climber if they fell, to ensure they landed on their feet rather than their head. Paige felt Taylor brace beside her. The climber gracefully pushed off the wall and landed with a soft thud, squatting down into a crouch position to absorb the impact, before standing up. They brushed some excess chalk off their hands before gesturing that their spotter should take his turn. Taylor turned to Paige, giving her her full attention now.

'I'm glad you could make it,' Taylor said with a smile, her cheeks turning a lovely shade of pink. It reminded Paige of sunsets.

'Yeah, me too. I think it's what I needed after being in the office all day.'

'All day? Try all month!' Taylor joked. She was right, though. Paige had barely been climbing for the last month, focusing more on her work and editing the first draft of her book. She became so fixated on it, that sometimes she forgot to eat or drink, and it had got to the point where Maya was sending her text reminders to shower.

'Have you had a go yet?' Paige asked, knowing Taylor was still nervous about climbing outside, especially without ropes.

'No, not yet,' Taylor said, turning back to the wall.

'You should. Even if you only get a metre off the ground, that's still something. You can jump down whenever you want.'

'Yeah, that's the bit that scares me,' Taylor said nervously.

'What can I do to help?'

'Hmm...' Taylor lifted a hand to her chin and furrowed her brows. 'Talk me through it as I'm going? That might help?'

'Sure. Look, he's nearly done,' Paige said, pointing to the climbers they had been watching. 'Mind if we cut in?' she said to them. The person on the wall had just jumped down and was breathing heavily. They nodded, putting their hands behind their head to open their lungs up. Taylor looked at Paige before taking a step forward, showing her intention, but not progressing any further.

'Go on...' Paige said, giving her a very gentle prod in the back, making her laugh.

'Alright, alright, I'm going...' she said, walking up to the base of the rock. Paige could see her hands were shaking, and followed her, ready to spot her if she needed it. Taylor began climbing, very gingerly moving her limbs one at a time. Paige watched as she pinched her fingers into a small crevice, wondering if she had the grip strength yet to maintain that hold. Paige talked her through each move, giving her descriptions of where the various hand and foot holds were, and the further Taylor climbed the more smoothly she moved. Slowly but surely, Taylor made her way to the top. She turned her head slightly to shout down to Paige, and her proud grin quickly turned into a wide-eyed grimace. Her face immediately turned white.

'I shouldn't have done that!' she said, turning back to face the wall, hugging it tightly.

'It's OK, I've got you,' Paige shouted up, arms outstretched.

'I'm good here!' Taylor said, scrunching her eyes closed and gripping the wall even tighter.

'You've got to come down sometime!'

'I know. OK... hooo... deep breath' Taylor coached herself, before pushing off the wall and heading towards the crash mat. Her positioning was fine, but Paige couldn't help reaching out to her, her hands gently touching the sides of her torso as she plummeted downward. Taylor absorbed the impact by bending her knees, but lost her balance at the last minute and fell over sideways onto the mat.

'Well done!' Paige said grinning and offering her a hand up.

'Thanks,' Taylor said, using Paige's hand to pull herself to her feet, before dusting herself off. 'I still think I prefer using ropes!'

'You get used to it,' Paige said, as she approached the wall for her turn. 'You got me?' she said, looking over her shoulder at Taylor. Taylor jolted forward as if the request was unexpected, raising her arms to the sky before Paige had even left the ground. Paige laughed to herself and started climbing. She could feel the grainy texture of the rock under her fingertips, and smell the slightly metallic scent they always had when it had rained recently. The sound of other climbers chatting away drifted up to her, and she could feel the tension radiating off Taylor, even if she couldn't see her. Paige knew she was more than capable, and it was just an issue of confidence. The higher she climbed the quieter it got, until she could hear the wind whispering as it came over the top of the rock face, bringing with it the scent of grass and pollen. The cloudless blue sky beckoned to her as she made her way upwards, reaching the top of the rock face in no time at all.

'Ready?' she shouted down to Taylor.

'Ready!'

So she jumped. But as she did so, she caught her foot on a rock that was jutting out of the rock face, and it tilted her dangerously horizontally. She tried to correct her positioning in the air but as it was such a low wall there wasn't enough time. Suddenly Paige felt warm hands on her back, guiding her body back to vertical, and she landed on her heels, completely off-balance, falling backwards. The warm hands, more callused than they had been nine months ago, slid up her back and cradled her head to make sure she didn't hit it on any protruding stones. Eventually her momentum stopped.

'Ooof! Thanks,' she smiled at Taylor before springing to her feet, the hibernating butterflies in her stomach waking up from the close physical contact. It must have been written across her face, because Taylor quickly turned red and muttered, 'No problem,' grinning sheepishly.

They climbed for another hour or so after that, until the light began to fade, and safety became an issue; though a few brave (or foolish) souls carried on. Paige and Taylor walked back to the car park together, walking much closer than necessary. A couple of times their hands swung so close together Paige could have sworn electricity jumped from one woman to the other. By the time they reached the cars the sun was just teasing the horizon and the sky had started to change into beautiful pinks and purples. Paige opened her car boot and sat down on the edge of it, taking out her water bottle and having a drink, watching the sunset. Taylor sat down next to her at a respectful distance. Both women rested their hands on the lip of the boot.

'How come you changed your mind about tonight?' Taylor asked, still looking at the multi-coloured sky.

'I needed to see you, to ask a favour,' Paige said, turning her head to look at Taylor. Taylor's face turned towards her as if magnetised.

'What's up?'

'You know I mentioned maybe being autistic?' Paige said hesitantly. They hadn't really talked about the A word since the day the argued, other than when Taylor briefly skirted around it when apologising.

'I remember, and once again I'm sorry -'

'I know,' Paige said, earnestly, reaching out and putting her hand over Taylor's. 'I know.' She could see Taylor's eyes shimmer slightly in the sunset, and her shoulders relaxed as if a rubber band inside her had finally broken.

'They've moved my assessment from November to tomorrow. You may not have noticed, because I am good at hiding it,' Paige said sarcastically, 'but I really struggle with new places and people. Maya was supposed to be coming with me, but she is in Japan...' Paige trailed off, hoping Taylor would understand what she was asking. She hated having to ask for help with things like this. But Taylor just watched her, waiting for her to finish her sentence.

'Would you come with me?' she said helplessly, a slight quiver in her voice.

Taylor put her free hand on top of Paige's and squeezed tight.

'Yes, of course. Just let me know the time and place.'

CHAPTER TWENTY-FOUR
The Assessment

The Blue Forest Centre waiting room was cold and quiet. The stained blue carpet had patches where rips had been duct taped over. Mismatched chairs were lined up in rows; injured soldiers about to go on parade. Every now and again the water cooler bubbled, almost like it was drowning and gulping for air. At the far end of the room there was a low table, with even lower, brightly coloured chairs, and an eclectic assortment of toys in various states of disrepair. There were only two other people waiting, sat diagonally from each other, trying to distance themselves from the situation. The windowpanes had a thin grid sandwiched in between them to prevent the glass shattering if broken, almost like the imprint of a cage. There was no annoying background music. Just the occasional shuffling in seats or deep sigh.

Paige had arranged for her and Taylor to arrive fifteen minutes before her allotted appointment time. Taylor had picked Paige up on the way. The two women sat next to each other in the front row of the chairs, waiting for the show to start. Paige was aware of every single movement

Taylor made; every sly glance, every parting of the lips when she tried to speak but then thought better of it. Paige un-crossed and re-crossed her legs multiple times, shifting in her seat, unable to settle. The heavy door creaked open as a smartly dressed young doctor came to retrieve one of the other people in the room. They didn't use words. They just smiled politely at their patient and nodded. The patient slowly got to their feet and dragged themselves out of the room, a condemned prisoner accepting their fate.

Paige took out her phone, ostensibly to see if Maya or Brandon had texted, but really it was just to distract herself from the situation she was in. She had read quite a bit about the assessment process when she had first gone to the doctors, and she knew it was likely this was the first of multiple appointments, each of which would take in the region of two hours. Her insides felt like they were twisted, contorted by some unseen force beyond her control. She felt a jolt travel down her arm, a surge commanding her to take Taylor's hand, but she resisted, taking a deep breath instead.

'Are you OK?' Taylor asked, for the twentieth time that afternoon.

'Yes, fine,' Paige lied, grinding her teeth together. She knew she wasn't fooling anyone.

The heavy door into the room swung open once more, and an older-looking lady came in with a clipboard, peering at it through small-lensed glasses balanced on the end of her nose. A beaded glasses chain swung underneath each slender metal arm.

'Paige Spencer?' the older lady called out, looking up, eyes darting between Paige and Taylor.

'That's me,' Paige said, standing up reluctantly. She took a couple of steps before realising Taylor wasn't following her. 'Coming?'

'Oh, yes, of course, sorry,' she replied, immediately scrambling for her jacket and bag. Taylor quickly fell into stride beside Paige as they followed the older woman down a long corridor.

'They said on the phone I had to bring someone with me,' Paige whispered to Taylor. 'I think they want to ask you questions, too'

'What do you want me to say, or not say?'

'Just the truth is fine,' Paige said, forcing herself to smile. She hadn't meant to spring this on Taylor, she had just sort of assumed Taylor understood she would be involved in the appointment itself.

The corridor seemed to stretch on for miles, and they had to make their way through several sets of heavy doors, each one opened by key card and locking loudly behind them as they went. Eventually they rounded a corner and the older lady led them through an open door, into a sparse consulting room. There were two soft chairs sat facing each other, with a table in the middle. There was a primed and ready box of tissues prominently placed on the table's centre. Taylor took a seat on the third chair which was off to the side, shifting it slightly before she sat down, so Paige would still be able to see her. Paige sat down in the corner-most seat, assuming that the psychologist would want the one by her desk. She looked around, taking in all the mental health and learning disability posters dotted all over the walls. There were some crude artworks on the wall opposite the desk. Paige assumed they were there to offer distraction to those who needed it; she thought they just looked ugly.

'Right, Paige, my name is Pamela, I'm a psychologist specialising in autism.' The older woman took out a notepad and rested it on top of the clip board, pen poised and ready. 'And who do you have with you today?' she asked with a sickly smile.

'Taylor. She's a friend,' Paige replied, addressing the floor.

'Mmm-hmm, no family members today? It really is

helpful if we can speak to a family member. Your parents perhaps?'

'My parents live hours away.'

'Ah, OK, you no longer live with your parents' Pamela said, jotting that down like it was vital.

Pamela spent the next ten minutes confirming all the information she had on her form about Paige, such as address, occupation, and other medical conditions. It was then that it dawned on Paige how personal this was likely to get, and she looked across hesitantly at Taylor. Taylor smiled back reassuringly. Soon the actual assessment started, beginning with Pamela slowly reading out all the questions on the online test Paige had already done. The questions were so badly worded, but when Paige tried to answer them more accurately than the test allowed, Pamela insisted on giving her all the options, from strongly disagree to strongly agree, for every single question. There were over fifty of them. Paige was struggling to keep the frustration out of her voice. Her hands were balled into fists resting on top of her thighs. She risked a glance at Taylor, who rolled her eyes, making Paige have to stifle a laugh.

After they had run through this test, and a couple of others, Pamela started asking Paige about her childhood.

Had she had many friends growing up? Had she partaken in imaginative play? Did she remember enjoying lining up her toys? Paige answered as best she could, but her memories from the ages Pamela was asking about were hazy. Pamela then asked about special interests as a child, and if she had any now as an adult.

'I don't think so,' Paige said, shrugging her shoulders.

'What about...'Pamela said, riffling through the paper on her clipboard. 'You're a history teacher, right?'

'Lecturer.'

'Right, lecturer. It sounds to me like history is a special interest. And you climb multiple times a week?'

'Yes, but as far as I am aware, that is called a hobby,' Paige said sarcastically. Taylor snorted and unsuccessfully tried to hide it with a cough. Pamela didn't say anything, instead she scribbled furiously on her notepad. Paige took that opportunity to straighten out her expression into one of seriousness.

'And how did you find school?' Pamela ask, the sweetness in her voice having a sour undertone.

'It was alright,' Paige said, unsure of what she was really asking.

'Did you have many friends? Did you do well, or did you struggle? How did you get on with the teachers? Were you last picked for teams?' Pamela probed with rapid-fire questioning. Paige folded her arms over her chest and resisted the temptation to tuck her legs up in front of her. School had been OK, really. She wasn't bullied *that* badly, she tried to rationalise. And so what if she felt she got on better with her teachers than her peers? That didn't mean anything. She did often get picked last for teams, even though she was one of the fastest runners in her year. She excelled academically, working way above what was expected of her age group, but that was a good thing, wasn't it? Why did it feel like Pamela was accusing her of something? She tried explaining all of this to Pamela, but the words were coming out of her mouth in fits and starts, creating a jumbled mess that the psychologist would have to sift through. Paige pulled at the neckline of her T-shirt and noticed how dry her throat felt.

'We've been at this nearly an hour now, do you need a break?' Pamela asked, putting her clipboard down and trying to make eye contact with Paige. It felt like a violent intrusion.

'I just need a drink, that's all,' Paige said, springing out of her seat as if it was suddenly electrified.

'There's a water cooler at the end of the hall.'

Paige was almost through the door by the time she

finished speaking. She looked pointedly at Taylor before disappearing.

Taylor caught up with her by the water cooler, where Paige was chugging water as if she had just come back from the desert.

'Are you OK?' Taylor asked once again.

'Fine. It was just warm in there,' Paige said, glancing across at a jacket-wearing Taylor.

'I'm not sure I like her,' Taylor said, leaning casually against the wall. 'I don't like the way she speaks to you.'

'Me neither. I am not a child.'

'I know, right? She tried to get me to stay when you left, so she could talk to me in private. I said I wasn't comfortable talking about you behind your back, and left.'

'Thank you,' Paige said earnestly.

'What are friends for?' Taylor replied, giving Paige a gentle nudge, her eyes twinkling.

Paige gave herself a few minutes' break by the water cooler, staff members smiling politely at her as they passed, Taylor smiling back but looking like she would square up to anyone who challenged them. Eventually Paige took a deep breath and began the short walk back to the consulting room.

'Ready for round two?' Pamela said as they walked in. Paige smiled weakly. That was exactly how it felt. Like the very essence of who she was had been unwittingly transported into a boxing ring, and in the red corner there was Pamela with her clipboard. Paige had barely sat down by the time Pamela re-started the interrogation.

'So, tell me about your family?'

Paige stared at the wall and tried to work through her family tree as systematically as she could, starting with her grandparents. All of them had been wonderful, warm, and caring people. She remembered spending many a summer holiday with them, going to the beach or to local museums. Both of her parents worked, and her grandparents relished the time they got to spend with the grandkids, even though having four of them all running in different directions could be a little stressful. Paige talked about her dad and how he was like her, in that he liked routine and things being in their place. Her mum had tried to get him to be more flexible, but even after forty years of marriage, he still ate the same breakfast at the same time every morning. When Paige started the process of running through her siblings her voice hitched as she remembered that her niece and nephew had just been diagnosed. She didn't know why, but she hesitated before telling Pamela this.

She didn't want to give the psychologist more ammunition, even though the whole reason she organised this assessment was because she thought she *did* have autism, not so she could convince someone else she didn't. Pamela made copious notes about the similarities Paige recognised between herself and Cayden and Susie. She tried not to think about what Pamela was writing, and instead looked vaguely in Taylor's direction and started reminiscing about their trip to the forest. How Susie had got a tiny speck of mud on her hand and started freaking out, until Taylor came to her rescue. How Brandon had called her a week later saying that Cayden refused to leave the house without his magnifying glass.

Eventually Pamela swivelled her chair slightly so she could see both Paige and Taylor.

'OK. Taylor, was it?' Pamela said, looking down at her notes through her glasses, so close to the end of her nose they looked like they would fall off at any minute.

'How long have you known Paige?'

'Oh, just under a year now, I think?' Taylor said, looking at Paige for reassurance. Paige nodded.

'Hmm, not ideal, but it will have to do,' Pamela said with a sigh. Paige stared at her with daggers in her eyes.

'I'm going to run through some of the questions I asked

at the beginning, and I want you to tell me how much you feel they apply to Paige, OK?

For the second time Paige was listening to the same fifty questions being read out, the ones she herself had found months ago. This time, at least, Pamela didn't give Taylor all of the possible answers for every single question. Taylor hesitated when answering a couple of them, such as 'Does Paige think she's been polite when you think she's been a bit rude?' Taylor looked across at Paige and fidgeted with her fingers on her lap. Paige gave her a small smile and a quick nod. At this point she was genuinely curious as to what Taylor's answers would be; she wondered how Taylor saw her, and whether their answers would match up. Despite less talking from Pamela, it actually took longer for Taylor to answer all the questions, due to how uncomfortable they clearly made her.

After Taylor answered the last question, the psychologist quickly moved on to asking about any social interactions Taylor had been part of with Paige, what she had witnessed, how she thought Paige had done. Once again Taylor was looking to Paige for reassurance.

'I'm just going to go get another drink,' Paige said standing up. She saw Taylor's expression change from discomfort to sheer panic, so she placed a gentle hand on her shoulder before leaving. Paige hoped this would be over soon.

Once in the empty corridor Paige dawdled as best she could. The blue carpet that she had seen in the waiting room seemed to run the entire way through the building, though this section didn't have any haphazard repairs. She tried to smile politely at anyone she passed, imitating what she had seen Taylor do earlier. She filled up another one of those disposable plastic cups and took a sip of water. At the end of the corridor was a set of glass doors looking out towards a river estuary. Paige watched as birds swooped and dived in the sky, sometimes skimming the water, looking for food. She took another sip. Taylor had been so kind in agreeing to come with her today, even if Paige hadn't managed to successfully communicate what it would entail. She was glad they were friends again.

After about a quarter of an hour Paige made her way back to the consulting room, not wanting to abandon Taylor for too long. When she walked in, she saw Taylor sat with her arms folded and her legs crossed, her elevated foot bouncing slightly.

'Ah, Paige, there you are,' the psychologist said, putting her pen down for the first time. 'I think we're pretty much done here for today. Same time next week?' she said, spinning around to her desk and opening up her appointment calendar.

'You have to come back?' Taylor said standing up. She had gone slightly pale.

'Yes, but I can probably manage on my own.'

'Not a chance' Taylor said, leaning close to whisper to Paige. So close in fact that the gentle breeze of her breath made the hairs on the back of her neck stand on end. She shivered slightly and tried to re-focus her attention on Pamela, who looked like she was expecting an answer.

'Err, yes, I can do the same time next week,' Paige said, grabbing her hoodie from the chair.

'See you then!' Pamela said, returning to the sickly-sweet tone that she had had at the beginning of the appointment.

Paige and Taylor looked at each other like naughty children who were about to bunk off school, before bolting out the door. They walked quickly back down the long corridor, having to press a small green button to be buzzed through each door, making Paige feel like they were in a jail rather than a medical facility.

By the time they got outside it was around half past three and the local school had opened its gates. Dozens of children filtered past them in matching green uniforms, shouting and joshing about, one child even stumbling into the road.

'Well...' Taylor said, finally breaking the silence. 'That was an experience.'

'You could say that.'

'Was she trying to help you or frame you for something?'

'Both, I think,' Paige said laughing. 'It's pretty much what I expected.'

'You expected that! And still walked in there of your own volition?'

'Yeah. I read a few blogs online of other autistic adults having similar interactions when trying to get a diagnosis.'

Taylor stopped walking and just looked at Paige. 'This must be really important to you, to knowingly put yourself through that.'

'It is. My whole life I've been blaming myself for making social mistakes, for messing up, calling myself stupid for not understand the jokes that everyone else gets. It would be nice to stop.'

'You don't need a diagnosis to not bully yourself for things you have done in the past,' Taylor said gently.

'But, it would help,' Paige said, honestly. 'When you

can vividly remember being seven years old and having no one turn up at your birthday party because they don't like you and their parents don't want their child associating with you, it's hard to not blame yourself.' Paige finished with a nonchalant shrug. It was a part of her life she had accepted for so long, it was normal to her. She saw Taylor's arms twitch as if her instinct was to hug Paige. But, for whatever reason, she didn't.

'If there is anything I can do to make things easier for you, please will you tell me? No matter how "weird" you think it makes you.'

Paige didn't respond straight away, and Taylor reached out and gently grabbed her arm to stop them walking once more. 'I'm serious.'

'OK.'

'Promise?'

'I promise.'

The two women walked back to Taylor's car in relative silence. Paige had used all of her mental energy for the week on this one day and wasn't entirely sure she could get her brain to form words anymore. She was grateful to Taylor for not trying to force pointless chit-chat. She laughed to herself, realising that was probably one of the things she should tell her about, to make her life easier.

CHAPTER TWENTY-FIVE
Results

Three weeks after that initial appointment, Paige was back at the Blue Forest Centre for her final appointment. There were more people in the waiting room this time, and the sun beat through the windows heating up the room. Paige sat quietly in her seat. She had decided this was something she needed to do alone, so Taylor was doing her research at the university, or supposed to be; Paige didn't think she was concentrating on work with the number of texts she was sending her. Maya had called earlier that morning to check on her, and Brandon had texted her saying good luck. It felt more like she was going on trial for some heinous crime than getting a medical diagnosis - or not, as the case may be. All the extra people in the room created a background hum with their whispers, interspersed with the loud voices of a handful of children. The room vaguely smelt of cleaning fluid combined with dust, which seemed contradictory.

The heavy door swung open and Pamela appeared, smiling her sickly smile straight at Paige, aiming for a bullseye. Paige grimaced back and got to her feet. For the third time she followed Pamela down the long corridor, watching her ankle-length skirt sway from side to side. For the third time, Pamela did not say a single word until they reached the consulting room. Paige wondered if this was some kind of policy to deliberately try and make patients feel uncomfortable, or whether the psychologist left her voice in her office every time she left, marinating it in sugar.

The consulting room hadn't changed. The only difference was a fresh box of tissues in the middle of the table, its white tongue sticking straight up into the air, blowing raspberries at anyone who looked at it. Paige sat down on the chair and stared at the side of Pamela's desk; a piece of wood she had become quite familiar with over the last few weeks. Instead of the usual clipboard, the psychologist had a thick envelope in her hands, almost taunting Paige to ask her about it. Paige uncrossed and re-crossed her legs, waiting for the judge to pass down her sentence.

'So, Paige, how have you been the last couple of weeks?' Pamela asked

'Fine,' Paige said, wanting to move the conversation along as quickly as possible.

'It's alright to feel more worn out or sad than usual, the

assessment can take its toll on people, especially those on the spectrum.'

'I'm OK.'

'Right, well, let's get down to business,' Pamela started before pausing, as if a reality television show presenter trying to create drama and suspense. 'I can say with a high degree of confidence that I think you are indeed autistic,' she said slowly. Paige drastically sucked in air as if she hadn't taken a breath in days, before exhaling. Her neck, shoulders and jaw un-tensed and she uncrossed her legs. She wasn't entirely sure how she was supposed to feel right now.

'Under the old system you would have been diagnosed with Asperger's Syndrome, which means it doesn't affect you that badly,' Pamela continued. Paige folded her arms and felt her hackles rise. Who was this person to decide how much she was affected? She wasn't inside her head. Pamela had known her for literally four hours before today. Paige scowled.

'But as that is no longer a term we use, the diagnosis is autism. But that's OK, you've still achieved so much!' Pamela said patronisingly, as if congratulating a child for tying their own shoes. 'The world would be so much more *boring* without *people like you*,' she said, lifting the idea of

Paige up onto a pedestal for everyone to gawk at. 'And it's important to remember, it's not a DISability, it's a DIFFrability; you're just different!' At this point Paige felt like she was drowning in a vat of molten sugar while the psychologist poured baby toys in as if that would make it better. Pamela had taken her patronising tone to a whole new level after pronouncing Paige autistic.

'In this folder I have the full report, detailing the reasons for the diagnosis. I would suggest having someone read through it with you.' Why? No one knew Paige better than she knew herself, she did not need anything explaining to her. Paige held her hand out for the envelope and detected a slight hesitation in Pamela before she handed it over. Paige eventually snatched it out of her hand.

'Are there any resources or groups or anything I can access now?' Paige asked, still staring at the side of the desk.

'Erm, well, there is this website,' Pamela said, writing down a web address. 'I'm sure there is some information on there?' Paige did not have much confidence there would be anything useful, and when she saw the address she realised she had already read everything on that website.

'Right,' she said, staring at the slip of paper.

'Do you have any questions?' Pamela asked stickily. 'Is there anything you don't understand?'

'No. Can I go now?' Paige said, not trusting herself to bite her tongue for much longer.

'Yes, of course, if you think you're ready?'

Paige did not respond, but simply got up and left, grateful she would never have to hear Pamela's overly sweet voice ever again. She walked quickly down the corridors, impatiently pressing the green buttons at each set of doors repeatedly, annoyed at the amount of time it was taking for the unknown security being to buzz her through each set. The envelope burnt in her hand. Her desire to devour its contents almost overwhelming her; but she wanted to be somewhere private before she opened it. Eventually she made it back to her car and couldn't wait any longer. Ripping the envelope open she pulled out a thick wad of paper; her entire personality and history splayed over the white pages. She speed-read the report, and words like 'deficit' and 'difficulty' jumped out at her, along with 'socially isolated' and 'cold'. There was very little reference to any of the positive things that made her, her. Her incredible memory for dates that had served her so well throughout her education and subsequent career.

Or how the many systems she used to organise her life were so efficient that even her parents and siblings asked her for help when facing any organisational task. Or how she saw every detail in every situation, noticing the smallest change in others, often making her the first to realise when something was wrong. Though she did admit to herself she didn't always know how to try and make them feel better, and that unless she had been through something similar, she had no idea how to put herself in their shoes.

About three-quarters of the way through she got to the section where Pamela had written about Taylor's responses to questions. The psychologist had written a caveat at the beginning, saying that Taylor's opinions were biased due to her relationship with Paige. But it also said that Taylor thought that maybe Paige's brain was just wired differently, and that that didn't have to be a bad thing. Paige smiled for the first time that day.

In the last quarter of the document there were all the results of the various tests Pamela had conducted on her. On all of them she had scored highly, well above the cut off for 'clinical significance'. Paige did not understand how, if she had scored at the extreme end of all of these tests, Pamela could say it didn't affect her that much. It seemed like a contradiction. But which was wrong? The psychologist or the tests?

Paige roughly closed the report, threw it onto the passenger seat, put both hands on the steering wheel, and leant forward until her forehead rested on the fake leather. She felt like all of the energy and light had been siphoned out of her. Her phone started ringing and she didn't even take it out of her pocket, letting it go to voicemail. She took a deep breath as tears started slowly trickling down her cheeks. She had no idea what she was feeling; sad, happy, relieved, angry... she just knew she was intensely *feeling*. Her phone buzzed again, indicating a text message. She reluctantly sat back upright to check the message; it was from Taylor: '*How did it go? X*' Paige guessed the phone call had been from her too.

'*It was hard. Got the Diagnosis. I think I hate Pamela.*' she texted back, putting her phone in her lap and wiping her eyes, taking a few steadying breaths.

Taylor texted again: '*Meet me at the pub later for drinks, loooooots of drinks. I'm buying.*' Another text came through quickly, stating, '*If you want to and are up to it of course. No pressure.*'

Paige laughed and texted back saying she would meet her at seven; for now, she just wanted to go home and sleep.

The pub was packed by the time Paige got there. All of the booths were full to the brim, with many people standing around tables in groups, bumping into each other and sloshing drinks everywhere. The landlord had opened the French doors out into the beer garden where many people lounged in the chairs, their noses and ears red from the sun, inebriation preventing them from feeling the burns. Taylor sat on a stool at the bar, gingerly leaning away from a group of men who didn't seem to understand what personal space meant. She had managed to save the seat next to her for Paige. As soon as Taylor saw her friend, she jumped down off the stool and wrapped her in a tight hug. It was the most physical contact they had ever had, but Paige found she didn't mind. In fact, she melted into the hug, squeezing Taylor tight, finding comfort in being squeezed back. Eventually they pulled apart and took their seats, Taylor blushing slightly and Paige not quite meeting her eyes.

'What are you drinking?' Taylor asked, pulling out her purse.

'Gin.'

'And tonic?' Taylor asked.

'No. Just gin.'

'Coming up.' Taylor got the bartender's attention and ordered Paige a large gin, and herself a lemonade. Paige took a large gulp, the alcohol burning her mouth and throat as it went down. She finally felt able to breathe again.

'How was it?' Taylor asked, sipping her lemonade. Paige explained how Pamela had somehow became even more patronising once she had told her she was autistic. How she felt like all her faults had been laid out and examined under a microscope, and how the report had made out like her brain was broken. Taylor took Paige's hand and held it tight. Paige just let their hands dangle in between them, relaying the whole appointment while staring at her drink, alternating between spinning the glass around and lifting it to her mouth, the cool ice occasionally touching her lips.

The group of men behind Taylor knocked into her, almost knocking her off the bar stool. Paige helped steady her and checked she was alright.

'Yes, fine,' Taylor said, rubbing her lower back where she had been elbowed. Paige picked up her drink and downed the rest of it.

'Let's get out of here,' she said, using their still joined hands to pull Taylor off the stool. Taylor tried drinking as much of her lemonade as she could before being forced to place it down on the bar as she was whisked away, Paige leading her through the crowds of people until they got outside. Paige suddenly became very conscious of their interlaced fingers and let go, embarrassed. Taylor took half a step away to give her space.

'Do you want me to take you home?' Taylor asked, putting her hands in her pockets.

'No.'

'Do you want to find another pub?'

'No.'

'What do you want to do?'

Paige thought for a moment, trying to work out what she needed in that moment.

'Walk. The river is about a mile that way,' she said, pointing down the road.

'Then let's walk,' Taylor said, stepping into line with her friend as they strolled towards the river. Paige was still trying to organise her thoughts, so used it as an opportunity to check in on Taylor, asking how Dylan was.

'He's OK, still sober, and he passed his first year at university.' Paige could see Taylor's chest swell with pride, so she let her carry on talking about her brother and how proud she was of him, and how living with him had worked out so much better than she expected. How if anything their relationship was stronger than ever, even if Dylan did insist on interfering in her personal life. And she was grateful that he had gotten her back into climbing; she hadn't realised how much she had missed it.

By the time she had finished talking about him they could hear the river gurgling behind the trees and shrubs. Taylor tried to lead them down the pavement that ran parallel to the river until they found a way through, but Paige said she knew a shortcut and disappeared into the shrubbery. From amongst the greenery she extended an arm back out, beckoning for Taylor to take her hand, and pulled her through. The leaves stroked their bare skin as they navigated through the shrubbery and twigs snapped underneath their feet. Eventually they broke through to the other side, the darkness of the vegetation changing into a cool light, and the sounds of the city behind them dying away.

The path by the river was fairly quiet. The trees and shrubs provided some welcome shade, acting as a wall between them and the outside world. In the few minutes it took them to walk to Paige's favourite clearing they only saw two other people; a dog walker and a cyclist. They sat down on the tree trunk and gazed across the river. The field on the other side was full of tall grass swaying lazily in the wind. Paige pointed out all the various wildlife, relishing in Taylor's excitement each time they saw a new animal. She had to reach out and put her hand on Taylor's leg to stop her jumping up when they saw the heron.

'Shhhh! You'll scare him off!' she whispered, letting her hand linger on Taylor's thigh. A fuzzy warmth radiated up from her fingers and her heart rate increased; she wondered if Taylor could hear her pulse, it was so loud in her ears. Paige withdrew her hand, worrying her heart was beating so hard it would jump out of her chest. They sat in silence, painfully aware of how small the gap was between them. Taylor seemed to be concentrating hard on keeping her eyes facing forward. Paige couldn't help stealing some sideways glances at her.

'Thank you, for helping me through this,' Paige said eventually, still watching the ducks as they drifted by. 'Not many people would have done that.'

'Maya would have, if she was here, wouldn't she?' Taylor asked.

'Yes, but I have known Maya for a long time. We're basically sisters at this point.'

'That's true,' Taylor said, picking up a loose twig from the floor, peeling off a couple of leaves and scratching at the bark. 'Has it changed anything, do you think?'

'Like what?'

'Well, do you feel different?'

'I mean... I do have a DIFFrability' Paige joked. Taylor laughed, making the butterflies in Paige's stomach flutter even harder.

'Seriously, though?' Taylor asked, still concentrating on the twig.

'I don't know. I don't feel any different. I might approach things differently now though, and not give myself a hard time over things like needing quiet and not liking being touched.'

Taylor subtly slid slightly further down the trunk, increasing the gap between them.

'By most people,' Paige clarified quietly, making Taylor blush. They watched a wagtail ride an invisible rollercoaster in the air, spontaneously dipping and diving before climbing even higher than before. The trees around them rustled with the breeze. An open water swimmer slowly made their way down the river, their high visibility float trailing behind them, almost like a submarine's periscope peering out of the water. Taylor had braced her hands on either side of herself, her fingers caressing the bark on the tree trunk. Paige could feel the butterflies trying to burst out of her as she reached down and put her hand over Taylor's. Taylor turned towards her questioningly. Paige didn't say anything, but instead leaned towards her, softly placing her lips on Taylor's. It felt like someone had set off a fireworks display to rival London on New Year's Eve as the warmth spread across her lips. Paige's brain started going so fast, like all the trains in the world were running through it at full steam, pulling on their whistles as they passed. Taylor parted her lips slightly as she kissed back, overcoming her initial hesitation, allowing Paige to kiss her more fully. In that second, in that moment, the rest of the world melted away. Even the little wagtail no longer existed. It was just Paige, and Taylor, and the deep current of electricity flowing through them.

After a few seconds they pulled apart, Taylor's cheeks as red as poppies as she blushed. She almost seemed like she wanted to hide. Paige just smiled softly at her, trying not to laugh.

'Are you OK?' Paige asked gently, trying to catch Taylor's gaze.

'Umm… I think so… I mean…' she stammered, her gaze flicking up to Paige's face.

'Do you want me to have not done that?' Paige asked, a

slight tremble in her voice.

'I never want you to *stop* doing that,' Taylor said, finally raising her eyes to meet Paige's.

'Good,' Paige said, kissing her again. She felt Taylor raise her hand and gently hold her cheek, deepening their kiss, drowning in each other. When they came up for air they could not help grinning at each other, chests heaving, nervous giggles drifting out over the river.

'I do have a question, though,' Taylor said finally.

'Shoot.'

'Are you going to tell Dylan, or am I?'

CHAPTER TWENTY-SIX
Epilogue

Two years (and a few months) later...

Taylor, Dylan, and Maya were spread out at the bottom of a sheer rock face, with Paige getting ready to start her climb. Maya, who didn't have quite the same enthusiasm towards climbing as the others, was lying down on a nearby patch of grass, soaking up the French August sun. This was the first holiday she had taken with Paige getting back from Japan and she was determined to make the most of it, even if the other three 'insisted on climbing'. She had bought a flat just a few miles from Paige, in the centre of the city, taking her boss up on their offer of choosing where to go next. She chose home. The city she was most familiar with and the friend she had missed so badly while on the other side of the world - and the man who kept stealing glances at her when he thought she wasn't looking.

The grass around her bent to the contours of her body, and the sun hat she had been wearing was pulled low over her eyes. The blue skies overhead seemed to go on forever and they could see green and gold vineyards in the distance. Dylan, wanting to make sure she hadn't fallen asleep, flicked water in her direction. She sat up and threw the travel pillow at him, nearly knocking him off the rock he was sitting on. He jerked his head subtly towards Taylor, who appeared to be shaking.

Dylan had just finished his third and final year of university, gaining a first class honours degree. He had decided to take the summer off to do some travelling and to take a 'well-earned break' before he started work writing for an online news outlet in the autumn. His console game collection had overflowed onto another bookcase. He was now sub-letting Taylor's old house on his own, enjoying the freedom of bachelor life and the fact his sister wasn't constantly nagging him to get his dirty socks out of the bathroom.

Dr Taylor Watkins had moved into Paige's house last autumn. It had taken them a while to adjust to their new living situation. Taylor, who often held conversations with herself and enjoyed blaring her music as loud as she could tolerate, learnt to be quieter when Paige was at home. Paige, in turn, was slowly learning to be more flexible and spontaneous, even agreeing to this last-minute holiday suggested by Taylor.

Paige's first book had been taken on by a publishing company, who had warned her that the niche market meant it might only sell a few hundred copies, only taking it on so they could diversify their portfolio. It had instead sold consistently well for many months, and her second novel did even better. She was currently writing her third, whilst juggling her teaching commitments, climbing, and spending as much time with Taylor as she could.

Paige started her climb, the yellowy-brown rock slightly crumbly in the French heat. Out the corner of her eye she saw Maya drag herself to her feet to come and watch, and even Dylan descended from his perch. She didn't understand why, it wasn't even that difficult a climb. She wedged her foot onto a small ledge, sending some dust trickling down the rock face. In some of the nooks and crannies, flowers had made their home. As a result the wall was speckled with colour, just like at the climbing centre, except the flowers danced with any light breeze. She could feel the heat beaming down onto her back as a trickle of sweat ran down the side of her face. Pausing to re-chalk her hands she looked over the nearby trees to the views beyond. Blue sky met patchwork fields in a beautiful duet. All she could hear was the slight breeze and the birds singing.

Eventually she made it to the topmost cam she had placed earlier in the day. Happily topping out, she signalled to Taylor that she was coming down, and started walking herself slowly down the wall. As she got closer to the ground she could hear the other three whispering between themselves, but couldn't make out what they were saying. She landed gracefully on the ground, looking up at the rock face in front of her as she untied from the rope.

'You know, Maya, I reckon you would be able to manage this. I know you think you're not "really a climber" but the views from the top are amazing.' Paige turned her head sideways to look for her friend, who was stood next to the wall, hands clasped in front of her and bouncing up and down.

'Maya, what -?' she began, turning to face her. The words were stolen from her mid sentence as she saw what Maya was so excited about. Taylor was no longer standing behind her, from where she had been belaying Paige. Instead, she had one knee on the floor, burning red cheeks, and held a small open box. Paige was aware of Taylor incoherently stammering some words, but all she could focus on was the simple, yet beautiful, diamond ring. The white gold circle rested in a purple velvet cushion, and supported a beautiful rectangular diamond, flanked by two smaller ones on each side. Paige had never seen anything so beautiful. Suddenly her hearing started working properly again, and she was finally able to understand what her girlfriend was saying.

'Paige… will you?' Taylor managed, her throat sounding as dry as the wall behind her, her nervous dimples shivering in anticipation. Paige was unable to form anything resembling words. She just nodded, gentle tears slowly beginning to fall down her cheeks.

'Eeeeeeeeeeeeeeee!' Maya screamed, jumping up and down, waterfalls cascading form her eyes. Dylan stood off to the side behind his sister, fists raised in the air in celebration. He would later say his eyes were watering from looking too hard at the sun.

Taylor scrambled to her feet and took the ring out of the box, and with trembling hands gently slid it on to Paige's finger. It fitted perfectly.

Paige pulled her fiancée towards her, rapidly alternating between kissing and hugging her, not really knowing what to do with the bubbling joy that was overflowing inside of her. Eventually she calmed down enough to remember how to form words. She took both of Taylor's hands in her own and looked into her eyes.

'I love you,' she whispered, squeezing her hands

tightly.

'I love you too,' Taylor whispered back, her voice croaking, making them both laugh.

Dylan and Maya quickly demanded hugs off both of them, Dylan picking Paige up by the waist and spinning her around, Maya bombarding Taylor with a high-pitched flood of gibberish. Paige couldn't stop grinning. Taylor kept trying to cover her burning cheeks and wipe away her tears, only for them to be replaced moments later. Dylan quickly ran over to the cool box and retrieved a bottle of champagne and glasses, making quick work of sending the cork into the air like a rocket.

'So that's why you wouldn't let me help make lunch today!' Paige said, pushing Dylan gently on the shoulder. He just grinned in response. Dylan filled up three glasses with champagne and handed them to the girls, using his water bottle to fill up a fourth for himself.

'To love!' he said, raising his glass.

'To love!' they all said in unison.

'And to interfering younger brothers,' Taylor added.

'By nine minutes! Our age difference is nine. Freaking. Minutes!' he said exasperatedly, while the others laughed. They drank and talked, Paige asking many questions about how long the other two knew for, and how long Taylor had

had this planned. Maya was still communicating in decibels only bats could hear, and Dylan could not wipe the smug look off his face. Eventually, Paige turned to Taylor.

'So,' she said in mock seriousness. 'Did you ever think you'd end up marrying a secret agent?'

About the Author

Rosie Williams lives in the South Wales valleys with her wife and two cats. Rosie first got into writing at a very young age, penning poems and self-illustrated stories. This passion for writing was fostered in school, before becoming an escape from the real world as an adult.

Now in her thirties, Rosie writes about the magic of romance allowing young and old to live vicariously through her characters. To get updates and access to exclusive content, sign up to Rosie's newsletter via her website: www.rosiewilliamsauthor.com.

Printed in Great Britain
by Amazon